MAJOR EVENTS

Anvil Lodge, a retirement home in The Chilterns, is run by the seemingly formidable Daphne Currer-Spriggs. Those who choose Anvil Lodge are fortunate. Their home is luxurious, with a sometimes eccentric staff, and friendship abounds. The effective king-pin of the establishment is the self-effacing but single-minded Major Llenots-Jones, who refers to his hostess as the C.O. His fellow residents are a group of characters whose experiences, and involvements with his activities, form the substance of this unusual and entertaining novel.

MAJOR EVENTS

MAJOR EVENTS

by

Bob Stonell

Dales Large Print Books
Long Preston, North Yorkshire,
BD23 4ND, England.

British Library Cataloguing in Publication Data.

Stonell, Bob
  Major events.

    A catalogue record of this book is
    available from the British Library

    ISBN   978-1-84262-883-6 pbk

First published in Great Britain in 2006 by The Book Guild Ltd.

Published in Large Print 2012 by arrangement with
Mr R. A. Stonell

Dales Large Print is an imprint of Library Magna Books Ltd.

Printed and bound in Great Britain by
T.J. (International) Ltd., Cornwall, PL28 8RW

To my old friend Walter (Smiler) Townend, whose cheery company so enhanced the days of National Service. Also in memory of our late mutual 'oppo', George Wake.

CONTENTS

INTRODUCTION

We spend the latter part of our working life innocently looking forward to the joyful release of retirement, assuming it to represent the unwritten pages of life, to be happily filled with unfettered pursuit of cherished ambitions – doing what we want to, for once.

When the time comes, however, the first thing we realise is that we no longer get days off. Suddenly, every day is a working day making the office seem like a lost escape. Furthermore, time seems to accelerate; leaving us little chance of indulging ourselves quite as imagined. Nevertheless, we have come up through a trapdoor of life to stand on the roof and see the world in true perspective for the first time. There we can perceive and appreciate the richness of existence and the abundance of benefits that life affords. All the scientists, great composers, and creators of every sort throughout the ages, have contributed to the quality of our little individual existence; a free inheritance which we ignore to our shame.

While all is right with the world, and good health is maintained, we see life as being normal; but that normality can be so taken for granted that by the time we realise the value of it we may be too old to take full advantage of it. We owe it to that inheritance to make the most of life by living our retirement to the decent full; trusting never to hear the fateful words of the physician saying, 'Sorry old chap, but...'; whereupon we fall through a trapdoor of a different kind of existence, to where the tenuous thread of attachment to our cosy life of well-being has parted, and we begin the despairing drift away from all that is dear and familiar to us, towards the darkness where no hand can reach to hold us back.

Some, who finding themselves virtually alone in the world and can afford to do so, elect to spend the remainder of their lives without the burdens of home and property. They divest themselves of all but their capital and retreat to the ease and comfort of a retirement home where others do the work and worrying. There they find their normality, while it lasts.

May 2005

Chapter 1

Revelations

A knock on the door interrupted his meditations.

'Come in Ramiro,' he called across the room.

'Coffee! Major,' announced the young Spanish attendant, pushing a trolley through the door towards the small antique table next to the major.

'Hang on, old boy,' said the major reaching for a coaster from the window sill. 'We'll shove that under it – better safe than sorry, eh!'

Ramiro set the coffee down together with a digestive biscuit and pulled from his overall pocket a slightly creased envelope which he handed to the major.

'Is for you,' he said in a cheery but deliberate manner which seemed to the major to carry a slight inference that some sort of reward would not be out of order.

'Where's the C.O.?' he enquired, fending off the hint.

'She gone to post office and bank,' replied Ramiro, backing out of the door; the trolley colliding with the door frame and leaving a small dent in the paintwork.

He glanced anxiously at the major through the diminishing gap of the door.

'Shan't say a word, old boy,' said the major, who was well aware of the value of keeping the staff on-side as much as possible.

Ramiro continued his tour of the rooms whose occupiers happened to be within.

The C.O., as the major referred to her, was Mrs Currer-Spriggs, who had been the proprietress of The Anvil Lodge Retirement Home for a number of years, having inherited the very substantial country residence from her father. She embodied the attributes for success both physically and intellectually. Medically trained, and weighty in all senses of the word including a commanding voice which had the qualities of a raven in its depth and volume, she was eminently qualified for her chosen career and revelled in her established 'command'. As sweeping radar precedes a warship, the rich low register of her voice reverberated along the corridors, leaving no doubts as to her whereabouts.

Although Daphne Currer-Spriggs was happy to use the married title in her professional role, she had in fact remained single. At quite an early age she had come to the conclusion that she would never entrust

16

her life to any man who in her assessment failed to achieve such an ascendancy over her as to overcome what she knew would otherwise remain a too-powerful urge to control her own affairs. Subsequent to a few unfulfilling involvements which fell decidedly short of those parameters, she was adequately fulfilled by the demanding occupation to which she had committed herself.

Being genuinely dedicated to achieving the utmost satisfaction of her 22 guests, within the scope of the income they afforded, she believed that a high standard of care could be maintained provided that she was careful to curb, when necessary, the natural altruism to which she knew she was prone.

The fees that she required were substantial but more than fair for the service provided. Each guest was furnished with a private bathroom, bedroom and a small sitting room, to equal the standards of a high-quality hotel. This standard of accommodation was achieved by the skilful adaptation of the two upper floors by her old friend Alan Staple, a fine architect with a small practice at Amersham. The work absorbed the larger part of her inherited capital, though without realistic expectation of its ultimate recovery.

She was careful to ensure that hers was a community of like-minded guests who would best benefit from the standards offered, while forming a harmonious relationship with each other. Crucially, she was keenly aware that the real happiness of the individual depended on the smallest details of comfort and preference being acknowledged and conceded if at all possible.

Losing their independence and importance to the world through one reason or another had reduced most of the residents to a simplified existence which magnified their perception of the pleasures remaining to them. All of which was subject to the understanding that the establishment was a retirement home, not a care home which would call for different services and a disturbing ambience. Sooner or later, of course, all might reach that regrettable stage in life and be obliged to move on.

In short, 'A good time while it lasted' was the underlying principle of the regime. Mrs Currer-Spriggs regarded her guests as being above the realms of regulation and accordingly engendered awareness that the only rule of the house was, 'There shall be no rules'.

The beneficiaries of this ideal were thus brought to an appreciation of the inscription above the drawing-room door which declared that – 'Contentment is the ultimate achievement, beyond which lie only vanity and avarice.' As the author of this observation, Mrs Currer-Spriggs maintained anonymity.

Major Llenots-Jones, known to his friends as L.-J., was content to believe that his rank accorded him equality with his formidable hostess; though possessing the wit to trust that circumstances would never call the matter into question. It was his belief that everyone inescapably relates by natural instinct to everyone else, in terms of social standing, irrespective of class or qualification; and conceded that rank, *per se* not being a natural endowment, afforded no assurance against the principle. It could be confronted by anyone in an inferior position, imagining his superior to be bereft of his trousers, provided that convictions of his own status were real and justified.

The major had been aware of such realities since his younger days; observing that each individual, consciously or not, betrayed his or her acknowledgement of another's higher or lower standing, by discernible body language and facial expression. Furthermore, the tone, and quality even, of that person's speech could change entirely according to whom they joined with in conversation.

Such phenomena were plainly comparable with the social behaviour of animals such as wolves, where each individual accepts, without question, its place in the hierarchy as part of the natural order of things necessary for the species' survival. It was, however, characteristic of humanity to strive against such actuality by specious aspiration.

The major further observed to what degree top dogs would manifest their superiority, even in such simple circumstance as driving away from social events. Those regarding themselves as most ascendant would rush off at great speed, determined to show a clean pair of heels to the remainder while being hotly pursued by admiring disciples subconsciously satisfied to maintain close contact, dutifully astern of them.

The front runners would reiterate their status by ostentatiously overtaking their lesser brethren on the road, usually eschewing recognition while passing them; or by overtly falling back to dissociate themselves by distance.

The major's further experience over the years confirmed the reality of this curious social behaviour which he came to regard as a sort of subconscious game from which no one was wholly exempt; the dissenter's part being played for him.

Drizzle, drizzle, drizzle. One of those words, the sound of which is exactly in accord with its meaning. Drizzle! The molten misery that dribbles down the window to mar the view and cast a feeling of gloom upon the day. From his swivelling armchair by the window, the major could make out the nut cage suspended in the willow tree, swinging slightly.

Moving his head from side to side, he sought a better line of sight through the writhing patches of clearer glass. With mounting irritation he tried to distinguish the species of bird clinging to the far side of the cage. By its size it was probably a blue tit, but the possibility of it being something more exotic attached a compulsive importance to knowing, which in itself he found annoying.

Trivialities assumed too much importance in his mind these days, he mused, putting it down as a consequence of his situation. Perhaps it was a good thing, desirable even, to have nothing more serious to concern himself with in his retirement. The bird was joined on the near side of the cage by what was, even as a distorted image, obviously a robin. He felt there was something a bit strange about a robin eating nuts. Perhaps, even the bird world was subject to change, as well as so many other things in life. Like many of his generation he had a profound dislike of 'change', finding it disturbing and too often brought about for its own sake rather than for any laudable reason.

Marketing people, for instance, were in his view the worst offenders in that respect, being responsible for much of the deterioration in the real quality of life these days. All the best products were fast disappearing, mostly by way of changes wrought by marketing executives, desperate to justify their existence simply by finding things to change.

The oldest and most familiar products that were the essence of a sane and comfortable world were the likeliest targets. Beware the sudden change of a label or packaging which often follows the temporary disappearance of a sound traditional product. Its return to the shelves will reveal a change of style, having a nice oblique line across the box in place of the former nasty horizontal one; all, so we are told, as demanded by the customer in response to exhaustive and costly market research. Most of such changes are accompanied by assurances that the product itself remains unchanged, with the inference that any reduction of quality, taste, or efficacy could only be imaginary.

With these convictions re-aired, the major resumed his contemplation of the natural world. Robins used not to be associated with nuts; neither were starlings or sparrows which now tended to dominate the nut feeders rather than dispose of breadcrumbs and what not! In fact he had noticed that bread no longer seemed acceptable to wild birds: perhaps something to do with the quality of grain used these days, he concluded. Like much else it probably boiled down to more interference from Europe.

In more natural terms, it had not escaped his notice that even birdsong seemed to be changing. Repertoires of some birds such as blackbirds now appeared to include mimicry of all sorts, telephone warbles, car alarms, wheeling cries of the red kites, which had become established in the district, and so on.

The thought put him in mind of an old hotel near Ross, which he had come upon by chance some years ago while looking for somewhere to stay for the weekend. Being at a quiet time of the year there were only two or three other guests present and he found himself alone for much of the time while in the dining room.

From his allotted table he could not quite see the doorway through which the staff emerged from the kitchen, sweeping aside the ringed curtain that served more conveniently than a door, and which made a fairly loud metallic 'swishing' noise.

During the first 24 hours or so he was often puzzled to hear not only a great variety of voices including a cultured throaty voice brightly proclaiming 'good morning', apparently emanating from the kitchen, but also the repeated swishing of the curtain without anyone coming in or going out of the room.

He spent the Sunday evening in the sitting room in company with, by then, the sole fellow guest who was a well-known critic and broadcaster. Together they watched the Leeds Festival on television, the winner of which was a newcomer to the music world, named Vladimir Ashkenazi. At the end of the programme his companion retired, wishing him a good night and safe journey home the following day.

Finding the waiter, the major ordered a brandy as a nightcap, and at the same time remembered to make enquiry in regard to the unaccountable medley of sounds heard in the dining room. The amused waiter explained to him that in the passageway immediately outside the kitchen there was a substantial cage suspended from the ceiling in which resided a particularly gifted mynah bird. He was further enlightened to the effect that the owner of the impressive voice, so often flattered by the bird, was a frequent guest at the hotel, by the name of General Roberts.

On expressing his admiration of the performances, he was offered an introduction to the artiste, there and then. The bird's response was to reverse its position on the perch and face away, refusing to communicate any kind of sound whatsoever pending the intruder's withdrawal.

The major finished his coffee and settled back in his chair. The soporific comfort of his surroundings relaxed his mind and his thoughts wandered away from the drizzle, back to his schooldays in north London. There, almost every master held the rank of major, including several M.C.s, although the school prospectus represented them all by the title of Mister. With the exception of one, Major Wood, who had just returned from the Second World War armed with campaign maps which never failed to impress the boys in geography class; all owed their rank to the 'Great War'.

The school was graced with three masters who were also school chaplains, the chief of whom was a senior wrangler named Thompson, who having dominion over the books and stationery store, was known as 'Booky-T'. The major's third-form master was a jovial ecclesiastic, the Reverend Whiteside, whose rosy smiling visage earned him the affection both of the boys and of the lunchtime regulars at the tavern across the road from the school.

Of the countless schoolboys who had, for over 400 years, successively worn down the wide stone stairs in 'big hall', from six inches at the sides to just one inch at the middle; most, like the major, had moved on to careers of relative obscurity, while others had fulfilled their mother's dreams and achieved eminence in the great affairs of the nation.

Dozing fitfully, the major's thoughts continually returned to those days, long gone but rich in memories; even more so, he fancied, than those of the army which had not afforded him a particularly distinguished career. He saw himself again in the biology class before the towering figure of Professor Heimer of Berlin University who, on occasion, thundered in his Germanic tones, 'Llenots-Jones, you ave ze mind like ze lavatory seat; everything goes straight through.'

He recalled watching his large physics notebook arcing across the classroom to land on his desk without a page opening; a skill developed over many years by Major Hough, the physics master, for whom the young Llenots-Jones had a warm regard. Llenots-Jones was pursuing the science rather than the classical or modern courses through the school.

The resonant bass tones of Major Hough, issuing strangely from such a slight figure, were redolent of Sunday evensong in the school chapel. Reverberating from the back of the choir as it processed solemnly along the aisle to the choir stalls, they seemed to define 'the system', signifying the communion of social and academic worlds ordered to the production of leaders of men.

As he thought about it, it occurred to the major that his physics master's voice was probably the most distinguishable to be heard worldwide on those occasions when the service was broadcast on the 'wireless'. He remembered the moving letter of appreciation received by the school on one occasion from a lonely soul employed on a weather station in the Arctic.

An inordinate amount of coughing invariably occurred during these services as, contrary to instructions, boys had written to advise their families to both listen in and to listen out for a loud cough at a particular point in the proceedings. The visible embarrassment of the staff was commensurate with the frustration of the engineers whose great, bronze, B.B.C. microphones responded splendidly to the frequencies and frequency of coughing.

The major's family, though loosely C. of E., had not truly been 'churchgoers' and his first experience of evensong in the school chapel was still clear in his mind. The anthem had been delivered with such soaring magnificence that at its conclusion he was on the point of rendering enthusiastic applause, but by a fraction of a second stayed his hands short of impact, though not without notice.

The major's head gradually tipped forward until abruptly jerking back as he was restored to the 'present' by a noise in the garden. The window view had cleared as the drizzle finally eased off and the distant sky was warming to the colour of custard powder, promising a change for the better.

The nut cage was now in the sole possession of a large black, white and red woodpecker that brooked no division of spoils, seeing off all comers, including a persistent starling, with sharp thrusts of its martial beak.

The major was impressed by the strikingly handsome newcomer whose vigorous authoritative air commanded universal respect. It dawned on him that he could well develop an interest in 'bird watching'; there were certainly things to be said in its favour. Clearly, much could be learned by simple observation without foregoing the comfort of his easy chair when the weather was as untoward as today's had been so far. He could even start a journal of his observations. Yes indeed, the more he thought about it the more he was enthused. It was time he did something besides exist and it would precipitate getting out in the fresh air more, as the C.O. was frequently telling him he should do.

It would be doing something to actually improve the quality of life rather than just moaning about its steady deterioration. It was only the day before that he was discussing with his breakfast companions the declining standards of life in the face of rampant commercialism.

'The higher the standard of living the lower the quality of life,' he had proclaimed to a startled audience, leaving them to ponder the veracity of the assertion.

Who knows? he mused, he might eventually succeed in contributing to the sum of ornithological knowledge! He could begin by noting which species actually fed on nuts. He would need a few things with which to get started, of course; such as a good book on birds and a notebook. He must jot down things as they occurred to him. Swinging round in his chair, his gaze swept the room in search of something to write on. He smiled to himself at the thought of needing a notebook to make note of needing one; rather like needing one's glasses to look for them!

Seeing nothing of use, his hands went instinctively to his pockets where his right hand closed on the unopened letter.

'Good lord! Completely forgot that,' he said aloud.

Never mind, he thought, whatever it was it would do well for making his short list on before anything slipped his mind; he did not want to negotiate extra trips to the town which was several miles distant. He had to hold the bottom of his jacket in order to drag the envelope free from the pocket.

Placing it face down on the table he flattened out as best he could the now well crumpled envelope and drew from his inside pocket the Parker 51 that his mother had presented him with on his nineteenth birthday. He still derived the utmost pleasure from using it, and had been astounded to learn from the woman at the sub-post office that its value was probably well in excess of £200. He found it almost impossible to steer a ballpoint pen, which modern methods of signing increasingly demanded, and threatening his treasured pen with obsolescence.

Having composed his list, which included by then, field glasses and knapsack, he began to wonder if he was being at all precipitate in incurring no small expense on a mere impulse, but soon regained his resolve.

He turned the envelope over, looked at the postmark and considered the handwriting; neither rang any bells in his mind. Despite the small pile of post that usually arrived for him, it was some time since he had received anything that was worth opening. Envelopes with a percentage on the front, or marked 'Urgent Open Immediately,' went straight in the bin along with anything that was ostentatiously overprinted with official looking frank marks. The word 'Congratulations' appearing on anything was enough to induce audible fury at the way 'these people' were free persistently to persecute the populace with their damned schemes.

The last time he'd received a gratuitous 'winner's cheque' for ten pounds, he actually sent it back with a stiff note asking if they were capable of comprehending that he, for one, probably among millions, preferred to be left alone to winning their 'blasted money'. Communications from 'Officialdom', on the other hand, were unmistakably plain with a vaguely 'foreboding' appearance.

He pushed his thumbnail under the end of the flap and tore a piece up, slipped his thumb inside and ripped open the top to find a short letter enclosing, to his astonishment, a cheque in his favour for £5,000.

'I don't suppose that you will remember me,' he read 'but we met briefly about three years ago, in the bar at The Eagle in Old Amersham. You found my wallet and gave me a "ring" to return same.'

The major remembered the incident clearly, as he'd only been in Amersham a few times. While he was living in London, he'd caught the through-train from Marylebone to Amersham on his way to Chesham to visit an elderly aunt in the cottage hospital. He had got into a taxi outside the station at Amersham and noticed the wallet on the floor. He attempted to hand it to the driver who declined to take charge of it and so, settling back in the seat, he opened it.

It appeared to contain nothing more than some scraps of paper.

'No cash?' queried the driver.

'No,' said the major.

'There you are then, he won't be back – don't leave it in here, mate, if you don't mind; chuck it in a bin somewhere.'

The major put the wallet into his pocket and forgot about it for the time being.

As the taxi turned into the steep hill leading up to the hospital he had an unaccountable feeling that perhaps all was not well. He dismissed the thought as irrational, paid the driver and walked into the reception area to be told that his aunt had died quite peacefully, scarcely an hour before.

He had telephoned The Crown Hotel in Old Amersham, as the nearest accommodation he could find to book a room for the night, having agreed to be on-hand the following day, at the request of the doctor in order to deal with formalities arising from his aunt's death. After dinner he stepped down into the comfortable sitting room and settled into one of the roomy floral armchairs. Gently swirling a small brandy, he gazed absently out of the window, across the narrow street to the arches of the old town hall, and reviewed the day.

Was it only this morning? he thought, that he locked the door of his Kensington flat and hailed a taxi to take him to Fortnum and Mason's to look for a suitable gift for an 88-year old lady? No mean task, he realised at the outset, and had been puzzling over it for most of the previous day. Chocolates, however expensive, seemed a bit trite; she would regard them as lacking in effort on his part, surely.

Flowers looked a bit pathetic, and certainly would do by the time he got them there! Anything requiring intellectual effort would not do either, as the ward sister told him on the telephone the day before that his aunt was unable to concentrate on anything for more than a few minutes.

No one was able to suggest anything to fill the bill satisfactorily, so he thanked them all for their efforts on his behalf and made his way to the exit. Just inside, he noticed a display of special and very expensive honey. Why not? he thought and settled his dilemma with a simple and possibly beneficial gift.

After an early lunch he made his way to Marylebone station and bought a day-return ticket to Amersham. The next train left at ten minutes past three, stopping only at Harrow-on-the-Hill, where the platform looked almost deserted. No one entered the major's compartment and the train pulled smoothly and quietly away, heading for its next stop, Amersham, where it was due at three thirty-nine.

The major removed his coat and, placing it on the seat beside him, gazed out of the window at the procession of changing views. As the vista became leafier, and Hertfordshire gave way to Buckinghamshire, a slight thud drew his attention inboard again to where his coat was lying on the floor, the weight of the jar of honey in the pocket causing it gradually to slide off the edge of the seat, pulling the rest with it.

As he retrieved his coat he wondered whether or not honey had any medicinal or even nutritional value; he really had no idea, but was confident that it would do no harm and he'd never met anyone who disliked it. He recalled being a guest at a Round Table Club dinner in Missenden and being seated next to a member who introduced himself as a bee-keeper. His companion told him that he would never find mould on honey because nothing could grow on it, as it had no food value, and would therefore remain in its original state indefinitely.

He pondered the phenomenon, wondering why honey was so attractive to certain creatures such as bears, if it had no food value; furthermore, what did bees use it for if not for food? Perhaps he was missing a point somewhere; he would endeavour to find out in due course.

Now that he was thinking about it, he felt sure that he'd been told at some time or other by an erudite friend that honey was packed with calories and was in fact, very fattening. Whatever the truth, he considered the subject exhausted for the time being at least.

The sudden blast of a car horn passing the window brought his thoughts back to The Crown Hotel. Remembering the lost wallet, he placed his drink on the window sill, fished out the wallet from his side pocket and glanced through the oddments of paper. One piece was a dog-eared card with a name and telephone number printed on it, which he thought might be the owner's calling card.

In addition, there was a piece of paper bearing a pencilled name and telephone number and, tucked down in a deep fold, a credit card, the discovery of which, he realised, changed the complexion of the situation somewhat, which he regarded as being a bit of a 'bind'. Firstly, he would have to try telephoning the number on the card and to gauge the response, if any.

He finished his drink, and made his way up the stairs and along the landing to his room, the sixteenth-century oak floor creaking and groaning all the way. He sat on the bed and dialled the number.

'Dingwall!' announced a tired voice.

The major was glad to hear the name coincide with the one on the card and introduced himself before explaining his purpose.

'Oh thank God for that,' said Dingwall in a brighter and evidently much relieved tone. 'Where are you, old bean?'

The major accepted the familiarity, putting it down to relief on the part of his respondent. 'I'm at The Crown.' 'Overnight,' he added. 'You can collect it straightaway if you like, or I can leave it with reception.'

'Ah! bit of a snag there, old bean,' replied Dingwall, pausing, 'Tell you the truth – don't get on too well at The Crown these days – mind if I make a suggestion?'

'Go ahead,' said the major, beginning to feel a slight unease with this new acquaintance.

'I wonder if you would mind stepping a few yards along to The Eagle, it's on the right, just up the street. I'd be jolly obliged to you.'

The major, in truth, jolly well did mind, but decided to go along with it; firstly, because he had intended to stretch his legs before turning in for the night and, secondly he was beginning to think that the sooner he got rid of the damned wallet the better.

Minutes later he scanned the few faces in the bar of The Eagle, and settled his gaze on a lone figure rising from a nearby table, who advanced towards him with outstretched hand. 'Dingwall,' announced the figure. 'Very good of you to come,' he said, grasping the major's hand and shaking it vigorously.

'First things first though, let me get you something,' Dingwall offered.

'Thank you, but I've just had a brandy,' began the major.

'Splendid. Large brandy and the usual please, Laura,' Dingwall called across to the bar. 'Water?' he queried, looking at his guest.

'Thank you,' said the major.

'And bring a jug of "aqua" too, Pet,' Dingwall added, glancing back at Laura.

They sat down at the small table.

'Perhaps I should explain,' started Dingwall, hesitantly.

'No need at all,' interjected the major, having a rough idea of what was about to be disclosed and suspecting that his host was gaining a reputation that was erasing his welcome in the local venues.

Laura brought the drinks and set them down, with a sideways look at Dingwall, which plainly meant 'the usual arrangement I suppose.' He returned the look with one of mixed pleading and gratitude.

'Thanks, Laura, see you later.'

Reading clearly between the lines, the major was anxious to hasten the proceedings and return to his normal affairs.

He took out the wallet and passed it to Dingwall saying, 'If there was any money in it, I'm afraid it had gone when I found it.'

'Good Lord, no, old bean, nothing of the sort, not a cent – don't worry!' came the instant reply.

The major gave an inaudible sigh of relief; it had not occurred to him until that moment just what a nasty situation it could have been. In fact, it crossed his mind what a first-rate 'scam' could be devised by the unscrupulous; to leave an old wallet on the bus with just a clue of identity inside and then charge the finder with theft of an imaginary £50 or so. There were plenty of people, particularly the honest or elderly sort, who would return the wallet in good faith and then feel intimidated into 'paying up'.

Dingwall anxiously looked inside the wallet and grinned with satisfaction as he retrieved the piece of paper with the name and number on.

'I can't tell you what a relief it is to get this back,' he told the major. 'In the taxi, eh! Of course; I should have realised.'

'Glad to have been of service,' said the

major, 'but now, if you'll excuse me, I must be getting back. I promised to phone my wife about this time,' he lied, being unmarried. Downing the rest of his brandy, he stood up to go.

'Well! I jolly well hope to see you again, old bean, chance to pay you back eh?' effused Dingwall.

'Who knows?' replied the major, managing a smile while shaking hands again and, giving a wave to the smiling Laura, he made for the door.

And that was that, he thought to himself three years later, as he read on: 'Thanks to you, things took a big turn for the better. I won't bore you with the details, suffice it to say, old chap, (that was a turn for the better, the major thought, remembering old bean with some displeasure), I haven't looked back since. Some weeks ago I told my people to find you at all costs, which they have now done, and I hope you won't take offence at the enclosed. It will be a load off my conscience to see it appear on my next statement. God bless! And thanks again. Dingwall,' the letter concluded.

The major was at a loss as to how to react. 'My people', he thought, that was pretty casual, weighty stuff, eh! How many people did Dingwall employ? he wondered. To tear up the cheque would show ingratitude for no really tangible reason beyond superficial impressions, gained at a time when his would-be benefactor was obviously at a pretty low ebb. He couldn't return it with any kind of excuse anyway, because the sender had obviously deliberately omitted his address.

Furthermore, there was little doubt that Dingwall would be very disappointed if his generosity were declined. The major was satisfied in his mind that there was no better course than to accept the gift which was, to say the least, timely. 'Where there's a will there's a legacy,' he concluded aloud; and, placing the cheque in the back of his chequebook, added the word 'bank' to his list.

Chapter 2

Circumstances

Suggestions that Mrs Currer-Spriggs should employ a chef, at least for the sake of appearance, were dismissed with the comment that as far as she was concerned a good cook free of fads and fashions was worth several chefs. She regarded most chefs as 'failed cooks' who possessed no more than superficial skills and fancy ideas. They were lost when it came to the simple arts of making decent toast, or preparing a grapefruit properly, as against bringing it to ruin by slashing at it with a knife in a gung-ho flourish. Few of them seemed aware of what a genuine roast potato should look and taste like, or appeared to think that it mattered. Mrs Currer-Spriggs was determined to protect her flock from such ineptitudes by employing a thoroughly experienced professional cook who offered the best traditions of English food in addition to an aptitude with foreign dishes as occasion demanded. Mrs Robertson, the cook, was just such a woman and in whom Mrs Currer-Spriggs placed her entire confidence.

Medical pronouncements on the suitability or otherwise of particular foods carried no weight with either woman since they believed it was only a matter of time before such assertions were disproved by subsequent tests revealing the contrary. Thus was trendiness ousted by enjoyment within a well-balanced diet as the order of things; besides which, none of the residents was of an age to worry about such matters.

The major had a particular fancy for stewed kidneys in a rich gravy on fried bread, always his favourite breakfast in the Army, and Mrs Robertson could be relied upon to get it right for him. Her soups were another trump card as far as he was concerned. They were rich in taste and substance, without the commercial trend to make everything possible 'cream of', or 'creamy', which was, to him, the ruin of honest provender, but all that could now be bought from shops. One well-known supermarket did, in fact, offer a range of 'gourmet' soups for a time, which were plain and of excellent quality, but they soon disappeared from the shelves; perhaps for want of wide enough margins or sufficient discerning customers.

One of the privileges enjoyed by the residents was that meals could be taken, by prior arrangement, in their own rooms, if preferred. Such factors were among the 'little things' that C.S. (as the staff referred to their employer), regarded as important. However, it was, to say the least, hard work for the cook to maintain such a demanding regime. Mrs Robertson was privately inclined to the opinion that it was all a bit overdone, although she revelled in the praise heaped upon her by her appreciative consumers.

Robina Robertson was affectionately addressed by her employer as Robbie. The manner of their first meeting was fortuitous for both, in as much as, six years after losing her husband in the Falklands War where he was serving with the Royal Marines, Robina was struggling to maintain the mortgage on their small semi-detached house in Chinnor.

From the age of 16 she had been employed in the household of an aristocratic family whose head was a minor ambassador. Starting as a maid, she travelled the world with the family until her employer retired and the family settled back in their country seat, Armanda Park.

During their time at an embassy in South America she met her husband, Ken Robertson, while he was a Royal Marine private attached to the embassy on special duties. They corresponded until the family returned to England, by which time Ken was a corporal and when he finished his current tour he too returned home and they decided to get married. That was in 1967 when they were both 24. They were greatly assisted by the family who had come to regard Robina almost as one of their own.

In addition to a fine wedding arranged by the family and held at the park, they were given the use of a cottage on the park estate. In due course, Ken was rated 'sergeant' and they decided that they could afford to start a home of their own while Robina continued as assistant cook, gaining much valuable experience and eventually taking the place of her retiring superior.

Ken was planning to retire from the Marines after 22 years, at the age of 40, which would have been in 1983. When the

Falklands' campaign came about in 1982 his experience and expertise were needed. Accordingly he was drafted to an assault ship and sailed south.

Had he returned, their plans for the following year would have included trying for a late family, or adoption if necessary. Supported by the family, Robina survived the next five years immersed in her work until the next wave of circumstance engulfed both her and the family.

Her ageing employer, plagued with financial problems and declining health, was advised to move abroad to live in a more temperate climate; all of which inevitably added up to selling the estate and the virtual splitting up of the family.

It was about that time that Daphne, then aged 33, was conceiving her plans in regard to what to do with Anvil Lodge. Being well connected with most of the county society, she was having tea one afternoon with the family at Armanda Park and being apprised of their unfolding circumstances.

She was struck by the antithesis that her own affairs presented, having virtually the opposite problems to resolve. As it had become obvious to her during tea that the staff must soon be given notice, Daphne suggested to her hostess that a stroll round the gardens would be a great joy to her before she departed for home.

The idea was welcomed, giving Daphne the opportunity she was seeking to outline her own plans, which would be greatly advanced by the recruitment of such a key member of staff as Mrs Robertson, should she be agreeable to it. She was already acquainted with Mrs Robertson from former visits when she had been greatly impressed by the high standard of the meals.

Daphne was assured that not only would she be welcome to approach Mrs Robertson on the matter, but that it would be an immense relief to the family to know that such a salvation was at hand, since none of the family could yet formulate personal plans whereby any of the staff might be retained. Furthermore, they themselves would take the greatest pleasure in being allowed to put the proposal to her. Such was the intensity of discussion of each other's affairs that the two women became quite lost in it.

It was the sudden chill in the air that brought their attention to how long they had been walking, and even how far. Consequently, Daphne was persuaded to stay to dinner on the assurance that dress could be informal. When it came time for her to depart, she arranged to take Robina back to Chinnor on her way home, having ascertained that Robina had been apprised of the offer of employment at some point during the evening.

It had been left to Robina herself to inform Daphne of her feelings in regard to the proposal, which she attempted to do as soon as they were underway. However, she was so choked with emotion that Daphne began to wonder if the woman was inarticulate, until passing lights revealed that Robina's eyes were brimming with tears.

'Oh my dear!' said Daphne. 'Whatever is the matter?'

'I can't tell you what a relief it's been; I couldn't believe it when they told me. Not having to worry about the mortgage or anything.'

'Listen to me,' said Daphne. 'Once you come to the Lodge you will have everything you need. And that means everything; a good salary, your own rooms, telephone.'

'Rooms?' Robbie queried.

'Of course; bedroom, bathroom, sitting room,' replied Daphne. 'All you have to do is what you do best.'

'Oh lor!' Robbie whispered, unbelievingly. 'What about the house?' she asked.

'Forget it,' said Daphne. 'As soon as you finish at the Park we'll put it on the market and pay off the mortgage. Oh! I'm so sorry. I'm forgetting it has memories for you,' Daphne apologised.

'Don't worry Ma'm, I'm used to that now. It'll be nice not to be on my own so much,'

Robina replied.

'Incidentally,' Daphne said, looking at Robina with a slight frown, 'if you don't mind me asking, how many people do you think you can cope with for one meal?'

'Oh! I don't know really, Ma'm, I've never had to do more than about a hundred I suppose; with some help, of course.' Daphne looked away, smiling.

'Goodness!' she said.

'The family call you Robbie, don't they?'

'Yes, Ma'm, but that's because my name is Robina.'

'Oh I see!' said Daphne. 'That's a lovely name, unusual. What do you prefer?'

'Oh Robbie does me,' said Robina.

'Robbie it is then.'

'Turn left here, Ma'm, if you don't mind, and it's the third on the left, by the lamp-post.'

As Daphne drove away, Robbie groped in her bag for the key and opened the door. As she stepped inside she had a strange feeling looking back at the so-familiar stained glass panel in the front door, the colours glowing in the light from the street lamp. It was as though it was no longer hers. She pushed the door to, lifted the night latch and switched on the hall light. Removing her hat and coat, she hung them on the mirrored hallstand that she and Ken had bought, with most of the other furniture, at Thame auction rooms.

With a little sigh she went into the front room and flopped back in the huge leather armchair which was part of the three-piece suite that they had acquired, through the local newspaper, for five pounds. With the events of the day crowding into her thoughts, and the overwhelming feeling of relief, she buried her face in her hands and burst into tears.

To the major, it was a matter of courtesy towards the staff to be punctual at meals, if he could, and not cause them to be late finishing their work; and at one o'clock precisely, he made his appearance through the dining-room door. He took a seat where he thought he could talk easily to as many others as possible, in the hope that he could find someone going into Thame that afternoon, although scarcely any of them possessed transport of their own; perhaps, he thought, he might be able to share a taxi.

'Hello, Major, you're going to sit there are you?' said the rhetorically gifted Tracey. 'What would you like today – soup as usual, eh! Major?'

Without answering, he took the teenager's hand and drew her confidentially closer.

'Try and find out if anyone's going into Thame this afternoon,' he muttered, winking archly.

'If you hear of anyone, just give me the tip,

dear,' he added, without need; then, 'By the by, what is the soup?' he queried.

'Onion,' she replied, 'and Ramiro's going in to the town as soon as he's finished.'

'Oh, good! Ask him to come and see me before he goes, there's a good girl.'

Back in his room, the major filled his pipe and, striking a match, leaned back in his chair. He had definitely decided to put his plans into effect and was looking forward to it.

It was happy timing, he thought, that the windfall coincided with his new plans; a sort of omen, an encouragement to get on with it.

His thoughts lingered on the subject of 'coincidence'. Where chance was concerned, and contrary to popular philosophy, he had long regarded coincidence as the best odds to choose, when available, since there was no reason to choose any other and as coincidences 'do' occur, he would always put his money on them as the best if not the only chance.

The weather had cleared up to a pretty good afternoon. The sun was dancing in and out as the clouds thinned, making a much better prospect of 'shopping'. By and large he was feeling quite perky when Ramiro knocked on the door.

'Come in, Ramiro,' he called, and the boy entered.

'All finished?' asked the major.

'*Si*, Major,' replied Ramiro.

The major registered the 'pun', but said nothing; it occurred all the time, such as Tracey's 'Eh! Major.'

'Off to Thame, I hear,' he observed to Ramiro.

'*Si, Si*,' enthused Ramiro smiling widely.

'Wouldn't care to give me a lift would you, old boy?' enquired the major hopefully.'

'*Si, claro que si*,' said Ramiro in some confusion, being taken aback by the sudden honour of having the major as passenger in his aged M.G. which had gained the epithet of 'The Hornet', for reasons the major would soon discover.

Twenty-five minutes later they turned into the car park across from the Spreadeagle Hotel. As Ramiro had only one call to make, they decided to stay together rather than invite complication by splitting up. Ramiro obtained his requirements from the auto-spares shop close by the car before they set off in search of the major's listed items, calling first at the bank.

As they walked past the town hall, his new interest in birds reminded him of the big Christmas tree, normally located at that point and lit with white lights from top to bottom, which one year attracted a huge flock of wagtails, perhaps 70 or 80 in number. They adopted the upper reaches of the tree, as a nice warm overnight roost for the holidays; boisterously commuting with the surrounding rooftops throughout the hours of illumination and adding to the festive life of the town.

While paying in the precious cheque, the major took the precaution of asking the clerk to confirm its validity, which took a few minutes, during which time the major's pulse crept up as his thoughts fluttered between opposing emotions as to whether Dingwall would prove to be benefactor or bounder.

The clerk returned, squirming back on to his high stool, and, with an affirmative smile, nodded confirmation. Being £5,000 to the better, the major would have opted for new binoculars rather than second-hand, as he had at first intended. However, Ramiro spotted a pair in the window of a second-hand shop and suggested having a look; they might just as well 'as they were there', he proposed. The major was dubious, but agreed there was nothing to lose by looking at them as they appeared to be as good as new.

The proprietor pointed out that the glasses were in perfect condition, of the highest quality, and while seemingly expensive, would cost, as new, far more than most people could afford to contemplate. Furthermore, he explained, he had been entrusted with their disposal, by the widow of the former owner – a naturalist of wide repute. By this provenance he was entirely confident in offering them as ideal for the purpose intended; being remarkably light-weight for 'Nine-fifties' – an unusual specification. They were sure to prove much superior in performance to the more commonly used 'Eight-forties', and – 'importantly' – scarcely more in weight.

The major agreed to try them outside and was astonished at the clarity and brightness of the images. He swept his gaze along the rooftops, resting variously on a pigeon preening its breast, a group of jackdaws squabbling over a scrap of food, and a sparrow basking in the sun between two chimney pots. His spirits rose at the very feel of the glasses. Such was the balance and comfort afforded by the rubberised finish that he felt quite desperate to use them in earnest and, despite the cost, resolved not to part with them. He paid the proprietor the required amount adding, in a rush of enthusiasm, a further ten pounds to be passed on to the widow, with his compliments and condolences.

Visiting the bookshop, the major purchased a compact textbook on British birds, recommended by the bookseller as being the most popular among local ornithologists. They spent some time in the sports' shop selecting a light haversack before calling at Glynswood's for a notebook and then crossing the road back to the car park. They set off for home with the new possessions safely stowed in the haversack and much kindly advice to bear in mind.

Ramiro, anxious to impress the major with his driving prowess, achieved the opposite, taking bends and straights with equal disdain. The major had contained his alarm during the outward journey, but 'broke' on the way back.

As Haddenham was passed, seemingly in a few seconds, he felt compelled to observe, 'You know, old boy, a man cannot go far wrong with his driving if he keeps his mind on the tyres!'

Ramiro, however, appeared not to interpret that pearl of wisdom as being either relevant to the moment or anything more than a general observation and continued the remaining part of the journey with equal zest.

'Steady, old boy, you'll have the C.O. after you,' said the major, as the wheels locked and slid for two feet in the gravel outside the Lodge entrance.

The major thankfully hauled himself and baggage out of the low seat and made his way stiffly towards the stone-framed entrance porch. Ramiro made himself and car scarce, before either could be caught on dangerous ground; he had been told to keep his rusty wreck out of sight round the back in the stable block.

'Good afternoon, Major,' rumbled Mrs Currer-Spriggs, greeting him from her sitting room doorway as he was passing through the broad, panelled hall. 'Have you time for a cup of tea?' she enquired.

'That would be delightful – thank you,' the major replied, with genuine relish, and altered course to follow her into the focus of her very comfortable world.

'Do sit down, Major,' she purred, like a huge cat, sinking into her usual chair.

The major felt just a bit awkward, wondering what to do with his shopping, and, signifying an armchair said, 'May I?'

'Of course, where you like. Don't worry about those. Just drop them by the door,' she said, picking up the telephone from a small elegant table at her side. 'Oh! Robbie, be a dear and send Tracey through with some tea would you? Two cups, please. Thank you. Has the order arrived from Budgen's yet?' she added. 'Well could you let me know when it does, they're bringing something for me. Thank you, Robbie.'

She dropped the phone gently down and smiled at the major.

'I heard that you'd gone out; had I known you were going shopping you could have come with me this morning,' she said warmly.

The major described the events of the day, explaining that the timing precluded that opportunity.

'What a charming idea,' she said, referring to his new plans, 'I'm so pleased – it will do you the world of good, I'm sure.'

A discreet knock announced the arrival of Tracey with the tea trolley.

'Come in, dear,' Daphne called.

Tracey wheeled the trolley over to where Mrs Currer-Spriggs was sitting.

'I've brought the tea, Ma'm, would you like me to pour out?'

'No, we'll manage all right, thank you, dear. I'm sure Mrs Robertson needs you more than we do.'

'Thank you, ma'm,' said Tracey, glad to be spared, and made for the door.

'Oh Tracey, dear, before you go, would you mind taking those things for the major?' she said, indicating the bags. 'Just put them in his room, please.'

'Awfully kind,' muttered the major awkwardly, 'really no need.'

He was glad, nevertheless, to be free of the encumbrances.

'Can't help feeling I'm in for a dressing-down, Mrs Currer-Spriggs,' he said, when the door had closed.

'What on earth makes you say that?' she said, laughing.

'Well! Hauled up before the C.O? Dunno

what to think.'

'Oh! Major, really!' she purred. 'How could you imagine such a thing?'

With a quizzical look at the major she went on, 'We've known each other for long enough now not to fall into any misunderstandings; I would much prefer it if you called me Daphne. Would you mind? It's such a bother otherwise.'

'Well! Thank you, Mrs ... er, Daphne, absolutely fine by me. In private, of course,' he replied, adding, 'as long as you're happy with "Major".'

'Oh! yes, it suits you very well I think. There we are then, that's nice! Have some more cake, Major.'

'Ah! Better not; don't want Mrs Robertson after me for eating cake before dinner, do I?'

'Well, she made it,' replied Daphne.

'Were you successful with your shopping?' she enquired.

'Yes very, had a bit of luck in fact, thanks to Ramiro.'

'Indeed?' Daphne responded.

The major outlined their progress in Thame, with some enigmatic comment on Ramiro's driving style, which prompted her to add that she intended to make a few observations of her own to him.

'Well, if you'll forgive me,' the major said, standing up after some 15 minutes of discourse, 'I must be getting on with things or I shall be late on parade.'

'Of course, Major, thank you so much for joining me, it was kind of you. I'll look forward to seeing you later.'

'Yes indeed, er, Daphne, and thank you for the very welcome "cuppa".'

'Not a bad day, one way and another,' observed the major to himself while shaving before dinner.

Saturday, even for the elderly, still remained special somehow, engendering the feeling that it shouldn't be wasted. The notion that it was intended for enjoyment, as an entitlement, seemed to persist into retirement when there was no longer any practical difference between one day and another. Sunday also maintained its peculiar character: one of sombre restraint, with a dark velvety background by tradition, as though to atone for the naughtiness of Saturday, before a clean sheet was started on Monday.

Perhaps each of the seven days should be accorded a colour from the rainbow as best suited its character. Seven colours for seven days, he frivolously mused. Saturday would certainly be red, Sunday indigo, Monday blue and so on. Such trivial notions can be occasioned by mild euphoria, he supposed, dragging his mind back to the present. He was looking forward greatly to the steak suet roll he had selected for dinner and, donning his comfortable well-worn dinner jacket, set off for the sitting room, with a warm sense of wellbeing.

It was the custom of the 'House' for everyone to dress formally for dinner on the first Saturday of the month. The tables would be arranged in a broad oblong, to encourage a festive atmosphere. Daphne Currer-Spriggs liked nothing better than a party and ensured that no one's pleasure was neglected. The residents were invited to make an appearance in the sitting room between seven and seven-thirty, where Ramiro acted as barman, serving pre-prandials to order from the portable bar trolley that was his joyful responsibility.

Wine was freely provided 'on the house,' during the meal, with good port and brandy as desired afterwards. The guests were of an age to appreciate the old-style pleasures afforded them and while smoking was taboo prior to the loyal toast, those who preferred to, took coffee and petits fours etc. in the drawing room, which was acknowledged to be a smoke-free area. While 30 or 40 years ago the meal would have included courses such as fish and Welsh rarebit, in addition to the usual four or five courses, advancing age reduced appetites considerably, though adding relish to what there was.

These occasions were invariably a great success and the major strode into the sitting room, glowing with anticipation. It seemed to him that Ramiro was looking uncharacteristically nervous and being not a little ham-fisted.

'You all right, old boy?' he enquired quietly.

'*Si*, Major, thank you.'

'If you say so.'

The major shrugged his shoulders.

'Gin and tonic, Major?'

'Thanks, old boy.'

The major carried his drink to where Daphne was chatting to Tom Beardmore.

'Good evening, Major,' they chorused.

'My dear, you look magnificent as always,' he said to Daphne. 'How're things, Tom?' he enquired, smiling at Tom who replied, grinning, 'O.K. thanks. I hear you're about to become a "twitcher".'

At this, Daphne excused herself saying, 'I must have a word with Robbie, before we start,' and slid away to the kitchen, before having to explain the leak of information

'Twitcher?' enquired the major, mystified.

'People who chase after birds,' said Tom, wringing extra inference from the expression. 'That's what they call them these days.'

'Damned if I fancy that,' replied the major. 'Pack it in before I start,' he said looking slightly put out.

'No, no, no,' said Tom. 'Forget it – sorry I mentioned it – never another word,' he promised.

'I should think not,' said the major.

'By the by, old boy,' he continued, leaning confidentially to Tom's ear, 'what's up with Ramiro? Doesn't seem himself at all somehow.'

'Yes,' replied Tom, 'I noticed that – mentioned it to the boss just now, thinking he was in the doghouse for some reason, but she said nothing.'

Couldn't have been to do with parking at the front this afternoon, the major thought; he wasn't there more than a minute; never mind, we'd no doubt hear all about it soon enough.

Conversation was gradually growing louder as the company continued to mingle and at twenty-five past seven a resounding bang on the gong served notice that dinner would be announced by a further wallop five minutes later. Daphne left it to the guests themselves to sort out the seating arrangements, without the formality of place cards, on the basis that conversations and preferred associations could be continued into the dining room. It seemed to work well enough and any little awkwardness was soon ironed out in the atmosphere of jollity. Being ultra-sensitive to any sign of friction, and a genius at reconciliation, she was able to keep her chosen 'band' relaxed and communally contented at all times.

It escaped no one's notice that Ramiro was wearing thin white gloves while attending to wines 'at table'; which was assumed to be a new refinement. When someone remarked on the point to Daphne, she passed it off with a seraphic smile, allowing a suspicion of 'intrigue' to germinate. A touch of mystery would add interest to the evening, and where Ramiro was concerned, perhaps the lesson would sink in and he would take better care of his hands in future.

The circumstances arose after Ramiro had released the captive major and driven round to the stables where he kept his car. Thinking he had sufficient time to fit the new part to the engine, he set about the job there and then, only to find after an hour's labour that he was nowhere near finished. Realising that he was due to report to Mrs Robertson for duty in a few minutes, he raced up to his room above the stables, to scrub up and change.

After a frantic session of scrubbing with hot water and soap, he looked desperately at the results and cursed himself for starting the job instead of leaving it until Sunday afternoon. His hands were an even grey colour when he walked into the kitchen at five o'clock to join the general bustle of activity.

'Better not let "Madam" see you with your hands in your pockets,' said Mrs Robertson. 'Slovenly, she'll call it. Go and help Tracey to lay the table.'

Ramiro was glad of an early escape from closer scrutiny, and disappeared into the dining room.

'Goodness!' exclaimed Tracey, 'look at your hands; she'll go mad if she sees them like that.'

'*Si, Si,*' lamented Ramiro. 'What can I do? Nothing.'

He contrived to avoid revealing his shame whenever Mrs Robertson looked in to supervise the table layout, but when they finished the table at six-thirty, he knew the moment of truth could arrive when he collected the key to the wine room.

His luck held a while longer when Mrs Robertson, seeing him come in to the kitchen, pointed to the far end of the long worktop, saying 'The key's on the end there, Ramiro; hurry up, you haven't got long.'

He grabbed the key and shot off to prepare his mobile bar.

He almost survived his stint in the sitting room, but luck deserted him just as the second gong sounded and people surged towards the dining room. Daphne smiled at Ramiro as she put her glass on the trolley on the way out. The smile froze for an instant as Ramiro stretched down to catch something falling off the trolley; then a look of horror took its place as the discoloured palm came into view. She stifled a shriek.

'Oh my God,' she said quietly as the last guest passed through the doorway towards the dining room.

'What!' she began to say to the petrified Ramiro, 'How in God's name did you get into that state?'

'*Lo siento*,' stammered Ramiro, struggling to orientate his thoughts into coherent English.

He attempted to explain his trouble with the car.

'Don't move,' she interrupted, and rushed away, returning shortly. 'Put these on,' she commanded, proffering the white gloves. 'I'll see you later,' she hissed and hurried towards the dining room, furious at having to keep the company waiting.

She took her place at the head of the table and beamed radiantly as the male guests sat down, oblivious of any crisis.

As a matter of damage limitation Ramiro had composed himself and resolved to be extra cautious and attentive in his duties. Consequently, no wine was spilt, no glasses clashed and no complaints were incurred. He quailed whenever Daphne caught his eye, but as the evening wore on he dared to fancy that her glances were progressively softer, and even persuaded himself that a hint of sympathy was forming in the steely smiles.

It was after the cheese and port were exploited to the full that the major suggested leaving the table free for Tracey and her helper to get on with clearing away. Most of the ladies had moved to the drawing room, from where peals of laughter were emanating as Minnie Caple recalled some of her experiences in the Land Army. In the sitting room Joyce Kingham was finishing a miniature cigar and chatting to Sandy Balfour, who was gradually disappearing, with a large brandy, behind a cloud of his own cigar smoke.

'What ho! L.-J.,' he called, from the depths of his armchair, as the major came in brandishing his pipe and followed by Tom Beardmore and others.

'Who's that?' queried the major, peering through the haze.

'Oh! It's you, old boy.'

Joyce decided to retire to bed while she could still get there and, downing the remains of her Cointreau, rose to her feet saying,

'Goodnight everyone, lovely evening,' and fell straight back into the chair again. 'Oops!' she said and made another attempt.

'Steady! old girl,' said Tom Beardmore, as she swayed on her feet, slightly. 'I'd better see you to your room, I think.'

Supporting her elbow, he steered her through the door.

'Brandy for me,' he mouthed, glancing back at the major. 'See you shortly.'

'So I should hope!' quipped the major.

Ramiro was thankful that it was the one occasion in the month when he didn't have to keep note of the drinks ordered. It was tedious enough at the best of times and he had discovered that it was almost impossible to write properly with gloves on.

As the drinks were distributed to the late arrivals, Ramiro struggled to cope with the discomfort of the gloves, until Sam Willoughby said, 'Why don't you take those damned gloves off, Ramiro, they must be driving you potty!'

'Yes, take them off,' said Daphne, gliding into the room and motioning the occupants to remain seated.

'Time to come clean eh, Ramiro,' she said, putting an arm round his shoulder and giving him a little squeeze.

'*Si Señora,*' he said, peeling-off the, by then, saturated and discoloured gloves to reveal the subject of his minor guilt.

'Goodnight, gentlemen,' said Daphne with a broad smile and, before anyone could get up, swished out again, heading for a good night's sleep.

'Listen to me, old boy,' the major said to Ramiro. 'I suppose you washed your hands in hot water, did you?'

'*Si, claro* – of course,' said Ramiro.

'Well you take my tip, never wash your hands in hot water! The blacker, the oilier, and the greasier they are, the colder the water should be. Stick your hands in hot water and what happens? The pores of your skin open up and the oil and grease thin out to soak through your skin. With cold water,' he went on, 'your skin stays smooth, the soap gets under the "muck" which slides off. Nine times out of ten you'll end up with pink hands instead of grey ones. Do you understand me?'

'*Si*, Major,' replied Ramiro, suitably abashed.

'Remember, hard soap, a good brush and cold water,' ended the major.

The logic of this homily left the audience as profoundly impressed as it had Ramiro and seemed to signify a natural conclusion to the evening's events. Half an hour later, all but Sandy and the major had retired. Having secured a 'nightcap' from Ramiro, they suggested that he should park his trolley and get off to bed, which he was thankful to do.

'How long have you been here now?' the major enquired casually.

'Ah, about four years I suppose. Arrived not long before Sam I believe. Three years after Pat died, and a year after I packed in the business.'

'Do you miss the business much?' asked the major.

'No, not really,' Sandy replied. 'It's satisfying enough to just look back on it all and ponder the changes over the years. Since my father started business in our old town in the late twenties, the electrical and radio trade has undergone astonishing changes.

'To begin with, half of the cottages had no electricity at all; others had basic lighting circuits with no provision of plug sockets for any kind of appliance; not that there were many to have anyway. An early type of supplementary heating appeared in the form of a four hundred and fifty watt cylindrical element plugged into a circular reflector on a stand: it was called a bowl-fire, cost twenty-two shillings, and could be plugged into a lamp holder. That gave rise to the use of the "two-way adaptor"; known generally as a "heat and light" adaptor; forming two sockets; one for a light bulb which was separately switched; and one for an appliance. Another increasingly used device was the electric iron, designed to the same wattage. I suppose the reason for rating the appliances at four hundred and fifty watts lay in the fact that two together amounted to nine hundred; which left room for a couple of lamps to be used at the same time without the fuse blowing; the limit for lighting circuits being a thousand watts as, indeed, it still is.

'Up to that time, it was rare for a fuse to blow; but from then on, it was a regular call out, costing a shilling to have the fuse wire replaced: people didn't do things for themselves in those days, especially where the mysterious and hazardous electricity was concerned. An electric iron lead, constantly pulling on the light pendant, was a sure source of trouble; otherwise it was usually due to overload.

'There was always plenty of work, wiring houses that had no electricity, and adding power points to those that had. Sales of battery radios were increasing rapidly; followed by battery eliminators, for those who later acquired mains wiring. The worst problem we had was the existence of two electricity suppliers in the area. One supplied at two hundred volts, while the other was two hundred and thirty. Appliances rated at two-thirty wouldn't work on two hundred and those at two hundred would burn-out on two-thirty. That meant that we had to keep twice as many lamp-bulbs, fire elements, irons, toasters, and so on.'

'You should write a book about it,' the major interjected.

'No thanks,' replied Sandy, 'that would mean spending my time worrying, when I'm supposed to be resting from my labours, not reliving them!'

'You could always give after-dinner talks,' persisted the major.

'Give me a break, L.-J. I just want to die in peace. I'll leave all that to others if you don't mind. In any case, I've given quite enough "talks" as it is, to Round Table and others.'

'Well, I expect you enjoyed doing it, didn't you?'

'I suppose so,' Sandy conceded.

'I wonder who's been here the longest,' he added after a pause.

'I've really no idea,' replied the major. 'Jane and Elsie have done fourteen years.'

'Good God!' said Sandy. 'Really?'

'I believe so. Maisie is the oldest resident, as far as I know, but she hasn't been here as long as they have.'

'Why does time seem to pass so much more quickly than it used to?' the major posed. 'My perception of time is just about fifty per cent of reality. If I have to assess when an event took place, it will invariably prove to be twice as long ago as I thought; whether in weeks or in years. Everyone repeatedly says "Doesn't the time fly by?" And why do people look younger than they are, these days, does time pass too quickly to keep up with it?'

'Maybe the universe is speeding up and because of relativity only the human mind can detect the difference,' offered Sandy.

'I don't know whether it's relevant to your

point,' he continued, 'but one thing that puzzles me is why it now takes six minutes to boil an egg, starting from boiling, when in the old days it used to take three, as far as I remember. You can't tell me it's because eggs are bigger, or because they're kept in a fridge!'

'There's very little difference in temperature, between a fridge and a cold pantry. Actually, I've had it in mind to look out for an old egg-timer, to find out how long it takes to run out, in case I've got it all wrong.'

'Why bother when you can probably look it up?' suggested the major. 'I believe there's a Pears in the bookcase.'

'I shouldn't think it would be in that, would it?' said Sandy.

'Why not? You never know; you can't be bothered to go and see can you?' the major taunted.

He was, in fact, quite intrigued to know the answer himself. Sandy made no reply, but pushed himself up stiffly and shuffled off to the drawing room, returning shortly with the Pears Encyclopaedia. He flopped back in his chair and searched through General Information.

'Nothing under "egg", or "timer". I told you,' Sandy concluded, closing the book.

'Look under hourglass, it seems more likely to me,' said the major.

Sandy re-opened the book and quickly

found, to his surprise, 'Hour-glass', followed by a description, and ending with 'egg-glass' a smaller version which runs out in three minutes.

'There you are, I was absolutely right,' he pronounced triumphantly, slamming the book shut. 'Anyway, I've never really believed in time as a dimension,' he went on. 'If you ask me, it's all to do with the rate of change; the universe is running on the spot and going nowhere so to speak, despite the pace changing.'

'I don't think you know what you're talking about, do you?' suggested the major.

'No, not at this time of night,' said Sandy. 'But you did ask! Anyway, as far as today is concerned, I'm for bed.'

'Hear, hear, old boy!' said the major, levering himself out of his chair. 'See you tomorrow.'

Chapter 3

Tribulations

A bright morning dawned, with frost covering the lawns and flowerbeds. Chattering magpies and the harsh squawks of jays failed to rouse the recovering revellers from their slumbers. A clatter of pans revealed the presence of Mrs Robertson in the kitchen, for whom lying in meant not getting up until six-thirty. Come what may, she would be found putting the kettle on at a quarter to six, long before the sky responded to the returning sun.

The milk float came whining quietly round to the back of the house and Marge Watts came through the kitchen door to plonk the first crate on the floor. As she returned with the second, to 'plink' on top, Robbie pushed a large breakfast cup of tea across the scrubbed wood table and sat down for the brief morning chinwag. Marge pulled off her mitten gloves and dropped them on the table, blowing her cold fingers as she sat down.

She looked across at Robbie, with a broad wrinkly smile, and winked.

'Ta,' she said, placing her palms close to the hot cup.

'I've put a bit of cold in it,' said Robbie.

'Ta,' repeated Marge. 'It's beginning to get a bit lighter, of a morning,' she added, stirring her tea and blowing across the top of the cup.

'Yes, it'll be spring again before we know it,' Robbie declared.

'I know, don't that old time go fast!' Marge replied 'Funny how everybody says that, these days.'

With a concerned look, Robbie said, 'Do you feel safe, driving around in the dark on your own?'

'Oh yeah!' replied Marge, 'I'd like to see anybody get the better of me,' she said, with defiant conviction and a knowing wink.

'That's all very well for you to say,' returned Robbie. 'You never know what's going to happen these days; you read such dreadful things in the papers now; I don't think anybody's safe anymore. I expect your mum worries, don't she? How is she anyway, she out yet?'

'No, they're keeping her in till her pressure's down a bit. They reckon she'll be all right by Tuesday; then Bill's going to fetch her when they ring.'

Marge gazed round the kitchen.

'I can't think how you manage all that lot,' she said, indicating with her thumb towards the dining room door.

'A bit of discipline and a lot of practice,' replied Robbie.

'Well, this wunt buy the baby a new 'at,' said Marge, standing up and pulling on her gloves. She took the empty cup to the sink. 'Thanks very much,' she said, making for the door, and throwing a 'Tatta!' towards Robbie, disappeared back into the gloom of the yard.

By daylight, Robbie was well on with the breakfast arrangements. She anticipated that, by the sound of things last night, a good few would be having breakfast late, and most of them in bed at that. She looked at the list that Tracey had pinned up the night before. Yes, she thought, they would have their work cut out when she and Ramiro turned up at eight o'clock. There would be no extra staff in for breakfast. Glancing out of the window, by chance, she caught sight of the major crossing the gap between the corner of the house and the end of the stable block. Well, well, she thought – full marks for the major. I wonder where he's off to?

When the major had set his alarm clock for seven o'clock, it was in a surge of enthusiasm, before going to dinner, in case he later forgot to do it. As it was, he woke up to find it a bit darker than he had anticipated, not being used to the world at that hour. He, nevertheless, rose and dressed in eager preparation for his first foray into the wild. It was much lighter by the time he set off at seven-thirty, exiting by the French windows of his room.

Ah, this is the life, he thought, breathing in the sharp morning air, as he followed the curving line of rhododendrons crossing the lawn towards the little wooden gate that led into the meadow beyond. Despite the evening before, he felt surprisingly fresh and energetic. The gate was really more of a door and was collapsing with age; he had to lift it by the handle to move it on the hinges as a bit more of the fading green paint flaked off.

The sunshine glittered on the water of the small chalk stream that crossed the meadow, heading down towards the road where it disappeared into a large section of pipe running under the road. He remembered hearing talk of rats being seen around the culvert and supposed that that was where it referred to.

He was startled out of his wits by the sudden loud 'Cloik, cloik, cloik' of a largish olive-green bird that rose from the grass nearby and sped away to the cover of some trees on the edge of the meadow.

To his astonishment, the utter surprise of it set his heart pounding. He could still see the bird in the top branches and squinted to make out more of it. It was a full 20 seconds of screwing his eyes up in an endeavour to discern more detail before he thought of the binoculars round his neck, and feeling an idiot, raised them up to focus them just as the bird flew off farther, out of sight.

Damned fool, he thought to himself. Realising he was shaking with tension, he started to laugh and resolved to get a grip of himself and take things easy. This was supposed to be a pleasure not a bloody battle. It was a kind of baptism, he thought; so be it, he could now pull himself together and start to enjoy it. He followed the little stream up towards the scarp to where its spring emerged from the ground with a rippling sound. Along the foot of the scarp there were many such springs that ran through fields and gardens in the area.

Two small birds with long tails and yellow breasts were flitting and bobbing about at the water's edge. He stopped to have a closer look at them through the glasses. He guessed that they were probably wagtails, from what little he knew, and soon found from the book that they were, in fact, grey wagtails. He'd heard of yellow wagtails and these were certainly yellow, so why grey? he thought. He looked in the book again and found, on the following page, yellow wagtail, having even more yellow on it. He would soon become an expert, he thought to himself.

When he moved towards them, they skittered away about 20 yards and settled again on a rusty barbed-wire fence, twittering excitedly, their tails continually bobbing up and down. As he neared the spring, they took off again, one chasing after the other; fluttering and swooping low to the ground; right down the slope to drop down to the stream again close to the culvert.

He stood for a while gazing into the water and noticed some very small black objects appearing to defy the fairly fast flow of the water, but they were too small for their shape to be discerned.

The major was pondering the matter when he realised that his feet were getting not only freezing cold but he fancied they were also beginning to feel distinctly damp. Oh dear, he thought, there was much to learn about this game. Obviously shoes, however stout, were not the answer to standing around in frosty or damp places. Never mind, he would acquire some suitable boots anon and, undaunted, resumed his walk to learn whatever else was in store for him.

He was mounting a stile when he both heard and saw the green bird again, about 200 yards along the hedge to his right. Gotcha, he thought, and calmly raising his glasses, focused on what he supposed was a green woodpecker. He was amazed and thrilled at how close it seemed to be and he studied it for some time, taking in as much detail as he could. Settling himself on the stile, he sat there referring to his new book. Sure enough, he had guessed right – a green woodpecker. Furthermore, on the following page was the great-spotted woodpecker he had seen on the nut cage the day before.

What next? he thought, feeling that a start had been made and his binoculars were all that he hoped for. He looked at his watch and was astonished to see that the half hour or so that he thought he'd been out, was, in fact, an hour and a quarter. He also realised that he was close to starving and had little time to get back for breakfast; everything seemed to have grown disappointingly quiet anyway.

At that point he suddenly felt an overwhelming desire to lie down somewhere and go to sleep in the warm sunshine. The delayed action of his true condition was beginning to take effect and he found himself quite unable to stop yawning.

The moment he started back, everything seemed to come alive around him, and he was tempted, time and again, to stop and look at things. How could it be so quiet one moment and lively the next? He was to learn, eventually, that it was almost a rule of nature for things to be that way.

'You're going to sit there then, Major,' observed Tracey, when he hurried into the dining room, and took his usual seat. 'What can I get you today?'

'Full house,' he replied eagerly, rubbing his hands together, 'Leave it to you, dear; sorry to be late.'

'You're not late,' she giggled. 'Coffee, Major?'

'On the double.'

'Right,' she said and hurried off to the kitchen.

He glanced out of the window and saw the

inseparable Mesdames Fuller and Redrup walking down the drive on their way to church. It was their 'little walk' as they called it, refusing all offers of a 'lift', whatever the weather; and besides, they would say, it gave them an appetite for lunch.

'Mrs Robertson says she hopes you had a nice walk, and thank you for sorting out Ramiro,' said Tracey, on her return.

'She's heard then?' said the major, looking up at her.

'Everybody's heard,' she replied. 'Though Mrs Robertson only found out this morning.'

'My compliments to her; let's hope he remembers what I said.'

'I'm sure he will, he thinks the world of you,' she confided.

Resisting the temptation to rest his elbows on the table and nod off, head in hands, the major opened his Saturday *Telegraph* which he hadn't read the day before.

He just had time to glance at his bank shares, and to take in the small shift downwards, when, 'Mind if I join you, L.-J.?' interrupted the slightly nasal voice of George Sargent.

The major folded his paper, saying, 'You're more than welcome, old boy; glad to see I'm not the only one late this morning.'

'We're not late, we're just not early!' George grinned. 'I expect most of them are still in bed.'

'Where's your namesake?' the major asked.

'Smiler? Still in his hammock I expect, unless he's gone off for a round of golf with Tom,' George suggested.

'No! I saw Tom sitting on the veranda a few minutes ago, swigging coffee: I expect the sun's pretty warm by now. Think I'll join him after,' the major replied.

'Morning, Mr Sargent; you'd like some breakfast too I expect?' said Tracey, unloading the major's coffee, toast and a plate with two sheets of fried bread piled with rich brown stewed kidney.

'There!' said Tracey, beaming, 'Mrs Robertson says you've earned it.'

'By Jove,' said the major. 'My thanks to Mrs Robertson.'

'Good show last night,' he said, pausing after a few mouthfuls; 'what with Smiler swinging the lamp and that Minnie Caple; as good as a music hall, I thought.'

'Well, you had everybody open-mouthed, over your lecture to Ramiro; I reckon we all learned something from that,' said George.

'I think he had a bit of a caning one way and another, figuratively speaking, poor chap,' said the major.

'Takes you back to school again, eh! Did you ever get the cane?' asked George, shifting the subject a degree.

'Quite often,' the major replied. 'It wasn't that difficult to incur where I was. It was always carried out by the housemaster. None of this Tom Brown nonsense about doing it in front of the whole school. I suppose the war changed a lot of things. They were enlightened enough to realise that, being physically painful, it served its purpose without the need for humiliation.'

'How many wallops did you get?' asked George.

'Three as a rule. The housemaster would tell you what time to report to the dormitory and there you would bend over the end of your bed to receive the sentence. The first whack would sting like billy-ho, but you were too numb to feel the third. Boys in the know would endeavour to find some sort of packing to reduce the effect; which was alright as long as it wasn't detected. What intrigued me though was the fact that we had to shake hands with the housemaster and say thank you afterwards, to show there were no hard feelings. Crying was fatal to the reputation and was no doubt borne in mind in character reports; though eye-watering was accepted as inevitable.'

'It never happened to me, I'm glad to say; I managed to avoid it, though I was for ever doing lines,' said George.

'Ah, yes, well for minor offences the standard form of punishment for us,' the major continued, 'was the award of P.C.'s, the dreaded penal-copies, which cost a penny and consisted of an A4 card on which was printed a row of script at the top which could be in one of various languages, with thirty or forty plain lines, below. The script had to be copied exactly on each line, and the completed card handed in to the author of the imposition, who could be a master or even a prefect, by a certain day and time.

'The number of cards meted out at a time reflected the magnitude of the crime. An unsatisfactory copy resulted in a repeat penalty. The worst thing about it was the depletion of your one and sixpence a week pocket money.

'There was a time when an acute national paper shortage occurred, whereupon PCs became unobtainable. Celebrations were short-lived though because some building work was in progress near the music school. As it happened, a pile of rubble had to be moved some distance from the building site to a place near the swimming pool. Thus was authority able to kill two birds by the imaginative substitution of one PC with one bucket of bricks. At least we weren't judged on the condition of the bricks when we dumped them,' concluded the major.

Smiler made a sudden appearance and, sitting down at the next table, turned the nearest chair to face them, saying, 'I've just come in for a cup of coffee, that's all. I'll hold out till lunch if I can, after last night. Have I been missing anything?' he asked looking at George.

'L.-J. says you're a music hall turn,' replied George.

'Does he now? By, it's a long time since I were in a music hall,' Smiler responded.

'Nineteen forty-nine to be exact, if memory serves.'

Tracey came with George's order, and looked at Smiler.

'Hello, Mr Townend, you sitting there are you?'

'Just a cup of coffee'll do, luv,' he replied with a twinkling smile.

'Aye,' he resumed, 'I were ashore in Chatham one night and thought I'd try the old Chatham Empire. Mind you, it were all films by then, even in those days, except for the interval when they'd an organ come up in the pit. Sometimes local talent would go up and perform all sorts. Anyway, it had got to the end of the programme and there were the usual rush to get to the exit before the National Anthem could start. There were an old couple sat behind me and the wife were about to join the general exodus when the old chap grabbed her arm and boomed in a loud Yorkshire voice, "Wait Mother – others mayn't."'

'I can well believe that,' said George

Sargent. 'It seems amazing now that the first notes of the anthem would stop everyone in their tracks, to face the screen and stand to attention until the last note sounded, before the rush resumed.'

'Aye!' Smiler added with a grin. 'And those caught halfway through the door had to make an instant decision; whether to stop and turn round, or carry on with their ears burning, all the way down the stairs.'

It was George Townend's natural and permanent broad smile which endeared him to all his acquaintances and earned him the nickname of Smiler which he had carried for most of his life including his National Service time as a signalman in the Royal Navy; and in the present circumstances to distinguish him from George Sargent. He was entirely devoid of social inhibitions and mixed easily in any company. Daphne had, at the outset, recognised him as a potentially colourful asset to her community, which he had proved to be.

When his wife died, George had sold his stationery business and come south from his home town of Leeds to live with his daughter before finding Anvil Lodge through an old navy friend, Bob Wake, who lived in the area. As a hobby, he had made a definitive study of the American Air Force presence in Britain during the last war and after extensive travel and research had become an authority on the subject. He had, furthermore, to his great credit, recently brought about, after immense effort, the erection of a memorial to the crew of a R.A.F. Halifax bomber that crashed near his home at Tingley during the war.

He was moved to do so by the memory that had stayed with him since boyhood, of seeing the wreckage from the bus on his way to grammar school. An annual service is still held at the memorial, and Smiler was the subject of an hour-long radio programme relating the story.

The patches of snowdrops, here and there amongst the shrubbery, were giving way to the vigorous clumps of crocus. Life was gradually returning to the dormant world as the earth drew, daily, nearer to the sun. Such thoughts occupied the major's mind as he was strolling round the grounds after his late breakfast, followed by a leisurely mid-morning coffee on the veranda.

He came upon the figure of Madge Russell who had found a quiet secluded spot and was sitting on an old wooden bench-seat, holding a letter and dabbing at her eyes with a handkerchief. The embroidered linen was saturated with tears and still she wept; nor could she stop when the major stood before her.

'Whatever's this, old girl,' was all he could

think of saying while taking the liberty of sitting beside her.

Madge, the youngest and newest resident, was an extremely well-preserved lady who retained that essential prettiness that can remain with some women for life, and occasions such comments as, 'She must have been a stunner in her day.' Seen from behind she would be perceived as much younger than her 62 years. The major took a handkerchief from his top pocket and placed it on her lap; removing the wet lump from her hand to his side pocket.

'This won't do,' he said taking her small hand. 'Care to tell me about it?'

She made no answer, but handed the letter to him, and started to hiccup away the little sobs that continued to well up. The major gave her hand a gentle squeeze as he held the letter to read. It was tersely written and conveyed its bleak news seemingly without the slightest regard for the effects of its import.

Madge's last surviving relative was her sister Ivy. She went to live with Ivy and her husband Bernard for a while, two years after her own dear husband Hugh had died from a sudden incurable illness. She and Ivy had been close since childhood, and had always depended on each other for support when needed. Poor Ivy, however, had married a man who was some years her junior and had proved to be the very antithesis of Hugh. Her health consequently deteriorated over the years through constant mental and physical ill-treatment.

Madge did what she could to make life easier for Ivy during the time she was with them by doing as much of the cooking and other housework as she could; knowing that it was the only reason why Bernard agreed to her staying there at all. When Madge began to receive similar treatment, Ivy begged her to leave, which she finally agreed to do on the understanding that Ivy would eventually join her wherever she went as soon as something could be arranged.

After a year at the Lodge, during which time Ivy's situation gradually worsened, Madge, having sufficient capital to do so, decided to lay the whole desperate story before Daphne, begging her to find a place for Ivy. Daphne was very sympathetic but was forced, by her own rules to say that Ivy was clearly in need of more care than could be provided at Anvil Lodge. She did, however, make immediate enquiries through her contacts and succeeded in securing a place in a care-home nearby, where Ivy would be well received and made as happy as her condition allowed. To Madge's intense relief and joy, this was to come about in two weeks' time.

'Your sister has left me in peace at long

last,' the major read, 'The funeral is next Thursday, you should be in time if this catches the post when I go up to the town on Monday. I can't remember what the doctor said it was, but you can ask him when you come down, if you want to know. If you want any of her things, bring something to put them in; not that she'd got much anyway.'

The letter was simply signed Bernard.

'The damned scoundrel,' the major said quietly, 'Can't believe it. The man deserves a good thrashing; tempted to go and do it m'self.'

'You're so kind, Major,' Madge said between sniffs. 'I can't stop wondering what poor Ivy went through before she passed away.'

She told the major all that had happened and what was about to happen had Ivy survived just a bit longer.

'Try to think of it as all for the best,' he said. 'She's better off where she is, perhaps,' he added.

'Do you really think so?'

She looked imploringly at the major, as though he would know. He was embarrassed and felt a bit on the spot.

'Come on, old girl,' he said, after a moment, and raising her up from the seat, added, 'You'll get rheumatics if you stay here. What you need is a good strong cup of

Robbie's coffee.'

They started back towards the house.

'You know we've all got to go before long,' he said, trying to put things in perspective. 'We know of far more people who've gone already than are still with us,' he said, wondering if he had got that quite right.

She took his arm and drew a little closer as they walked, wishing it was her Hughie with her.

'Don't worry about a thing, old girl; we'll arrange for someone to take you down for the funeral and make sure Ivy has a good send off, and if I get my hands on that...' He didn't finish. 'Meantime,' he went on, 'remember you've got your own life still to lead. Don't just make the best of life; try to make the most of it. None of us knows what's round the corner. When we're born, we take our place in the queue to die. Try and think of it as sleep without dreams.'

He felt a slight squeeze of gratitude on his arm.

Chapter 4

Trials

It was a few years since the major was behind the wheel of a car, having disposed of his old one before moving into Anvil Lodge, but had thought it prudent to retain his driving licence, at least for the time being. Following his recent good fortune, he had allowed the thought to grow in his mind that it might, for a number of reasons, be worth re-establishing his mobility; the forthcoming funeral presenting a possible case in point. After careful consideration he resolved to pursue the idea and accordingly took the train to visit the nearest agency.

'Listen to me, old boy; I may not be of this generation; but I didn't crew for Noah,' said the major, addressing the sharp young salesman. 'When I say a car doesn't feel right, it's because fifty-seven years of driving tells me so and I can assure you that "one owner" may sound impressive but it guarantees nothing; this car has been driven too hard.' The salesman, in his early thirties and feeling somewhat abashed in the face of the assertions, hastened to assure the major that his judgement was paramount in the matter.

After declining a second offer, the major drove the third 'absolute bargain' out from the forecourt and headed in the direction of Buckingham.

'Ah! that's more like it,' he said to the now rather subdued salesman. 'When can you have it ready, old boy?' he asked, ten minutes later. 'I'll try to arrange for somebody to bring me over; it's a bit of a bind coming by train.'

'Don't worry, sir, we'll deliver it to you,' said the relieved sales executive, adding, 'Thursday, all right?'

'Splendid! I suppose you want me to sign something, eh?' said the major bringing the two-year-old Rover to a stop, back on the forecourt.

'Yes, if you wouldn't mind, sir; come in and have some coffee while I sort things out; then I'll run you back to the station.'

'Good man,' replied the major.

Just before three-thirty the major alighted onto the single platform that constituted the local railway station, it being no more than a halt with no buildings of any sort. He fervently wished he'd had the foresight to wear a proper overcoat, the temperature having dropped to almost freezing level. It hadn't seemed nearly so cold in Aylesbury.

He pulled his collar tighter round his neck and stepped off boldly towards home. The first excited flurries of powdery snow came dancing round the bend towards him, carried on short gusts of wind. In the 15 minutes it would take him to reach the Lodge, he was going to end up pretty wet and dangerously cold, he knew. As he walked onward, head down, he brushed off the snow as best he could from the light coat and swore at himself for not at least bringing an umbrella. The top of his back was getting distinctly colder than anywhere else and beginning to feel damp. Because he was hurrying more than he would normally do, the top of his right leg was beginning to ache like fury; a condition that had been growing on him for several years; and now added considerably to his discomfort as he grew colder and wetter.

He was within 50 yards of the Lodge gates, with the snow stinging his ears, when the familiar noise of the Hornet made him look behind and to step back into the hedge.

'Get in quick, Major!' shouted Ramiro, revving the engine, as though rescuing the major in the nick of time from certain death.

The major pulled the door to as the car sped off, braking almost immediately to turn into the drive, sending a spray of gravel into the shrubbery and clattering against the gate.

He was, on balance, grateful for the few

moments of relief from the elements, stepped out at the Lodge entrance with a wave of thanks and hurried gratefully into the warmth of the hall. He was tempted by the familiar noisy clatter of teatime in the drawing room, but hurriedly turned right, along the corridor to his own room.

'Thank God,' he sighed, as he closed the door behind him, wishing he could just sit down and relax; but he had to get out of his soaking clothes.

He ran the bath in anticipation of a long hot soak; having an hour to spare before Ramiro opened up his mobile bar and he could attend to his next priority in the form of a large whisky.

The hot water was so relaxing that he almost nodded off. His mind drifted back to the fraught business of bathing at school. His boarding house had been endowed with a sophisticated electrical clock system, by dear old Mr Kitting, the housemaster, as a gift to the House before his retirement to the country, at the end of the major's first term.

Every room in the house had a wall clock which was electrically governed by a master clock in the housemaster's study. The second hand of each would move in unison every half-minute to regulate all formal activities. Each of the 42 boys was allotted two baths a week; to be taken during the two hours of evening prep which was carried out in the common room, between seven and nine o'clock. The common room was much like a classroom in the school, being largely filled with desks.

When the clock moved to the half-second before his stipulated 20 minutes' bathtime commenced, the boy held up his hand for the prefects' permission, and on the next half stroke raced off to begin the abulution in his allotted bathroom, before returning to his seat; hopefully by the time the second hand clicked audibly to complete the 20 minutes.

Spitting and spluttering, the major hauled himself upright in the water, which had crept up over his chin as he sank lower during his reverie.

'Damned fool!' he exclaimed, standing up to rinse-off with the shower, 'One of these days...' he thought.

Warmed, dried, and dressed, he felt restored to his normal good spirits and wandered round to the sitting room where he found a lively gathering, awaiting the arrival of Ramiro with essential supplies. As the major entered the room to a chorus of welcomes, the circle of armchairs was enlarged to accommodate a further place,

'Been far?' enquired Jim Witherspoon. 'Saw you going out, earlier.'

'Aylesbury,' came the reply. 'Got half drowned and frozen, as a matter of fact.'

'Was it worth it?' Jim asked.

'Oh, I think so; bought a car, as a matter of fact – Rover, couple of years old.'

'Goodness me! – hear that, Tom?' Jim said, leaning towards Tom Beardmore and thumbing towards the major. 'The old bugger's bought a car!'

'Never!' exclaimed Tom, looking up from the *Television Times*. 'What for?' he said, looking at the major with astonishment.

'To get away from the Hornet probably,' said Smiler, laughing.

'Perhaps he wants to start courting again,' suggested Sam Willoughby.

'Not on your life!' the major replied.

'Ah! Just the man!' said Jim, as Ramiro appeared with the bar trolley, having first looked into the drawing room to collect any orders from there.

'Let's drink to the ... what are we going to call it?' said Jim, searching for inspiration.

'Might as well call it The Bee,' said Smiler, relating it to The Hornet.

The suggestion was adopted and christened, when all were furnished with drinks; the major having no say in the matter beyond giving an account of the day's events.

Chapter 5

Despair

There are those who, perhaps wisely, can live life as it comes, accepting change as inevitable and sparing themselves the trouble of worrying about things of no practical consequence to them: which leaves the rest who, like the major, just cannot capitulate to the continual assaults on the native culture and customs without protest. The latter will contend that the English Language provides more than adequately for as near perfect communication as any in the world, without the need for the corrupting import of contemporary American styles.

As far as the major was concerned, Americans had a perfect right to adopt, adapt, or even improve on any language they cared to. What he abhorred was the avid adoption of all such influences by a populace increasingly devoid of national pride and who, metaphorically, got up every morning and bowed to the West. Not that the Americans would feel flattered by it; indeed they were more likely to despise it, as being pathetically symptomatic of a nation's once admired but rapidly declining character. Furthermore, it was typical of Americans, as individuals, to exhibit a fierce patriotism together with overt pride in their national flag and anthem, contrasting painfully with the outlook of today's average Briton.

It was not a matter of education, such as the general misuse of apostrophes, by those understandably lacking in formal knowledge; but the sheer lack of concern on the part of all sectors of society, that led to situations such as the major's visit to the post office. There, the lady sweetly requested the major to 'fill out' the proffered form.

While his toes bent painfully to the soles of his shoes, he wrestled with possible replies, before answering, 'I will certainly fill it "in", madam, as I would a hole in the garden, which would be as difficult to fill out.'

There were, however, areas of society with which the major was positively impressed. Whereas a few years ago, he recalled, the youth of Britain had seemingly become a pretty morose and discontented lot, unwilling to serve with good grace in any capacity, surly towards others, and the despair of their elders, it now seemed to him that for some reason (and thank God for it), those he came across, in the main, appeared to be the complete antithesis of their forebears: being altogether cheerful, courteous, willing, generous, and thoroughly praiseworthy;

allowing for exceptions as much for them as for their predecessors.

The nursing profession which had always been, perhaps, the finest example of selfless devotion to the welfare of others, and deserving of the utmost praise and gratitude, continued to provide expression of those qualities despite increasingly difficult conditions. The major was, in fact, inclined to the belief that the general moral standard of the best of today's youth was, if anything, higher than that of any foregoing generation, since it was set against a much wider awareness and understanding of the world through the inescapable media, including the baleful 'box'.

In an altogether different sector of society, as far as his experience had proved over recent times, the immigrants of his acquaintance had always proved to be entirely affable, efficient, and civilised people; certainly among those at the interface presented by commerce, where the most industrious and therefore most deserving of welcome, were to be met.

He was of the strong conviction that most of the population, whom he presumed typically to represent, harboured no resentment towards 'immigrants' as such, but were entirely against 'immigration', while it continued in its present unfettered manner. He believed that the extremists, correctists and other minority factions, to whom the Government preferred to listen and accommodate were ignoring the difference.

He further suspected that the newcomers were probably welcomed by authority, in their millions, more as sympathetic voters, than for any more laudable reason and it was time to pull up the gang-plank before the boat sank. Specious contentions in regard to the need for special skills such as doctors ignored the fact that unless the rest were to be excluded, the services of such skilled people would be entirely absorbed, in proportion, by those who came with them, thus doing nothing at all to alleviate the country's needs.

Furthermore, the consequent enormous increase in housing demands must be the underlying if not the sole motive for plans to impose ever more housing developments – blatantly ignoring the warnings of over-burdened service providers.

One way and another, the major was beginning to feel like the small boy on a garden fence. 'Could we have our England back, please?', and he was prepared to support anyone whose objective was to get it back, before what was left of a proud nation, was finally parcelled-up, and without the slightest support or approval of the majority, traded in payment for somebody's European ambitions.

To the devil with all extremists and correctists, European imposers on British liberty, anti-this and thats; especially anti-smokers, he thought, who clearly wouldn't stop at any reasonable accommodations, preferring to deprive the last pensioner of his pipe than to be thwarted over their personal persuasions.

How long, he wondered, before they turned their attentions to the cost of drinking to the National Health Service, or the passive smoking effects of log fires in pubs and cosy hotels, if they hadn't by then turned the pubs into milk bars. They should rejoice in their freedom to avoid pubs and leave them for the traditional use of those who are just as free to enjoy them. So-called passive smoking is no more imposed on anyone than is a television with a switch on it.

On the day of judgement, those who feed so avidly on a diet of interference with the conduct of others will have the opportunity on all counts of admonishing Winston Churchill for shortening his life to 90 years.

These and other weighty views were put by the major to the world at large, at any opportunity, although he was perfectly aware that he was wielding a cardboard sword; in company with millions of like-minded citizens whose voice counted for nothing in a country ruled by a government determined, in its myopic view, to remove all trace of the English culture.

He envisaged the day when all the historical county names would be replaced with regional numbers. The shires would go for certain. Arrogant bureaucracy had, for its own administrative convenience, already destroyed such proud names as Cumberland and Westmoreland.

'And that's another thing,' he said, over lunch, to Sandy Balfour and Tom Dangerfield, to whom it was clear that he was having one of his 'flag' days.

'If they're so damned keen to see us all ruled by Europe, what was the point of devolving Scotland? What's more to the point, now that the Scots have got their own parliament, what are they all doing down here running Westminster? They might as well move Parliament to Edinburgh; at least they could all get home for tea.'

'I see your point,' said Tom. 'It's hard to think of anyone of significance in parliament who isn't Scottish; how does it come about in the first place – who do they represent? They must have English constituencies.'

'I'm certain of one thing,' said Sandy, 'you won't find a Welshman, and certainly not an Englishman, representing a Scottish constituency.'

'Not in a thousand years,' the major added. 'Trouble is, the English electorate are unconcerned about who they're voting for as long as they represent a particular party.'

'Well, that's it isn't it,' said Tom, 'They've been quietly ferrying them all down here and slipping them in where they want them. Must have been at it for years.'

'It's unbelievable when you think about it,' continued the major. 'They sit there creating legislation for us while excluding Scotland from half of it.'

'Well, I don't know what we can do about it,' Tom concluded, 'apart from complaining to the Speaker of the House of Commons and he's Scottish.'

'Coffee in the sitting room, gentlemen?' Tracey offered, while clearing the plates.

'Thank you, m'dear,' said the major with an enquiring glance at the others.

They made their way to the sitting room where they found Joyce Kingham and Muriel Lewis, in earnest discussion over the siting of clematis plants. Muriel stood up as the three men came in.

She smiled at them saying, 'Nothing personal, boys, but we're going next door,' nodding towards the drawing room.

'So, when are we going to see the Bee, L.-J.?' enquired Tom, as they settled down.

The major, tapping out his pipe in the ashtray, said, 'Thursday, all being well. They're bringing it over. I've been to the post office this morning to get a new tax disc. Once that's put on, that's all there is to it.'

'I suppose you feel like Mr Toad, now,' said Sandy.

'I thought that was coming,' said the major, grinning.

'Well, don't start collecting speed tickets, you know what they're like around here,' added Sandy.

'You don't have to tell me,' retorted the major. 'The C.O. picked up a summons last month. Everybody seems to have fallen victim to that particular camera. The police must regard it as their star turn.'

'There's something peculiar about that one, if you ask me,' said Tom. 'Everyone seems to get the same speed recorded on the ticket.'

'Well, I don't know about that,' the major replied. 'What gets under my skin is that damned silly sign they use nowadays. Nothing would persuade me that the hideously ungrammatical exhortation to "Kill your speed" is any more effective than the straightforward "Go slow", or "Slow down"; in fact, it positively tempts me to put my foot down. What's wrong with plain English? It's just another example of bureaucratic change for its own sake,' he concluded.

'Here we are then,' said Tracey, putting the tray on the table, between them. 'I've put some extra mints on.'

'Good girl,' said Sandy.

'Have the afternoon off,' Tom added.

'Thank you, Mr Dangerfield, I'll tell Mrs Robertson, I'm sure she'll be very pleased for me,' replied Tracey, laughing and swinging her hips saucily away through the doorway.

When she returned for the tray, half an hour later, both the major and Sandy were sound asleep and Tom was trying to keep awake while struggling with the major's *Telegraph* crossword. She winked at Tom and quietly loaded the crockery onto the tray. Lifting it carefully, she tiptoed away.

'Hey! come and look at this,' whispered Smiler, beckoning to Sam Willoughby as they were crossing the hall.

They peered round the doorway of the sitting room and grinned at the dormant figures spread symmetrically outward in three directions, mouths agape and snoring peacefully.

Smiler pointed towards the dining room; Sam followed his gaze for a few seconds before nodding and stealing across the hall, returning with the dinner gong. He paused for a moment, lost his nerve and passed the gong to Smiler who crept forwards and took his stance behind the major; leaning over to hold the gong above the three heads. With teeth bared and a grin spreading from ear to ear, he drew back the striker with his right hand, closed his eyes and then froze.

'Don't – you – dare,' thundered Daphne from the doorway.

Not realising that she was standing beside him, Sam's heart almost stopped from the shock.

The grin on Smiler's face gave way to a reddening smirk, as he hastily withdrew the gong from his victims' notice before they could recover from the shock of Daphne's intervention, the effect of which probably rivalled that of the gong.

The major opened his eyes and remained motionless for some time as his mind attempted to decipher a situation that was wholly beyond his grasp. An instant before he had been driving his new Rover along a wide fast road, when a catastrophic noise snatched him away to be confronted by the terrifying image of an avenging angel framed in a doorway. Beside it stood a large figure whose vaguely familiar face was rigid with shock.

'Of course,' he concluded, 'an accident!'

His eyes glazed over again for an instant as he experienced the gradual awareness of encroaching reality that attends arousal from dreams. Tom and Sandy, being similarly transfixed by events, simply waited for someone to tell them what was happening and to reveal their role in it.

Smiler, correctly assuming responsibility for breaking the ice, began the long journey back to the door, attempting to conceal the gong from the 'sleeping party' and trusting that Daphne would be gracious enough to step aside and allow him the semblance of a dignified exit.

She was, however, having none of it, and nudging the hapless Sam farther into the room, released another peal of thunder, addressing the late diners with, 'Thank you, gentlemen?' before turning and leaving them to find their own enlightenment.

She regarded the incident as dealt with, in the knowledge that it would be instantly forgotten. They were responsible people, even though they might act like children at times. She was, if anything, content with the fact that they were obviously in good health and spirits despite their years.

What did surprise her, however, was the major's intention to acquire a car. He had spoken to her about it in regard to her finding him a convenient place to park it. As it happened, she was happy enough to oblige him although it would require having the last of the stables cleared out; which would mean waiting until Laurie Henderson could come in and do it. However, she was inclined to think that a car was an undertaking he might regret and had done her best, as subtly as she could, to dissuade him from the idea. She felt that at 73 he should be shedding such responsibilities, not adding them. However, he wasn't senile; he would obviously have given it plenty of thought and it was, after all, his business anyway.

Kathy Summers was the secretary and had been the trusted friend of Daphne over many years. They had known each other since they were nurses in training at the same hospital. Kathy moved on to be a practice nurse, gaining administrative experience in the process. When Daphne set up the home at Anvil Lodge she offered Kathy the post of secretary, which was accepted without hesitation. Kathy sold her flat and bought a cottage close to the home. Daphne allowed her free use of the guest-room on the ground floor for personal convenience as well as when standing in while Daphne was away.

As secretary, Kathy was fully stretched taking care of day-to-day administration, dealing with the small switchboard, liaising with Mrs Robertson and the housekeeper, in addition to diverse other responsibilities.

To ensure that Kathy wasn't over-burdened, Daphne assumed a freelance role dealing with incidental matters; supervising the gardeners and arranging extra-curricular events such as theatre visits, parties and similar diversions to keep both staff and residents happy.

Kathy was strikingly attractive and, at the age of 42 had, like Daphne, successfully evaded marriage. Having no particular urge to raise a family, she was content to live life to the full and leave marriage to the vagaries of chance. Meanwhile she had an 'understanding' with Geoffrey MacDonald, a widowed doctor who would be 49 on his next birthday; two weeks before that of his daughter Karen, who would be 23.

Kathy's attractions were not unappreciated by the male residents who, although being generally twice her age, regarded her as a very welcome adornment to the daily scene. The major in particular, regarded her as typical of womanhood at its best; having always contended that no woman attained her peak of attraction before the age of 40. He also approved of her relaxed attitude towards the opposite sex.

He certainly spared no time for the abrasiveness of feminism and its pointless aggressiveness which he saw as ugly and devoid of charm and humour. In his view, there was something missing in such women, who seemed to have a need for confrontation wherever men were concerned, as though fighting an undeclared war.

How did they reconcile their disdainful perception of the male world with their desperation to become part of it? What was it that led some women to campaign their way into male institutions, regarding every rational partition as a rampart to be torn down? Why would a normal woman want to be a member of a men's club? Should men feel at home in the Mothers' Union or Women's Institute? What kind of world would we be committing our grandchildren to if society was to become so homogenous, without contrast or shadow, and where we all appeared to be the same?

What was the attraction of mixed everything he wondered? Should we look forward to public 'Unilavs' as such logic suggests? Surely the women wouldn't. As the major saw it, that was the way things were going, completely over the top as usual, now that the loony correctists were leading them to batter their way into male preserves of every sort.

When the Pankhursts and others fought, at great cost, to establish women's rights, they were working on meaningful principles of justice, equality and freedom for all, not the iconoclastic strife now in train. If women, discontent with women's clubs wanted mixed clubs, they were free to create them, who would stop them? Why did they prefer to despoil the established retreats of the masculine world?

Femininity itself was being cast off. The

fashion world had gone completely to the dogs, the clothes, with few exceptions, being shapeless rags devoid of inspiration. Models, especially those at the top of their profession, appeared to be perpetually at odds with the world; maintaining sullen expressions, as they stared defiantly from the fashion pages, as though the ability to smile had been extracted from them. Maybe, to do them justice, they are merely reacting to some of the ridiculous creations that they are obliged to present!

Pretty girls were going to extremes of grotesqueness by adopting the most incongruous attire imaginable; which would have brought howls of laughter from their forebears, coming across such images in their comic papers.

Traditional courtesy towards women was becoming distinctly hazardous and often received with sour disdain. Where was the allure and seduction in modern woman? Were women mutating by some insidious biological disorder towards a complete dissociation from romance? Where it was all leading to the major didn't care to think, but thanked God there were still young women like Kathy to admire.

Daphne also employed a night porter, Reg Saunders, to come in at five-thirty or otherwise as Kathy required, to man the switchboard and provide overnight security. She had acquired Reg after he retired from the army where he had absorbed the discipline and tradition like a sponge; regarding such discipline and service as a true calling not the least related to subservience or obsequiousness.

He detected, with considerable regret, a lowering of standards in the evolving modern army as he perceived it through the occasional glimpses of military activities afforded by television. He positively squirmed to see N.C.O.s, issuing orders to the ranks while wandering about looking at the ground or elsewhere. Shouting abuse at the men was all very well, and traditionally practised, but respect and discipline could only be achieved by standing to attention and facing the ranks while doing so. However, Reg's strongest reactions were aroused by the spectacle of squads of men aping the American practice of 'sound-off' chanting while on the march. When Americans did it, it merely looked and sounded American. When our troops were led to copy it, it seemed to him to be sycophantic, childish and downright embarrassing to witness.

Like the major, Reg was too old-world to fit comfortably into changing society. He had been married for 20 years and divorced for 15; separation being inevitable following years of perpetual argument through his fun-loving wife's inability to cope with his punctilious approach to everything. In civilian life Reg was like a stray dog and beginning to despair of finding himself comfortably under orders of any sort again. When Daphne's advertisement for a well-disciplined and mature person came to his notice, Reg responded eagerly and their general compatibility was immediately evident.

He had rooms with a Mrs Barton, a widowed lady living about half a mile from the Lodge and with whom he enjoyed an affable relationship. He cycled to the Lodge daily; keeping his bicycle stowed in Ramiro's garage, and was able to render extremely useful service while offering infinitely flexible hours.

At Mrs Barton's, he lived an independent existence, his rooms being self-contained, although he would, from time to time, accept an invitation to join Mrs Barton for a 'proper meal' as she put it. She enjoyed those occasions as all too infrequent opportunities for company and genial conversation.

Having particular views on certain topics, she, like most others with strong convictions, had a lasting urge to express them. While she persistently held to religious tenets, she was less inclined to accept scientific principles, whatever the rational arguments offered to support them, when they conflicted with her notions of common sense.

Typically, nothing would dissuade her from the conviction that the earth must be getting progressively heavier on account of the enormous weight of trees growing up all the time. When she laid the conviction before Reg, over the roast pork one Sunday lunchtime, Reg instinctively forbore to take issue on the matter; affecting, instead, to support her belief as being obvious and to observe that she was probably the first and only person to realise it; a response that assured him of countless future meals. His further association with Mrs Barton was a matter of idle speculation with which few concerned themselves.

Chapter 6

Deliverance

At ten thirty-three on Thursday morning two cars came into view round the bend of the drive and crunched to a halt opposite Daphne's sitting room window. Daphne was sitting at her desk writing a letter and she paused to watch the arrival of the two

113

drivers, one of whom remained seated in the smaller of the two cars. The other driver eased himself out of the larger car, straightened up and smoothed back his hair which to his evident annoyance was immediately ruffled into disorder again by a capricious gust of wind. He braced his shoulders, giving the impression that he was conscious of possibly being observed.

Walking casually round the car, he opened the passenger door and leaned in to retrieve a clipboard from the seat with his right hand and, stepping back, slammed the door shut with his left. Dusting down the front of his stylish suit, he advanced deferentially towards the arching stonework that obviously guarded important people. There being no bar to his entry, he walked through into the hallway and knocked discreetly on the oak door marked 'office'.

'Oh! Hello! Have you brought the major's car?' enquired the blinding smile that opened the door and numbed his mind for several seconds. 'I'll let him know you're here,' said Kathy without waiting for a reply; the question being entirely rhetorical, as the office had a window onto the front drive.

She withdrew back into the office to ring through to the major's room.

The salesman started to tiptoe about the noisy oak floor, gazing at the watercolours. Peering at his reflection in the picture glass, he took the opportunity to pull a comb from his back pocket and quickly tidy up his hair.

'Ah! there you are, old boy,' said the major, rapidly crossing the hall to grasp the salesman's hand and propel him back outside to the cars. 'Found your way then,' he added.

'Yes, thanks, no problem. Did you get the tax disc all right, sir?' enquired the salesman, glancing back at the house for any further glimpse of Kathy.

''Course, old boy,' said the major, pulling the envelope from his inside pocket.

'Fantastic, shall I stick it in for you?' offered the salesman.

'If you wouldn't mind, thanks old man; jolly good of you.'

The salesman sat backwards onto the passenger seat and deftly tucked the licence in place on the windscreen.

'There you go, all done now. Insurance and all that stuff's in the glove box. Don't forget to read through the manual before you go far, always pays; all I need now is your signature and we're away,' he concluded, passing the clipboard to the major.

With the signature secured and another deal safely completed, the salesman got in beside the spare driver, saying, 'We'll stop for a coffee at that tea shop we passed.'

Without a word, the driver started up and drove away. His sole function was to deliver and collect cars; the tedium of which had more or less rendered him speechless during working hours, when he remained largely devoid of facial expression. He sat through the late proceedings with eyes glazed and mind 'in neutral', waiting to be re-activated.

The major caught Daphne's eye through the window and they exchanged a little wave. She was really quite impressed by the style and colour of the Rover and felt relieved that the major hadn't let the side down by acquiring anything too old or prosaic; the Hornet was quite enough to put up with whenever it appeared at the front. The major eased himself into the driving seat and decided to show admirable restraint by driving round to the stable yard to park the Rover, as though having more important things to do than to rush off to try it out. He stopped in the yard, switched off and sat for a moment gazing round his acquisition with the greatest satisfaction. He recalled a colleague asserting that Rovers were an old man's car. If so, he thought, it was a positive recommendation as far as he was concerned.

He leaned across and opened the glove box, taking out the black plastic folder containing the handbooks and documents. He would take them in and go right through them at his leisure. After adjusting the seat back and forth to set the best position he grasped the door handle with his right forefinger, levering it back to release the lock, and pushed the door open with his elbow. Stepping out onto the cobbled yard, he closed the door and pressed the key fob to lock the doors.

This was the signal for all the hidden eyes to come out from cover like natives on a tropical shore. First Smiler, then Sandy followed by Joyce and Tom Beardmore: all happened to be just round the corner.

'Aren't you going to try it out, L.-J.?' asked Tom in disappointed tone.

'It's a lovely colour,' observed Joyce, sliding fingertips along the wing.

'What is it called?' she asked.

'Metallic Copper Red,' replied the major with a hint of pride.

'I reckon it's the best design they ever produced,' opined Sandy, with the air of someone who knew about those things.

'So when are you going to try it out?' repeated Tom.

'I already have, the other day,' the major answered.

'Oh! come on, L.-J.' said Smiler, 'you know jolly well we're all dying to get in and try it.'

'I'm not going anywhere,' protested the major. 'I want a cup of coffee,' he said, hesitating for a moment and then adding, 'before I do anything else.'

'Right! Let's all have one, eh!' said Smiler sensing the weakness.

'Well, if you must,' said the major, as they finished their coffee in the sitting room. 'When I've had a pipe we'll have a ride down to the Swan for a "quick one" before lunch eh!'

'By! that's more like it,' said Smiler. 'A run ashore for "Up spirits" eh!'

'What's "Up spirits"?' Joyce asked.

'It's a long story, is that!' he replied.

'It always is with you,' she said.

Not wishing to delay the forthcoming trip, Smiler replied, 'I'll tell you when we get there.'

They reassembled at the Rover and Joyce was accorded the front seat while the three men crammed into the back. The major switched on for his first real trip and moved off gently round to the drive, arriving at the gates ready to turn into the lane.

He had barely nosed out a yard into the lane before he stabbed at the brake as a small blue van flashed by from the left. The Rover stalled and the major's mind went blank for a second, his heart pounding.

'Well, the seat-belts work,' observed Tom as they flopped back in their seats.

'Well done, L.-J.,' said Sandy from the back, anxious to recharge the major's confidence. 'Nothing wrong with *your* reactions. Another second and that madman would have written us all off,' he added.

'How are you, Joyce?' asked the major, restarting the engine, fully conscious of the fact that she would have been the first casualty in the event of an impact.

'Well,' she replied, looking a bit pale, 'I could do with a drink!'

They all cheered and continued on to the Swan.

'Well!' said Joyce looking at Smiler.

'Well what?' he replied, taking his pint from Sue the barmaid as she handed the drinks round.

'Up spirit'? Joyce prompted.

'Oh aye! spirits,' he said, 'with an "s". It's what the rum issue were called in the Andrew,' he began. 'It were piped every morning at eleven o'clock; if you were on-board that is. If you were on a shore station it would be issued at midday as you went into the dining hall for your dinner.'

'Wait a minute,' Joyce interrupted, 'what does "Andrew" mean?'

'It was just the common name for Royal Navy, but don't ask me why,' Smiler replied.

'Patron Saint?' offered the major.

'Perhaps, I don't really know.'

The subject, together with the strong Yorkshire tones, attracted some attention from others around the bar.

'You'd only a minute to get it down you!'

Smiler continued, warming to his narrative. 'You were moved on pretty quickly, out of the way, like; they needed your glass and there were a long queue of lads behind you.'

'Was there only one glass then?' Joyce asked.

'Good Lord, no, there'd be several of you drinking up at a time, obviously,' Smiler answered with a tolerant grin.

'It doesn't sound very hygienic,' observed Joyce.

'They didn't worry about that sort of thing in those days. You just dropped the glass back into a bowl of water ready for the next man.'

'Pretty strong stuff, I understand,' the major interjected.

'Well, no, not really; you've to remember it was watered down at the rum store when it was collected; so it was half strength before it was thinned again with three parts water. You had about two-thirds of a tumbler-full. Mind you,' he added, 'I'm not saying it was weak, in fact it had quite an effect, especially if you weren't used to it. It'd take about two and a half minutes, before the din began to subside and your ears begin to go funny. The first time, I thought I'd been given wooden cutlery,' he said, winking at Joyce, who began to giggle.

'By, though, it didn't half give you an

appetite. You'd eat anything they dished up; though I think that were probably the idea.'

The major laughed, Joyce giggled more, and a ripple of amusement set off round the bar.

'Sounds strong enough to me,' said Tom.

'Oh aye, it were,' agreed Smiler. 'If it had been any stronger we'd have not got much done in the afternoon!'

'What was it like neat, then?' asked someone from the other side of the room. Smiler raised his head to oblige.

'Very few people knew,' he started. 'One and ones, that's one measure from the barrel and one of water, was as strong as anyone could or would want to drink. You'd hear all sorts of stories of course.'

He paused as Vera did the rounds for a further order while Sue was busy in the other bar.

'Was it true that they poured away any left over?' someone else enquired.

'Oh aye, always! I've watched it many a time, they'd no option, you see. It were all very strict because of Customs; the Officer of the Watch were always there to make sure it were done properly.'

'There again, you see, the same thing applied to duty-free tobacco; when a packet of twenty cigarettes were normally about three bob, we were paying fourpence for naval issue, or pusser's as they called it, and that were in old money. A half pound tin of tobacco were three shillings and you could draw two tins a month. You could buy ordinary brands in the NAAFI where twenty Players, for instance, would cost about one and threepence. There were always politicians who were against the Navy having privileges like rum and duty-free tobacco; they'd use every excuse to stop it.'

'Which they did, didn't they?' said another voice.

'Aye, you're right,' confirmed Smiler.

'Well, you've got to admit it wasn't fair on the other services, was it?' said someone.

'No,' Smiler replied, 'but it were nothing to do with complaints by the other services; the Pongos and RAF weren't behind it. Whenever we came across them, on exercises for instance, their attitude was always "Good luck to you mate!" No, I'm afraid it were purely political.'

'Damned Lefties again,' the major murmured, 'sheer jealousy; couldn't bear privileges of any sort.'

'Aye, I'm afraid so,' confirmed Smiler who was now in full flow and, with an attentive audience, he carried on.

'The best thing was to be on watch so as to miss Up-spirits. That way you were entitled as a watchkeeper to be on what they called mis-muster. Then you'd to report to the rum store in the afternoon, at, er ... if memory serves, I believe it were quarter to four and you'd be issued with two and ones. By, that were good stuff. If you were going ashore for the evening, you'd draw your tot at quarter-to and then go ashore p****d as a handcart at four o'clock, at the end of the working day.'

'That sounds an incongruous term for the Navy to use,' observed the refined tones of an elegant girl in her late teens.

'Not at all, miss,' Smiler replied, facing her. 'The naval handcart was one of the commonest items of equipment in those days. They were on a par with forklift trucks in a factory or bicycles at a university. Every establishment, barracks or otherwise, had a fleet of handcarts. They were painted warship grey, had two large wheels and a shaft at the front with a crosspiece handle on the end. The body was about four foot by six and its principal use was for transporting kit bags and hammocks. The point is, that while it was easy to pull, whatever the load, it were completely hopeless trying to push it. You'd very little control of direction. Hence the expression "p****d as a handcart".'

He concluded his answer with a wide grin which was returned with a saucy wink and, 'Thank you, sailor!'

Smiler ploughed on with his narrative.

'It were a well-established custom at the time, as part of mess-deck lore if you like, to use your tot to pay off favours on a sort of token basis really. For instance, if you'd agreed to do someone's duty watch so that he could go ashore on a date, or perhaps you'd lent him something, he would just say, "Come round". That meant that at up spirits you would go round to his mess and he would hand you his tot which he'd save until you came, so you could have first go. Then he'd say either "sippers" or "gulpers", and you'd take a token sip or a good gulp, according to the size of favour you'd done for him. Of course, it only worked if you were onboard a ship.'

'Oh dear, I suppose I'm talking too much, as usual,' declared Smiler, looking at the others.

'Not at all, old boy, interesting stuff,' replied the major, finishing his shandy. 'Perhaps we ought to be making a move though if we're not to be late for lunch.'

They all rose with much scraping of chairs against the stone floor and, bidding their farewells to the remaining company, trooped out as Sue called after them, 'Mind how you go.'

They settled back in the Bee, the major started the engine and pulled away towards the main road.

'Stop!' shrieked Joyce.

The major stopped, jabbing on the brake, thinking he'd run over a cat or something.

His heart was pounding again, and he wondered if he could cope with this driving business after all.

Joyce unstrapped herself and leapt out of the car, shouting back, 'Sorry – handbag.'

She ran erratically over the stony ground towards the pub entrance to be met by Sue rushing out with the handbag.

'Thank you so much,' Joyce said, grasping the bag on the turn, like a relay runner, and hurried back to the car.

'I reckon the sooner you eat something the better,' said Smiler as she settled back in her seat.

'I'm afraid you're right,' she replied, turning to face him with a flushed smile.

Again, the major engaged first gear and gingerly turned into the main road, anxious to conclude the baptismal venture with his confidence at least partly intact. They bowled along the flat landscape, the Chiltern escarpment in the distance presenting a long panorama of steep sloping fields and beech woods, with peeping stone churches and the needle-like monument scratching the low clouds above Wendover.

The view, held by many to be unsurpassed, incorporated several strip-parishes, whereby each community was accorded by ancient charter an equal share of the differing terrain, stretching back from the plain of Aylesbury, up through the wooded scarp into the Chiltern region. Among these, the oldest parish in England, Monks Risborough, centred round St Dunstan's church, had just celebrated 1,100 years of existence and stretched from the hamlet of Owlswick, well out on the plain, back across the scarp and on to Hampden.

'You can see it now all right,' said the major, pointing towards the great white chalk cross carved into the hillside above the village of Whiteleaf.

The Cross had just been renovated as a Millennium project, having gradually become obscured by discoloration and erosion of the chalk. Its age and authors had yet to be determined by academics.

'It doesn't look very white to me,' said Tom.

'I expect it will when it's had time to dry out properly; in the summer it'll shine like a dollar up a sweep's backside,' assured Sandy, succumbing to the effects of what Sue had described as gentleman's measures of malt.

Back at the Lodge, they scattered to their rooms to tidy up before lunch. The major switched on his television set to see the weather report; and in consequence felt encouraged to contemplate a day's birdwatching on the morrow. At lunch, he had the company of Tessa Harry, Dick Baker and Mary Taylor.

126

He asked Tracey if she would arrange for a packed lunch for him to collect from the dining room at breakfast, in the morning.

'Nothing too heavy or bulky,' he added.

'Yes, major, you're going out somewhere then, are you?' She did not expect answers to her rhetorical observations, but merely said, 'I'll talk to Mrs Robertson in just a moment,' and departed to the kitchen.

'Going far?' enquired Tessa.

'No, not really. Depends on how the old leg holds up, mostly.'

'Walking then,' observed Dick.

'Yes. Spot of birdwatching, actually.'

'Used to do a good bit myself,' said Dick. 'Had to give it best though, when I moved after my wife died; wasn't the same without her anyway.'

'Damned sorry to hear that, old boy,' said the major. 'I say, if you still yearn for the outdoors, you'd be very welcome to join me sometime, if you'd care to. I could certainly do with some guidance, mind you. I'm probably ten years too late getting into it.'

'Nothing of the sort,' said Mary. 'You'll find at least half of the wildlife fraternity are our sort of age, these days. Like heritage societies for instance; the audiences are a sea of white hair and you'll see hordes of them walking the countryside in the summer.'

'She's right, L.-J. You're never too old for

127

exercise that you can cope with; just don't overdo it, that's all,' Dick advised him. 'Generally speaking, there's too much going on to wander too far anyway. It's just a matter of pace really; you can meander along all day without much wear and tear. In my seventies I would spend anything up to ten hours a day on the reserve where I was a warden, and not cover more than about three miles.'

'And don't be too hasty about joining things,' said Tessa, 'Once you start on these things it's so easy to go from one society to another with related interests.'

'That's true,' said Mary, 'I found myself paying eleven subscriptions at one point and cancelled half of them. My advice is, only join things that are essential to your main interests.'

'Oh, I don't belong to any societies,' replied the major, 'but I'll bear it in mind, thanks.'

'Mrs Robertson says, "Would you let her know by this evening, after dinner, what you would like for tomorrow?"' said Tracey, handing a list to the major. 'Anyone like coffee?' she enquired, with a glance round the table.

'Yes, please,' they chorused.

'Sitting room for me,' the major requested.

'And me,' said Dick.

'I'm going to the ladies'; I'll see you in the drawing room, Mary,' said Tessa, pushing her chair back under the table and reaching for her handbag.

'I expect you've got some field glasses,' said Dick as they sat down for their coffee.

The major, striking a match, waited for the flame to grow while he nodded vigorously at Dick.

When he'd finished drawing the pipe to life, he replied, 'Absolutely, old boy, damned good pair of nine-fifties.'

'A bit heavy, don't you find?' Dick asked.

'Not a bit; I tell you, you wouldn't believe it, you must try them; take 'em for a walk round the grounds some time.'

He described how he came by them in Thame, with due acknowledgement of Ramiro's part in it.

Tracey appeared with the coffee.

'Mrs Robertson says, will you want a thermos tomorrow?' she asked, looking at the major, who was looking at Dick, who was shaking his head meaningfully.

'Err ... no thank you, dear.'

As Tracey withdrew, Dick said, 'Sorry to interfere, L.-J. but take my tip, do everything to minimise weight; first of many rules and, while I think of it, bear in mind that you are there above all to enjoy yourself. Don't get bogged down with trivial worries about record keeping and identifying correctly. It's very easy to mar the day with that sort of thing. In fact, I would go so far as to say it's better not to keep records at all than let them dictate your life – which they can do – believe me! Stay loose, as they say these days.'

'I say, old boy, I'm jolly grateful for the benefit of your wisdom at this point. I'll certainly bear it all in mind; clearly, you know what it's all about; I really had no idea,' the major confessed.

'I could list a few tips for you before you go tomorrow, if it's not being too presumptuous; purely my own rules you understand,' Dick offered.

'I'd certainly appreciate it, if it's not too much trouble,' replied the major with enthusiasm.

'Well, let me give it some thought; I'll bring something with me at dinner, eh?' suggested Dick.

'First class, old man,' the major concluded.

'Only too glad to be of help, L.-J.'

True to his word, Dick arrived in the sitting room just after seven o'clock, waving his piece of paper like the triumphant Chamberlain and took the chair next to the major. Ramiro dispensed the orders, collected their signatures and moved on to other customers.

'Good heavens, Dickie,' the major ex-

130

claimed, 'didn't expect all this; you've really thought about it, haven't you?'

'Hope you can use it,' replied Dick.

'Cheers, old boy, and many thanks indeed.'

The major raised his glass towards Dick, who answered, with a grin, 'Good luck and don't get lost.'

The major glanced at the paper on which was written in two pencilled columns a list of things to take and a list of things to wear for summer and winter. Also, a short list of advice:

Walk slowly
Scan frequently from sky to ground
Pre-scan round corners
Stand still frequently.

'You wear long johns in the summer?' the major queried. 'Or is that a mistake?'

'No mistake,' replied Dick.

'A bit warm, surely.'

'No, they keep the heat out as well as in and you wait till you walk through a patch of heavy nettles; they can penetrate tough trousers to a surprising degree.'

'I shall have to find somewhere to get the extra gear,' said the major.

'I know the very place,' Dick replied. 'I'll come with you if you like.'

'That's very kind of you, old man; how far is it?'

'Amersham,' said Dick.

'Oh, what's that, half an hour's run?'

'Just about, I suppose,' agreed Dick. 'We'll go whenever you like then, L.-J.'

Chapter 7

Nature

As promised, the morning sky was almost cloudless. A full moon had reigned throughout the night and left a slight frost for the sun to clear up when it came on duty. The major was awakened by the whirring of his travelling alarm clock. As he moved his foot to slide from the bedclothes it was seized by a cramp. He had, over recent years, evolved a method of his own for dealing in minimal time with minor cramp pains, which had initially called for considerable faith and determination. Success had resulted from the paradoxical practice of forced relaxation, resisting all temptation to do anything but virtually ignore it. The pain quickly reached its full effect, which had to be endured anyway, before rapidly disappearing, taking some few seconds in all.

The method became easier with practice and proved to be far superior to the natural tendencies to screw up, shriek, hobble about, grab and maul about, seek cold surfaces to place against, or other desperate remedies that merely tended to prolong the agony. Thus the major was soon about and dressed, as far as he could be in accordance with his new mentor's instructions prior to obtaining the rest of his needs from Amersham.

Having not yet acted on his resolution to provide himself with proper boots following the salutary experiences of the last expedition, he had given his old heavy brogues a good thick polishing after they had dried out. However, conditions should be drier today by all accounts, he thought; furthermore, he would now benefit from Dick's advice in selecting the best sort of boots to buy.

Today, he mused, would be a day of learning the ropes and qualifying Dick's advices, some of which he found rather enigmatic. He had lots of questions in mind for Dick already, but they would be best put after some practical experience, he thought. Firstly, he would go and have a jolly good breakfast before collecting the lunch pack that he'd ordered last night; having chosen from Mrs Robertson's list of suggestions and added, small plastic bottle of water, please.

Back in his room, he put everything including an extra pullover, into the haversack, placed the strap over his head onto his left shoulder and pulled the sack round behind him. Hanging the binoculars round his neck, he glanced finally round the room before unlocking the French window and stepping out into the cold air. Locking the door behind him, he placed the key carefully into his hip pocket, turned and set off in the direction of the little green garden gate.

As he approached the stream, a magpie taking a morning dip flew up to perch on the nearby fence post where it commenced to preen its snowy white breast, intermittently shivering away the remaining drops of water from its wings. Paying proud attention to its long flowing black tail, it periodically sent rippling waves of agitation along its length, reminding the major of a housewife shaking crumbs from a tablecloth.

By nine-forty, the major was beyond the limit of his previous expedition and was gradually making his way up the steepening slope of the scarp. He was avoiding the shadier places, where the frost was still holding its own against the steadily rising temperature, in order to keep his shoes as dry as possible.

After the problems of wet shoes, he was soon to discover the problems of dry ones. Where the ground was steepest and driest, the short dead grass was difficult to grip with his smooth soles and once or twice he found himself slipping back and falling to his knees against the slope. He found the process sapping his energy, causing him to stop for a few seconds every two or three yards, to recover.

If it was this difficult to climb in shoes, he wondered, what must it be like in great boots? He would see what Dick had to say about that, later on. He judged that he must be pretty near to the top by now and turned his back to the ground to sit up for a while. The view before him was amazing. He scanned the horizon towards Oxford and Abingdon, some 25 miles away, as he guessed it must be. He could make out the white plumes of the cooling towers at Didcot power station, drifting to the left beyond the western slopes of the Chilterns where the M40 motorway traffic burst out of the hills to career across the plain northwards.

Closer to, the sound of the short train could be heard crawling along in the direction of Aylesbury, mainly invisible among the buildings and hedges along the shallow banks and cuttings. The major mused on the fact that in former days it would have been more than evidenced by the smoke trailing behind it.

By chance, it happened that Jim Witherspoon was gazing out of the window from one of the compartments of the same little train, with similar thoughts in mind, as the landscape of Kimble slid away behind. He tried to recognise the site of the county schools' camp that used to be located somewhere thereabouts. He failed to discern anything that even vaguely stirred his memory of it, although recollections of the hot sunny week he spent there as a schoolboy came readily into his mind even after 60 years. In an old worn scrapbook he still had the tinted postcard of Kimble which he bought on that occasion, but never got round to writing and posting home from the cottage post office.

He could still recall the smell of taut dry canvas, and grass, pervading the great marquee wherein such prosaic meals as mince and cabbage were dispensed with pungent distinction. Here and there, untrampled grass remained green within the shelter of the canvas while elsewhere it was arid and straw-coloured. Seating at the trestle tables consisted of forms, making a somewhat unstable arrangement on the uneven grass. Periodic upsets resulted in squabbles on the ground when someone stood up, tilting the rest backwards.

Sleeping facilities consisted of large brown bell tents, each sufficient for six or eight schoolboys, radiating from the central pole. Entrance flaps were situated on opposite sides, a feature which Jim recalled with some discomfiture. He had crawled into his bed one night and lain for a while looking out at the fading light through the open flaps to his right, before eventually nodding off.

At sometime during the night he had awakened with alarm, realising that the triangle of starlight was now on his left and immediately concluded that he had been sleepwalking with the result that he must now be in the wrong bed.

Had he been fully awake, he would have realised that, whatever the circumstance, it would have been better to stay put since he had no companion in the bed and all could be resolved in the morning. Instead, he felt compelled to correct the situation immediately and, forsaking the bed he was in, stumbled across to the opposite side, treading on limbs amidst violent protest. Eventually locating the opposite bed containing a contentedly slumbering close friend, he proceeded to slide down beside him while tersely informing his friend that he was in the wrong bed and should immediately effect a changeover to rectify the matter.

The friend would have none of it, demanding instead an explanation, loudly enough to awaken the other sleepers. Sensing that he might in some way be in error, the unfortunate Jim sought to account for his actions by rational explanation, defending in injured tones his interpretation of the disposition of the entrance.

When it was patiently pointed out that in order to avoid the night draught blowing straight into the open flaps, it was, by whispered agreement, resolved to close the one end and open the other. With soporific forbearance, Jim was permitted to retrace his erratic course back to his legitimate roost, his blushes mercifully lost in the night.

Sitting in the train, Jim couldn't help but ponder the effect of such an incident occurring now, with the awful interpretations bound to be adopted by the savage and unforgiving presumptions of society today. There would even be questions raised over the camp's visit to Whiteleaf Cross, when the more boisterous sector of the party elected to get too playful with the two straight-laced masters in charge, by knocking them to the ground and rolling them about, to the extreme outrage of the victims.

It was all so long ago, Jim mused; how different his career might have been had it not been for the fact that his parents were astute enough to seize the opportunity presented by the authorities, allowing narrow failures of the 'Scholarship' to go to the grammar school on condition that they subsequently trained as teachers. How many, he wondered, actually followed that undertaking. He could not recall that any others among the several who went with him actually honoured the intention, there being no contract to bind anyone against opportunism.

Thus he found himself eventually teaching general science in a secondary school, having achieved an ordinary degree in chemistry. His life had been fairly humdrum but comfortable. He married a girl of middle-class background who eventually inherited property and funds sufficient to ensure that their future existence was without financial concern. It was a situation unique to his generation, where inheritance had benefited from the enormous inflation of property values, as they grew up, with the result that division of estates between beneficiaries yielded capital far in excess of anything enjoyed by their forebears, thus creating a distinctly richer generation, apart from those whose parents were not home owners.

He would leave his estate to the two sons (now in their forties), as agreed with his wife Pauline just before she succumbed to her illness in her sixtieth year. One of the boys lived at Watersmead and Jim was on his way to pay his monthly visit as the train bore him farther and farther away from the nostalgic scene and the major's view.

Meanwhile, the major continued to scan the panorama which consisted of endless detail too densely telescoped into the view for him to distinguish anything familiar for certain. Even with his binoculars he was unable to find things where he thought they ought to be.

A herd of white cattle were grazing their way slowly across the grassy slope below him. He watched a pair of chattering magpies hopping from branch to branch in an oak tree at the end of a hedge beyond the herd. One of them flew off and he idly followed its flight until it stopped to perch again halfway along the hedge.

He noticed something in the field near to the bird. It was large and white, of a curious shape, and with what appeared to be a white post sticking out at an angle of 45 degrees or so. He focused the glasses onto the object and was startled to see that it was a cow lying on its side with its hind leg in the air; clearly an unsustainable attitude for a living beast.

The major, for some reason, felt ill at ease with the situation. He wondered how long the cow might have been there and whether anyone was aware of it, which he was inclined to doubt. It was quite a distance away from him and he had no idea what he could do about it anyway. He decided to mention it to Daphne or Kathy, on his return; they would know who the farmer was and would contact him.

He looked at his watch. It was ten-fifty and he felt surprisingly peckish already, but dismissed any idea of attacking his lunch so early. That, he concluded, was no doubt why Dick had included sweets in the list. He had put a small bag of barley sugars in the sack, and was surprised at the degree of comfort they afforded; somewhat like mid-air refuelling, he thought.

Continuing upward towards the top of the field which was bordered by a thick blackthorn hedge bearing the remnants of the previous year's crop of sloe berries, his further progress was hampered by the discovery of a barbed-wire fence skirting the field along the hedge which, he supposed, marked the edge of the summit. Not wishing to break any rules, he forbore to attempt any negotiation of the fence and followed it along towards a clump of trees where he found a stile. To his surprise, it led into a plantation sloping even farther upwards; thence into a wood which in turn appeared to continue the ascent yet more.

As he stepped into the plantation, a blood-curdling noise erupted in the woods at the top. The major thought it sounded like dogs fighting to the death. He stopped to scan the edge of the woods but could see nothing. He started to walk up through the plantation which consisted of saplings of oak, cherry and beech, generally about six feet in height. Each was supported by a post, and sheathed with a dull white plastic tube to prevent damage by the grazing muntjac deer that roamed abundantly throughout the area. The plantation was much strewn with bramble patches and young thorn, providing excellent cover for almost every kind of wildlife.

From a little way up the slope, the major caught a movement at the top and through the glasses he could distinctly see a large fox trotting down the slope towards him. He kept still to see what developed and was quite thrilled when the fox passed within two yards of him with no more than a casual sideways glance. The major felt quite gratified, as though privileged to be regarded as just part of the scene; it was real communion with nature.

He had just reached the wood when he was startled out of his wits by a loud whirring noise as a large round-shaped bird took off from the undergrowth within a yard of his feet. As it sped along the edge of the wood, away from him, he could see a long thin beak pointing directly down below its fat brown body. Rising gradually it curved away leftwards into the wood.

He took out the bird book and looked through the list of shapes at the back, finally tracking it down to being a woodcock. Before pressing on, he stopped to make a quick sketch of the shape as he remembered it, resembling a flying Christmas pudding.

Rounding the corner of the wood, he came face to face with a beautiful sharp-looking vixen, which stopped with a startled look, glanced behind it and cantered off into the undergrowth, shortly followed by a dog fox which came out of the wood to the left and, ignoring the major, crossed the path to follow the vixen.

From time to time the frantic noise of the vixens mating would break out again from different directions, as the chases progressed around the area during the rest of the morning. Occasionally the woods echoed with the sound of muntjacs barking, adding to the general concert of wild activity.

By one o'clock, the major felt justified in seeking a comfortable perch, to enjoy his well-deserved picnic, and looked about for somewhere to squat. He soon realised it was not as easy as one might think; to find a satisfactory seat could take considerable effort. He found that fallen tree trunks were too hard after less than a minute; anthills were plentiful and the right height but prone to the 'creeping damps' or the close attentions of any occupants.

He tried sitting at the base of various trees for the luxury of leaning back but concluded that trees are just not designed for the convenience of man; all attempted attitudes resulting in an inexorable sliding downwards like a playground chute and a growing ache in the outstretched legs. Furthermore, comfort demands that the knees are bent, for relaxation.

He found an area where several beech trees had been felled to form a clearing. The stumps were all at a perfect height for sitting, but not one had been cut without a 'slope' of some degree, despite appearing to be invitingly horizontal. The major discovered that any slope at all effected a gradual sliding forwards within his clothes, incurring unmentionable constrictive effects.

His desperate searching took him farther into the realms of starvation, until, frantic as he was for a good rest, and dismissing visions of deckchairs, he decided to wait no longer and, pulling his haversack round to the front, set about the thick corned-beef sandwiches liberally spread with good English mustard. The strong clean aroma of the beef made him ravenous with anticipation and he fell to with enthusiasm.

He walked on out of the wood into an area of sloping chalk grass sprinkled with large anthills and juniper bushes. A little to his left was a large spreading beech tree whose lower trunk divided unequally in a 'U' shape that reminded him of a saddle. It struck him as perhaps worth finding out to what degree it might serve like one. Walking across to the tree, he lifted his foot over the branch and sat down gingerly. Not only did it prove to be remarkably comfortable, but, also, his feet were resting on the ground. He leaned back against the trunk with a sumptuous feeling of grateful relaxation.

There were convenient gnarled projecting stubs on the branch in front of him whereon he was able to hang the sack and binoculars; thus relieving him of their encumbrance at last. He resumed his snack with as much comfort as if he were back in the dining room at Anvil Lodge.

The panorama before him and the warm sun on his face led him to conclude that there was surely no more rewarding place in the world to be than where he was. He swept the horizon through the glasses again, and this time he could see even farther than before. The mound of Wittenham Clumps in the direction of Didcot was easily discernible and the milky-blue haze of the farthest hills was probably beyond Abingdon, perhaps as far as Boar's Hill, west from Oxford itself.

A movement in the grass 50 yards away near the bottom of the plantation caught the major's attention. He trained the glasses onto an anthill where something green and white was busy digging into it. After a few seconds there was a flash of crimson as a large bird stepped back and stood erect, alerted by something. The major recognised his old acquaintance the green woodpecker, known to feed mainly on ants. He now understood why many of the anthills looked so mauled about. As he was to observe later, the pheasants also played their part in such disturbance.

Remembering the advice to 'watch the sky frequently', he made occasional sweeps below the scattered clouds, as far as he could from beneath the canopy of bare branches. Looking out over the plain, he saw a movement below the skyline where it was difficult to distinguish anything. He picked up the object with the glasses as it skimmed along blending with the background until suddenly swooping upwards to become a silhouette against the sky. The flight was lazy and graceful with large pinions spread and the tail distinctly forked.

The major guessed it to be a red kite; he'd heard much about them, especially the forked tail. He could hear it making a whirling-whistling sound as it gyrated round, moving gradually closer to the hillside where it was joined by another, swooping up from below. The two birds played together, making agile movements as though to curtsey towards each other and touch together. The display drew nearer until the major could see, without the glasses, the full rich colour of the bodies and underwings with their white patches.

146

Eventually the two raptors drifted out of sight above the woods behind him.

Away to his right beyond the trees he could hear a sound that reminded him of a seagull's cry which continued for some time until another large bird lifted above the trees and began to spiral slowly upward. It was soon joined by two more and after a minute or two by two more again; all following the spiral in turn. With mounting excitement the major searched through the raptor section of his book. While some of these newcomers had the brown and white under wings similar to the kites, the tails were rounded at the ends, not forked. After much checking against the possibilities, he decided that these could only be buzzards. He continued to watch as the number taking part in the now towering spiral grew eventually to nine.

Thinking that he must make a move, the major dismounted from his makeshift seat and glanced at his watch; two forty-six; how long would he need to get back he wondered? Standing for a moment, he tried to gauge how long he had been actually walking. He concluded that he needed about an hour and a half without hurrying.

That should be easy enough he thought and lifted the haversack from its peg, placing it round his shoulders again and, giving the tree a pat, said, 'Thanks, old boy, see you again perhaps,' and started to retrace his way back home.

The major had always been led to believe the wren to be the smallest British bird; but as he turned back into the wood, a tiny bird flitted into view on his left and, without the slightest concern, busied itself among the old-man's beard festooned on a derelict elder bush not above six feet from where he stood. As it searched about it faced towards him to reveal a reddish gold patch across its crown. A second bird then appeared, having a lighter, yellower mark. The major was delighted to be so close to the little charmers and kept quite still. When they foraged higher into the bush, he took out his book and tried to recall what they were, being sure that he'd seen them in the book somewhere as gold-something.

Goldfinches they were definitely not, as he could see by their size in the picture. Goldcrest – page 78, was certain to be it, he thought, correctly. Out of interest, he compared the size with that of the wren and found to his surprise that the goldcrest was almost half an inch smaller. He noted, for future interest, the similarity with the fire-crest, but then read that he wasn't likely to see one in that part of the country anyway.

About halfway through the wood, he began to realise just how far he'd wandered in search of a resting place and reiterated his gratification at eventually finding one. From the corner of the wood came a sudden quavering 'Hit who!' repeated after a few seconds, which the major knew very well to be an owl although he was unable to identify it. He had sometimes heard it in the grounds of the Lodge but had never heard one in the daytime before, a fact which he noted in his book.

As he emerged from the wood into the plantation he swore at himself when the great wings of a kite rose into the air almost immediately in front of him and arced away over the wood. Damn, he said to himself. He must learn not to break cover without first checking what was beyond the intevening bushes; that was where binoculars proved to be of more than obvious use. He had already discovered how effectively binoculars could penetrate through bushes, even those in leaf, to make all but the objects actually 'in focus' seem almost invisible. Even so, he thought, he could have peeped out before blundering out into the open. It was obviously what Dick meant by pre-scan round corners.

He could have had the thrill of watching a kite on the ground from close quarters and observed what it was doing there. Never mind, old son, he thought, don't forget the further advice, not to worry. He dismissed the incident from his mind and half an hour and a few minor species later, he found himself approaching the meadow down the slope where he'd noticed the cattle. There was, in fact, no sign of the herd; but where the dead cow was a tractor was manoeuvring a trailer into position just ahead of the dead animal.

The major stopped and watched the proceedings with interest. The driver tilted the trailer up until the back end was touching the ground. He walked round to the rear of the trailer and, taking a hawser from the back, pulled it out by the hooked end towards the carcass. He secured it around the hind quarters and clipped it back onto the line to form a noose. Clambering up onto the trailer, he commenced to wind the handle of a winch set into the front end. As it was hauled in, the carcass was dragged up the sloping trailer until it was mainly inboard.

The driver dismounted from the trailer, stepped up into the tractor, started the engine and the trailer began to descend back to the horizontal mode. He then returned to the winch to complete the easier hauling in. Returning once more to the tractor cab, the driver faced the front, pushed the gear into forward and set-off in a wide arc to head back to the farm. 'Just like that eh!' thought the major, lowering his binoculars. He later learned that the cow was in fact a heifer and had died from pneumonia early that morning. The farmer was unsurprised, having visited the field at first light and seen from the condition of the animal that it was near the end of its life.

During these proceedings the sky had rapidly gathered a few clouds together and formed a spectacular picture as the sun slid downwards into the western hills. It would not remain light for much longer the major mused, looking at his watch. It showed two minutes to five. Farther down the slope, and silhouetted against the sunset, a kestrel hung with motionless body, while the wings fluttered intermittently.

The major could see the towering boles of the beeches at the top of the eastern scarp bathed in the sun's last red rays, which were gradually sliding off as the sun sank behind a thin bank of black cloud along the western ridge. The air began to grow distinctly colder. Removing the haversack, the major dragged out his extra pullover and light windcheater, shivering slightly as he put them on, to feel instantly warmer. Ten minutes later he reached the door of his French window feeling extremely tired but gratified to look back on a most enjoyable day. Groping in his back pocket he took out the key and unlocked the door, to be greeted by his old German wall clock striking half past five.

Chapter 8

In Stitches

Maisie Metcalf and Gill Bolton had joined Daphne's 'brood' within a few weeks of each other and, as the newcomers at the time, had tended to talk more easily together as though needing no introduction, thus becoming close friends from that time onward. The liaison was furthered by their both being retired teachers and consequently seldom lost for a topic of discussion.

Maisie had arrived early in 1993 to assume occupation of second-floor rooms which had once been partly servant's quarters. Her bedroom was above her sitting room, both overlooking treetops to distant hills where the sun rose. She soon settled, and became much attached to her dear little rooms as she called them. On her first evening, while taking coffee in the drawing room, she became acquainted with a nice gentleman named Mr Beardmore, who endeavoured to make her feel at home. He told her of his close friendship with the old gentleman, Tom Bonner, who had been the former occupant of her rooms. He had remained sprightly to the end of his days, which came only a few weeks previously, at the age of 96. Born five years before Queen Victoria died, he had led a remarkable life, much of which Mr Beardmore retailed to Maisie over the ensuing weeks.

Old Tom was born in Aylesbury and, recalling his life as a boy, described being present at the railway station at the time of the great disaster when two trains collided just outside the station. He claimed to have seen one of the firemen draped over the signal gantry, following the impact.

Tom began his working life apprenticed to a bookbinder, mastering the art of gold blocking. At the outbreak of the Great War he enlisted in the army and at the age of 18 found himself in hospital with shrapnel wounds in the chest. The nurses informed him that he had been pronounced dead over a period of several minutes.

On his subsequent return to the front he was seconded to the Royal Flying Corps, with a temporary commission, to act as a courier between the Military and the French Resistance agents. Being regularly flown into occupied territory, he established a close relationship with a young couple who were his contacts in the resistance movement. From them he learned many useful skills including effective knife throwing, by which ability he was able to save himself following his capture by the enemy, killing the officer holding him captive in the process.

He was later accorded the assistance of a volunteer who, having a criminal record, was offered redemption through the dangerous missions they undertook together. The man proved his worth by many acts of courage and dependability. While Tom was awarded decorations from both British and Allied authorities, his worthy companion was, as an ex-criminal, excluded from such recognition, and at the cessation of hostilities Tom registered his outrage by returning his own British awards.

Much of his later life was spent working in the racing world at Newmarket where he became acquainted with the family of the leading jockey of the day, whose mother was, as a young girl, on one occasion, exercising horses, near the course. Tom was on hand when her mount bolted, carrying her towards a dangerous hazard. His instant reaction enabled him to arrest the horse just short of disaster, thereby earning the gratitude and lasting friendship of the family.

During the Second World War he was living at Westerham in Kent, and in minor official capacities became acquainted with Mr Churchill at Chartwell, which he often had occasion to visit. He was emboldened, in one instance, to criticise Winston's artistic efforts, face to face, naively suggesting more comprehensible detail. His observations were borne by the great man with generous tolerance, the artist having already made his philosophy widely known, using the phrase 'Audacity is the best ticket'.

Tom was moved to venture onto yet more hazardous ground when he discovered that the wine store in the town had run out of his particular label, on account of an order from Chartwell absorbing all available stocks. At the next opportunity, he confronted the offender, with a virtual accusation of selfishness. Fortunately for Tom, it was met with further magnanimity in the form of half a dozen bottles being delivered to his door, by the chauffeur.

Such anecdotes were relayed to Maisie during her various conversations with the solicitous Mr Beardmore, whose first name she discovered to be Tom, also. When Gill Bolton arrived to take up residence, and formed an attachment with Maisie, it was seen by Tom Beardmore as his cue to ease off from his duty of care.

Gill Bolton, possessing a natural inclination to creativity, had developed, to a high degree, the arts that she taught, particularly those of lacemaking and crochet work, which she continued to practise as the principal pleasure of her retirement. She often astounded her fellow residents with the gems of her output. When she presented Daphne with an exquisite lace table cover, of a colour between straw and gold, Daphne placed it for permanent display on a small antique table in the main hall, and no visitor was allowed to overlook her treasure.

Maisie, on the other hand, was content to bash away on a bit of knitting, as something to do while she chatted. Her skill in that quarter had remained little changed since she was six years old when, at school, she embarked on her initial instruction. Although she ultimately completed much of a chocolate-brown and yellow scarf, succeeding admirably with creating the stitches, she never quite mastered the critical requirement of coming back along the next row without, somehow, adding an extra stitch. Over the ensuing weeks, while the pleasing bands of yellow and brown appeared as properly required, the width of the scarf continued, despite the dedicated attentions of the mystified teacher, to increase from the initial four inches to about nine.

The two friends were sitting on the veranda in the afternoon sun, discussing The Dome, when the major appeared.

'Good afternoon Major, won't you join us? It's so lovely here,' Maisie invited.

'We always sit at this end, it seems less draughty somehow,' she continued.

'That's most kind of you,' he replied, touching his hat.

'I think I will, just for a few minutes.'

He was about to sit down but straightened up again, saying, 'Can I get you ladies anything?'

'No, thank you, Major, not just now; I expect we'll have some tea later on,' Gill replied.

He sat down and tilted his hat forwards to shade his eyes. He had just been talking to Laurie Henderson who was busy servicing the lawnmower ready for the coming season. Laurie intimated that he was working on Mrs Currer-Spriggs to change the old electrical mower for a petrol version, on the grounds that the lawns were too extensive for a mower that relied on miles of lead to reach everywhere.

The fact was that Daphne had never made the choice of an electric mower in the first place, the present one being the first prize in a gardening journal competition. She had failed to persuade any supplier to agree a fair deal in swapping it. Meanwhile, as Laurie described to the major, the damage inflicted on the plants by the flexible lead was hard to credit. It could perform the most astonishing feats, tying complex knots entirely unaided, to lasso such small plants as lobelias and snatch them out of the ground. It would invariably effect intricate engagement among the sword like leaves of the giant yuccas and achieve waist-high capture of rose bushes.

The major expressed his sympathy and undertook to use any influence he could in support of Laurie's pleas to the C.O.

'The water hose is almost as bad,' complained Laurie.

'Well there you have it, old boy,' said the major. 'There's nothing to be done about that, and when it comes to mischief, there is nothing more animated than the inanimate,' and leaving Laurie to ponder the profundity, he continued on his way.

'Have you seen the Dome, Major?' Maisie asked, glancing sideways, needles clattering.

'Can't say that I have actually,' he replied.

'We saw it from a distance once,' said Gill, 'my husband and I were on the Dockland Railway, just sightseeing while we were in St Katherine's Dock for a few days with the cruiser club. Most of the other boats had gone downriver to see the barrier and other sights that we had done before, so we decided to go ashore. The Dockland Railway seemed the obvious thing to do. I can't say that it was much of a thrill to see the Dome from where we were.'

'Have they decided what to do with it yet?' Maisie enquired, looking from one to the other.

'I know what I'd do with it,' said the major. 'In fact I wrote to *The Daily Telegraph*, about it once.'

'Oh, my goodness,' said Maisie, dropping the knitting to her lap and looking first to the left at Gill, with eyebrows lifting, and then at the major to her right.

'Did they print it?' asked Gill.

'No!' said the major ruefully. 'Just an acknowledgement card as usual.'

'You've written before then by the sound of it,' she added.

'From time to time on various topics; never had one printed yet though,' the major confessed.

'Well, I suppose they must receive thousands of letters,' Gill remarked.

'Yes, I'm sure they do,' the major agreed.

'So, what was your suggestion, Major?' asked Maisie, resuming her knitting.

'Well,' he paused, gazing into the distance, 'I think they should give the whole damned island to a special trust having complete autonomy, free of any interference from government or other authority including the police, and exempt from Customs duty and tax, to be developed and run as a venue for pop concerts. Those attending would do so knowing it to be entirely at their own risk while having the freedom to make as much noise as they liked and being entirely responsible for themselves, the law being neither threat nor salvation.

'Reasonable people are not opposed to

pop concerts as such, which are enjoyed by many, provided they are not imposed on the public at large, to many of whom they present an unbearable racket. Furthermore, I don't think that national monuments and historical sites are suitable venues for such events and I can't see the need for it.

'I wouldn't mind betting,' the major continued, 'that with the right people in charge, it would develop into an outstanding social and financial success. The place is absolutely ideal for it. Given the chance, with imagination and determination, the Dome could achieve real purpose instead of being a monument to failure. Probably too late now, of course. I've no doubt someone will knock it all down rather than see it put to laudable use. Avarice will doubtless be the governing factor with no benefit to the nation as a whole, I'm afraid!'

'I can't see how it could possibly work,' said Gill, 'think of the problems involved.'

'Think of the problems involved with the Golden Jubilee,' said the major. 'That show left the world gasping. Anything can be done with the right man in charge.'

'Well I must say, it's a novel idea,' said Maisie, 'We'll just have to wait and see, won't we?'

Gill glanced at the major to note the effect of Maisie's superficial comment. He met her gaze with the trace of a smile and stood up.

'Well, girls, better be on my way,' he said.

'Oh, won't you stay for a cup of tea?' said Gill, disappointed.

'Afraid not,' he replied. 'Must find old Dicky, before he goes out; see you later,' and off he went.

'Such a nice man,' said Maisie.

'M'mm,' said Gill, gazing after him.

'I think I'll go and find Tracey,' said Maisie, standing up.

'Good idea,' said Gill, 'I'm dying for a cup.'

Maisie put down her knitting on the chair; the ball of wool rolled straight onto the ground and headed for the flower border.

'Oh botheration,' said Maisie, stopping it with her foot.

'Push it on the ends,' said Gill strictly. 'I keep telling you, dear; you won't listen, will you?'

'I know!' said Maisie, with a trace of irritation.

Jabbing the needle points through the ball of wool and returning the bundle to the seat, she walked to the nearby doorway and entered the dining room just as Tracey came through the kitchen door, opposite.

'Hello, Mrs Metcalf, come in for some tea, have you?' enquired Tracey, 'Where are you, on the veranda? What about Mrs Bolton, she with you and all, I expect.'

'Yes,' was all Maisie managed to interject.

'Will you want biscuits?' Tracey continued.

'Just one or two, please, dear,' said Maisie, retreating.

'I expect it's lovely out there this afternoon,' Tracey went on. 'Laurie Henderson reckons it's fifty-eight, in the shade.'

'Goodness!' replied Maisie, slipping back out onto the veranda.

The sun was getting mixed up with the network of branches as it headed into the larger trees surrounding the main grass areas, thereby reducing its strength. Maisie gave a little shiver, as she sat down again.

'I think I'll go and get my cardigan,' she said, getting up once again. 'Won't be long, dear,' she added and disappeared round the end of the veranda.

Why on earth didn't she bring it with her in the first place? thought Gill, though not with any surprise. How she ever managed a class of children Gill couldn't imagine. Devoted as she was to Maisie, she wondered how the woman would manage without someone to keep her on the right path, all the time.

Tracey arrived with the tea tray.

'Oh,' she exclaimed, 'you haven't got a table, Mrs Bolton. I'll fetch one from down the end,' she said, putting the tray on the ground. 'Mrs Metcalf's coming back, is she?' Tracey conjectured adding 'Oh! there she is' as Maisie rounded the corner, deftly lifting the cast white table as she passed it. 'You shouldn't have bothered, Mrs Metcalf,' said Tracey, picking up the tray again and placing it on the table. 'I'd have done that.'

Maisie sat down once again and Tracey returned inside, bobbing back for an instant to enquire, with a smile, 'All O.K. then?' before vanishing, without pause for answer.

The sun sank lower, taking the temperature with it. The crocuses had made their first attempt to open during the day and the glimpses of yellow stood out like candle flames in the darkening air. Blackbirds around the edge of the shrubbery were starting up their evening chorus of captious piping, as they scattered dead leaves and bark mulch onto the grass, to the later annoyance of Laurie Henderson. The noise of table laying in the dining room, as lights were coming on, prompted the two women to adjourn to the drawing room, before the air turned any colder. Maisie pushed her knitting into the crumpled brown paper bag, 'Ready, dear?' she said, looking at Gill.

There was quite a gathering of ladies in the drawing room as usual. Tea trays were on most of the tables and voices were gradually increasing in volume as they competed for ascendancy over the ambient noise level. Gill and Maisie found seats by joining with Joyce Kingham and Minnie Caple. The latter was being entertained by Joyce's description of the outing in the Bee, as the Rover was now generally known. Minnie persuaded Joyce to repeat some of the story, for the benefit of the newcomers, and as the mood of the quartet gradually warmed, conversation became increasingly more animated.

Minnie said she was reminded of an occasion during her Land Army days when she was invited out for an evening by a local boyfriend whose father owned a large Austin car with a sliding sunroof. Borrowing the car for the evening, they had stopped on the way home, parking discreetly, to see what developed.

Rain was pouring down in torrents and as they reached a critical juncture, in the front seats, the sunroof gave way, releasing half a pint of cold water straight into her lap.

'I screamed blue murder and leaped into the back. I took my knickers off and wrung them out on the floor; it was no good trying to do them out of the window. I just put them in my bag with a hankie round them; there were no tissues or plastic bags, in those days. But, what really got me, was that it missed him altogether. At least he had the grace to give me his nice big clean handkerchief.'

Joyce was, by now, holding her sides. Gill

was trying not to laugh.

Maisie kept saying, 'Oh my goodness!' with her hand to her mouth.

'Then what?' giggled Joyce.

'I stayed in the back, in the dry; I just wanted to get back to my digs, I was in no mood for anything else,' said Minnie.

'So, you went home with your knickers in your bag, for the wrong reason then,' said Joyce, wiping her eyes.

'You could say that, I suppose,' Minnie concluded.

'I can't understand why the major would want to take on a car at his time of life, can you?' said Maisie, looking at the others in turn. 'After all, if he can't get a lift to wherever he wants to go, he can always get a taxi, can't he?'

'He's not all that old, is he?' Minnie enquired, 'What would you say, seventy?' she suggested.

'I don't think we should be discussing the major's age, or business,' commented Gill getting up from her armchair. 'Anyway, if you'll excuse me, I'm off to my room; it'll be dinnertime before we know it. I'll see you all later,' she said, and left the room, hoping that she wasn't offending anyone.

Minnie looked at the others, questioningly, lifting her shoulders, eyebrows arched.

'Well, I think it's very venturesome of the

major and as a matter of fact I happen to know that it's his birthday sometime next month and he'll be seventy-three,' said Joyce.

'Perhaps he's after someone,' suggested Minnie.

'Yes, and with your experience, it's probably you!' replied Joyce, laughing. 'What do you think, Maisie?'

'Goodness,' said Maisie, 'I'm sure I don't know,' and then with unaccustomed boldness, astonished the others by adding, 'I suppose a bonnet in his bee, would be a change from the usual bee in his bonnet.'

She clapped a hand to her mouth and looked at the others with a shocked expression; gradually giving way to a saucy grin, as though she'd overstepped the mark. The other two looked at each other briefly before collapsing with laughter.

'That was brilliant, Maisie,' said Joyce, waving to Ramiro who had just entered the room with his trolley.

'Something rich and cheery, Ramiro; what do you suggest?' she said, looking up at him with a twinkle in her eye.

'Bristol Creams?' he offered.

'Why not?' said Joyce, glancing at the others who nodded approval.

With the drinks poured, Joyce declared, 'Here's to you, Maisie, cheers!'

Maisie blushed and, feeling she was

getting slightly out of her depth without the shelter of her mentor's presence, drank her sherry as soon as she decently could and announced that she, too, really must go and get ready for dinner.

Meanwhile, the major had managed to find Dick and to arrange a morning expedition into the wild. Following their trip to Amersham, he was eager to try out his new gear.

'Just a quiet stroll really,' he said, bearing in mind that Dick was 80 years old.

'Whatever you like, L.-J.,' Dick replied easily.

'Shall we say nine o'clock in the boot room, then,' the major suggested.

'At the latest,' came the firm reply.

Chapter 9

Natural Histories

The following morning the major emerged into the hall carrying his haversack which contained, among other things, his new Brasher boots to be tried for the first time. The boot room, as it was generally referred to, led off the inner corner of the entrance hall. It was formerly used as a sort of small gunroom in the days of shooting parties. Two moth-eaten and faded trophy heads bore testament to how long ago that was, as from the high wall they stared across into space with infinite patience, awaiting their material doomsday. There was little else left to share their dusty world. One small tilting window with the remnants of its operating cord shed minimal light from the apex of the gabled end wall; sufficient only to reveal the traces of where gun cases and racks once lined the room. A few pairs of muddy walking shoes and gumboots, against the wall, betrayed occasional latter day intrusion.

Dick was sitting on the rickety old form seat along the wall, pulling on his boots as the major walked in.

'Ready L.-J.?' he asked as the major appeared.

'As soon as I've got my boots on I'm with you,' he replied, taking a seat at the other end of the form.

Dick sat back ready to go and gazed around the peeling white-washed walls of the dilapidated little room.

'You know, to me, this place reeks of history, scruffy as it is; it's the one corner of this building that remains as it was when it was first used. Look at that,' he said, pointing to the bare light bulb; bulbous toward the bottom where the sharp sealing pip pointed downward. 'That's at least seventy or eighty years old and still working. Just think, it could have been there during the Great War.'

'Well, in those days they didn't know how to make things that wouldn't last,' the major replied, rather cynically.

'Wouldn't it be marvellous if you could put your ear to the wall and still hear echoes of conversations in this room from all those years ago? Just imagine the noise and bustle; the loud, assertive, aristocratic voices.'

'Yes, I suppose you're right, old boy,' said the major, standing up and flexing his toes. 'By Jove, these boots feel marvellous. I wondered if I'd be able to stand up in them from the shape of them.'

'Ah, that's the secret,' said Dick, rising to his feet, 'they may seem damned expensive but they're worth every penny, you'll see. Shall we go?'

They clumped across the flagstones of the entrance hall to the outside and took the path left towards the meadow.

'Not such a good day today,' observed the major as they approached the steeper slope beyond the spring stream. 'Pity really,' he added.

'There are dry days, wet days, cold and windy days,' observed Dick, 'but there are no bad days. Whatever the weather the wildlife is still there and serious observation demands it all. Mind you, as I've said before, don't make hard work of it; if you don't enjoy traipsing about in a cold wind, for God's sake don't force yourself to do it. Leave that to the dedicated nutters like me.

'It depends on your depth of curiosity,' Dick continued. 'I would always go out if there had been a fall of snow. It's a different world then, with everything revealed by the tracks left. It shows just how much goes on that you would never be aware of otherwise.'

'I see what you mean,' said the major. 'I must try that, though I don't suppose it will snow again this year; the amount that fell the other day was soon gone.'

'You never know,' said Dick. 'I've seen snow fall in June, not that it settled, of course.

'Then there's the other end of the scale,' he continued. 'For instance, round about the end of May and early June, the midday weather can be at its hottest and everything seems to have gone to sleep. You might then be amazed to see lengths of dry grass stems, maybe six inches or so in length, apparently cruising unaided through the air a foot or two above the ground without a hint of breeze to carry them. The first time I saw that happening I thought I was having sunstroke, in fact you'll probably only see it in hot weather if the sun is actually out. You'll then notice that a tiny black bee with a reddish backside is carrying the stem like a witch on a broomstick. The odd thing is that they usually ride up-front with the stem drooping down behind them.

'If you see one, it won't be long before it drops down to the ground where you'll find the bee is building a sort of wigwam of stems in the grass. It's actually making a shelter over a snail shell. Whenever the sun goes in the bee will instantly disappear, though I've yet to see where it goes to, it happens so quickly. Obviously it drops into the grass somewhere.'

'Good Lord,' said the major. 'What's it all about?'

'Well, it starts with the bee finding a place to lay its eggs and it always uses an empty snail shell of a certain type and size. I'll try to find one to show you.

'The bees are quite rare, actually, but calcareous hillsides like this are typical habitat for them, so you stand a reasonable chance of coming across one. They're called Two-coloured Mason Bees, or Osmia Bicolor, to use its Sunday name. Most textbooks only show the commoner Osmia Rufa, which is less specialised. They're becoming better known at the moment. In fact, last summer I met a young girl student from Oxford University who was doing a thesis on them. Otherwise there's not an awful lot known or published apart from one or two old tracts and a fairly recent

German paper.

'I caught two of the bees, five or six years ago, which were passed on by the County Museum at Halton to the Natural History Museum who identified them and sent copies of the few references there were.'

'Well done, old boy,' said the major. 'Incidentally, I can't believe how much easier it is to walk up these steep slopes; these boots are absolutely first class. Sorry to interrupt, Dickie. Do go on.'

Dick resumed his narrative.

'When the bee finds a suitable empty shell, it heaves it over onto its back, crawls to the innermost recess and lays one or two eggs. It then seals the eggs in by making a mastic of chewed grass and mud. It repeats the process until the shell is filled up and a final layer finishes it flush to the outside. During the process the bee flies back and forth to a nearby patch of exposed earth, always one of the site conditions, I've noticed, for making the mastic. The bee then has to manoeuvre the shell which, by then, is quite heavy and several times bigger than the bee itself, into the upright position flat side down.

'Finally, it starts the business of covering the shell with the grass stems, presumably to disguise it from predators and perhaps to shade it from the sun.

'More flying back and forth as it collects

the stems of the lengths it requires to build the wig-wam structure; siting it in a tussock of grass well-camouflaged in itself. You're not likely to find one without seeing the bee at work.

'I managed to take a short video sequence of one, while the battery lasted. It was quite amusing to see the bee bringing in a length of stem and getting it caught up with some grass; being frustrated from placing it for some seconds before having to fly off and come in again backwards in order to thrust it down into place; which, to me, is more to do with intelligence than mere instinct.'

'That's absolutely fascinating,' said the major. 'You're not just an ornithologist, then.'

'I don't see how anybody can be,' replied Dick. 'With so much else going on around; you can't really ignore it all.'

'Well, no I suppose not,' the major concluded. He looked back at the view and realised how much easier the climb had been with proper footwear.

'Try the new glasses,' he said, handing the treasured binoculars to Dick.

'Thanks L.-J.,' said Dick, putting the strap over his head for safety. 'Lovely feel to them,' he observed.

He trained the glasses towards the sound of a train that was crawling across the landscape in the direction of High Wycombe.

'Where did you say you got them?' he enquired.

'Second-hand place in Thame,' said the major.

'They must have cost a fortune, new. You take good care of them; I've never seen better, or as good come to that,' said Dick, handing them back to the proud owner.

To the major, Dick seemed tireless. They reached the top of the scarp seemingly in no time and he again realised how much difference was made by not having to struggle along in shoes. The boots practically walked up by themselves, he thought.

'Ah!' exclaimed Dick, as they came to a gateway, 'Before we go through there, let's have a look under that,' he said, pointing to a rusted half sheet of corrugated iron lying in the grass at the bottom of the hedge.

'You never know your luck,' he said, as they walked over and squatted by the sheet. Dick glanced at the major as though to say 'ready,' and then lifted the end firmly and evenly upwards.

In the middle of the dry area was a neat round nest of dry grass in the midst of which something stirred for a second. Then a startled wood mouse emerged to sit up on its haunches quivering for a moment before streaking for the grounded end of the sheet and diving into the cover of the under-growth beyond.

'Look,' said Dick, pointing to something coiled up towards the end of the sheet.

'Lummy!' said the major. 'A snake.'

'No, it's a slow-worm,' returned Dick and after a moment or two he gently lowered the sheet back into its exact position.

'Well I'm damned,' said the major, grinning as they walked away. 'Do you think the mouse will return to its billet?'

'Perhaps; I hope so,' replied Dick. 'It's fairly safe from predators there. It will have to make a difficult decision I suppose.'

'Poor little devil,' remarked the major. 'Surely the slow-worm is a snake of some sort,' he added.

'Not at all,' said Dick. 'It's a lizard, actually, slowly evolved to the point where it still has the vestiges of legs under the skin, and it's still in three parts. The tail section can easily break off, and often does, leaving a square end. Actually, they're anything but slow when they want to move. If it had been roused, and it will come to any day now, it could move at a surprising speed.'

'What do they live on? Insects?'

'Yes,' Dick replied. 'Very largely those little white slugs that gardeners hate so much, and for that reason they should be made very welcome in the garden but I'm afraid there are many so-called, gardeners who are ignorant enough to kill them on sight without knowing why.'

'I shall test out Laurie, when I next see him; ask him what he does with slow-worms,' the major said, with a grin.

'I expect he takes them home,' suggested Dick, laughing.

'How's the time?' enquired the major looking at his watch. 'Perhaps we should be turning back; it's about eleven.'

'Yes, I reckon so,' said Dick.

They started back towards the gateway, pausing to rest against it for a few minutes. They reviewed the number of bird species they had seen so far and accounted for 15.

'Not bad for a couple of hours,' observed Dick.

'Pretty good if you ask me,' said the major.

'Winter and spring are the best times for bird counts,' said Dick. 'Late summer is the dullest, the opposite of butterflies,' he added. 'Talking of which, there's a male brimstone dancing along by that wire fence, look.'

'What, the other side of the field?' said the major, peering through his binoculars at a light-coloured speck dropping down into the long, dead grass.

'How on earth can you tell from here, Dickie?'

'First of all because they will appear out of hibernation for a fly round at any time of the year if it's a mild enough day, and the male is a light yellowish colour, while the female is white. The earliest I've recorded them is February the second, in fifty degrees; I remember seeing a bumblebee at the same time. There won't be much else about in the way of butterflies for another week or so.'

They had reached the lower slopes of the hill and the sound of the spring stream became audible again.

'The rabbits are having a high old time,' said the major, pointing towards the middle of the field.

'Hares, L.-J.,' corrected Dick. 'Notice the longer ears, with black patches at the ends, and the awkward angular look.'

'Yes, I see,' the major replied, looking through the glasses. 'I say, there are two of them squaring up, look, like kangaroos, almost. There are four altogether, dashing about like mad things.'

'Of course,' said Dick. 'It's that time of year isn't it?'

'Dickie, I really can't thank you enough,' said the major, as they crossed the grounds towards the house. 'It's been an education and such a pleasure for me.'

'Well, as I always say, "A pleasure shared, is a pleasure doubled",' replied Dick.

'Come through my room; save you walking all round,' said the major, groping in his back pocket for the key as they arrived at his French door. 'Oh dear!' he said, remembering their shoes were still in the boot room.

'We'll both have to go round to the front, anyway.'

There were two small libraries at the disposal of the residents. Books of an antique or reference nature were displayed in an appropriate setting in the hall. Housed in a long, glass-fronted mahogany case, they had remained a virtually undisturbed feature of the hall for as long as Daphne could remember and she believed them to have been there for probably 100 years or more. Although the contents were available to the residents, they were generally regarded as ornamental and consequently were rarely taken out.

The other source of literary diversion resided in the drawing room, in the form of a bookcase at each end, containing the customary collections of general interest. Privately sourced periodicals were liberally available, by abandonment, on the occasional tables in both reception rooms.

The major was not an avid reader beyond casual perusal of his daily paper. However, his attention was caught one afternoon by the title of a book about the Chilterns. Having briefly indulged in a pipe in the sitting room, he had wandered into the drawing room for a cup of tea and settled himself at a small table at the end of the room near the bookcase.

Prompted by his recent ventures into the wild, he withdrew the book and a quick glance through was enough to persuade him that it should prove well worth reading for background knowledge. He placed the open book on the table before him while he drank his tea.

At that moment Sandy Balfour came into the room and nodded to the major, as he poured some coffee.

He walked over to the major's table, but seeing the book, said, 'Hello, L.-J. I see you're busy, I'll leave you to it.'

'No, no, old boy, the book's for bedtime reading. Do take a seat,' replied the major, waving Sandy towards the adjacent chair.

'Book at bedtime, eh? I say. That looks familiar if you don't mind me saying,' said Sandy, as he sat down.

'What, the book?' asked the major.

'No, the picture,' replied Sandy.

'Oh, I see,' said the major, looking at the photograph of a white square-looking house. 'Somewhere in Amersham, apparently,' he said.

'I wondered if it might be,' Sandy observed.

'Do you know it?' asked the major.

'I believe so, let's have a closer squint,' said Sandy.

'Certainly, old chap,' replied the major, handing him the book.

Sandy had only to glance at the picture, for a smile to spread over his face.

'Number one, High and Over,' he said, 'otherwise known as the First Sun-house.'

'Obviously you do know it then,' said the major with some surprise.

'Oh yes,' said Sandy. 'A schoolfriend of mine lived there for a while in the mid-forties.'

'During the war, then,' observed the major.

'Yes,' replied Sandy. 'That's where I was on D-Day, I remember. The sky was filled with hundreds of planes droning over, from early morning. It went on for several hours; mainly Dakotas, half of them towing Hotspur and Horsa gliders. I can't recall the other types of aircraft; anything that would carry troops or tow gliders, I suppose. The noise was unbelievable, as you can imagine. One of the gliders became detached and skimmed along the Misbourne valley, coming to rest in a field.

'Everything seemed to happen along the Misbourne. A German fighter came down there once but by the time we arrived to look at it there was a marquee over it and the farmer was charging a shilling to see it, until the army arrived to remove it. A stick of bombs fell along there one night; you can still see some of the craters from the London road. I was eleven at the time and lying in bed listening to each bang, successively louder; frightened the life out of me, I can tell you. The Misbourne valley was also a regular route for Doodlebugs, one of which demolished two houses in Amersham.'

'But what was special about this place apart from being in the middle of a war zone?' the major asked, grinning.

'It was the first of a small estate of five houses built on the hillside leading up to the principal house called High and Over, which was situated at the top of the hill overlooking the town. They were built in the twenties and they're world famous for their *avant-garde* architecture. They were unique, principally because they were made of concrete. I expect it will tell you that in the book. Local people referred to them as the aeroplane houses because of the shape of High and Over itself. Actually, they're only a few hundred yards from where you and Dick went for your walking gear the other day.

'The thing I remember particularly about that house is the flat roof with a wall round it; we spent a lot of time playing up there. If you look at the picture you can see that the windows run continuously from the front door right up to the roof top, exposing the spiral staircase and landings. At the top, there's a door through onto the roof.

'Incidentally, between the kitchen and the dining room there was a revolving door with circular shelves on one side; exactly the same as the one in the kitchen here; I've often wondered which of them was the first. I've never come across one anywhere else. I must ask Daphne if she knows how long it's been here.'

'Oh yes, I know,' said the major, nodding. 'Between the kitchen and the passageway, you mean.'

'What about the big house at the top, did you ever see inside it?'

'Oh yes, my friend knew it well. I went up there with him for a swim once. There was a long flight of wide steps from the back of the house, down through an avenue of conifers to a circular swimming pool.

'In those days the house was a breathtaking place. Built on three floors, in three symmetrical wings radiating from a circular centre. The double entrance doors were stainless steel sheet and led into a large circular hallway, consisting of a black marble floor surrounding a central fountain set in a round illuminated fish pool. I remember our host turning up the fountain so that it passed through the first floor circular balcony that overlooked the hall.'

'By Jove! Sounds quite a place,' said the major.

'Well, bearing in mind that it was built nearly eighty years ago, I can't exaggerate the futuristic opulence of it,' continued

Sandy. 'It's still a world-famous building. The atmosphere of the place was extraordinary; like being in an airship, looking out at the clouds. The whole place was surrounded by gardens, radiating out, as soft fruit areas, stone fruit orchards, kitchen gardens, rose beds and Lord knows what else. Cars were garaged underground and water was supplied through a white concrete round tower standing in the grounds nearby, looking like a big cross on the hilltop.

'Apart from the building itself, it's all gone now. The house was converted into flats and the grounds became a housing estate. It must bring tears to the eyes of anyone who knew the place in its heyday.'

'Extraordinary,' the major exclaimed. 'What a waste, should have been preserved in its entirety.'

'Well there we are,' said Sandy. 'I remember it being on the market, in its prime, for thirteen thousand pounds, if you can believe it. My friend's father bought number one for a thousand pounds, early in the war and, following a family tragedy, sold it two or three years later for two thousand.

'I think I'll get another cup of coffee,' Sandy said, handing the book back to the major.

Well, well, the major thought, small world.

Chapter 10

Security

'Isn't that just typical!' exclaimed the major, lowering his *Telegraph* sufficiently to survey the immediate circle of midmorning companions in the sitting room.

All were preoccupied with their own literary distractions and none made reply until Smiler, reaching the end of the page that he was reading, said, 'If you say so. L.-J. What is?'

'This security business; gets worse by the week,' the major went on, glad of someone's attention. 'They've just let someone walk through Customs with a damned great packet of heroin in his jacket pocket; bold as brass!

'If it hadn't been for the fact that he unwisely made a fuss of someone's nice dog by patting it in a display of innocence and normality as he passed casually through Arrivals, he might yet be at large. The off-duty handler of a sniffer-dog had been sitting down quietly with the dog, awaiting the arrival of his wife off a flight from Belfast, when his boredom was abruptly relieved by the affable attentions to his dog. The spectacular reactions of the dog alerted the handler in time to make an arrest before the offender could fully appreciate the magnitude of his error.'

'The trouble is,' asserted Bob King, closing his book, over his thumb, 'the general psyche of the Western world, especially in this country, is innately naive. They make rules and regulations, and expect everybody to play the game.'

'That's a bit simple, isn't it?' said Sandy. 'How do you make that out?'

'Well, I'll give you an instance,' Bob replied. 'When I was visiting Ministry of Works depots on business, I sometimes had to call at top-security locations such as nuclear-bomber bases. On one occasion I was looking for a place a few miles outside a small town in Rutland. I took the main road out of the town hoping to recognise the place when I came to it.

'I'd only gone a couple of miles when I caught up with a small van beetling along in front which I recognised by the name on the back as belonging to the contractors holding the current two-year franchise for Ministry work at the base. I guessed he might be going to the same place and thought it might be worth following him.

'After a while, the fields on the left sloped upwards, forming a continuous bank that obscured the view from the road. I was rather surprised when a bit farther on he suddenly turned off to the left through a gap in the hedge and drove into the field.

'Thinking he was perhaps, after all, visiting a farm or something, I decided to follow just as far as the top, for a view point. We roared up the slope following a rough track. At the top, lo and behold, all was there before us; vast hangars in the distance, aircraft and buildings scattered about. As we had obviously arrived at the right place, I simply followed him until, reaching the middle of the airfield, we drove into the heavily-fenced works' compound where I parked beside the van; thinking "very nice, thank you."

'I got out, locked the car, and wandered into the offices to ask for Mr Such-and-such, the superintendent. He seemed very surprised to see me; saying something about "they didn't tell me you were here". "Never mind!" he said, "come with me and I'll take you over to the main hangar to look at the work. I must impress on you, though, we shall be passing some top-secret offices, so on no account stop by any windows especially if they're open,' he said.

'"Where's your badge?" he asked. "What badge?" I said. "The one they gave you at the guard room, with your car-sticker." "Ah," I said, "I didn't come in that way." "What do you mean?" he said. "Well, I just followed that van from the road," I replied, pointing. "Oh my Good heavens," he said. "Quick! We'll have to go in your car." I unlocked the car again and we got in and went tearing down to the guardhouse. "You must never do that again," he said, on the way. "Everybody has to go through the main gate to be properly checked in; otherwise we get into trouble if it's anybody to do with us; they're very strict about it all."This is cloud-cuckoo-land! I thought, they're all in a world of their own."'

His narrative occasioned frequent laughs and expressions of incredulity.

'Yes, but when was that?' the major asked, somewhat dubiously.

'Who cares when?' said Tom Dangerfield. 'Methods may have changed since but I doubt if people have!'

'There was one place though,' Bob went on, 'near Aylesbury, as it happens, where the security was very good. The perimeter fencing was absolutely impenetrable and you just had to go through the main gate; there was no other way. You were subject to a time-marked and signed card at every point and escorted everywhere by an armoured car if you were driving, or an armed guard if you were on foot.'

'There you are then,' concluded the major, anxious to defend the military case if he could.

'Well, that's my experience,' said Bob King, 'Perhaps it boils down to individual thinking; there seems to be a simple lack of imagination very often.'

'Oh! I'm sure things have improved by now, they must have,' said Sandy.

'I don't know about that,' countered Bob, 'it seems to me that all you need is cheek; as L.-J. was just telling us. People still walk into places like Buckingham Palace.'

'Ah, that's because we are a democracy,' Sandy added. 'No one would like it if such places were made completely secure.'

'Well, we may be a strange lot one way and another but I'm still glad to have been born British,' declared Smiler.

'That's all very well,' replied the major, 'but the fact remains that we're just all humans; we may differ as individuals, but every vice and virtue is inherent in the species wherever you look.

'You can take a cross-section of any community in the world, from the smallest village to any city, and you'll find the same spectrum of humanity: whatever their shape, size or colour, all the characters will be there. You might find a potential murderer in the smallest village in this country, just as in any other corner of the globe. Whether or not their character comes to the fore is purely a matter of circumstance. It's nothing to do with race or religion, it's just humanity.'

'I'll take your word for that,' said Sandy.

'What I can't understand, is how people can be so irrational,' the major went on. 'It seems to me that society has become completely over-emotional in its instinctive reactions, especially in cases of so-called disasters. Why, for instance, is it assumed that the degree of suffering on the part of victims and families depends on the number of people involved? No one person or family suffers any the more because someone else is killed at the same time. Or any the less if they're not.

'What is the magic number of fatalities necessary for the word disaster to be brought forth and the entire country to go out of its mind with expressions of grief? Government ministers rush to the scene to express the nation's sympathy; the queen advised to send a message and a decision made, on God knows what grounds, to set up a national fund for the relief of relatives who wouldn't warrant a second's thought had they been alone in their suffering. Must they be among twenty-eight others rather than twenty-seven, to be in need of support? It's all in the mind. Logic and common sense are displaced by sheer emotionalism.'

'Yes, but they only have disaster funds when victims suffer loss of homes or possessions, surely,' put in Sandy.

'So, what? It's still a question of numbers, isn't it?' the major persisted. 'I have every sympathy for victims, disaster or not; but if one house is blown to bits, it's nothing more than a matter of insurance as far as anyone else is concerned; if ten houses go, why are the victims more qualified for attention, and support?'

No one else seemed disposed to comment, either because they regarded the major's views as unworthy, though perhaps difficult to refute, or because they were disinclined to pursue an awkward subject.

Everyone returned to his reading apart from Smiler who went to the drawing room for a cup of coffee. Glancing round the room, he carried it over to where Elsie Redrup was sitting alone.

'Where's your Jane today, Elsie?' he enquired, pulling an armchair closer to hers.

'Hello, Mr Townend. Oh! she's cleaning out some cupboards this morning; I expect she'll pop in for some coffee before long; she never misses her "stand-easy".'

'I haven't heard that expression for a long time,' said Smiler, with a quizzical grin.

'What, stand-easy?' she queried.

'Aye. Were you in the services?'

'We both were; that's how I first knew Jane; we were in the WRNS together, mainly at Mercury, the signals' school.'

'When was that, Elsie?'

'About the end of the "forties" sometime. We were newly commissioned: I was more or less responsible for clothing stores, and Jane was in technical supplies.'

'Well, that's a coincidence,' exclaimed Smiler. 'I was there myself for about two weeks, doing an A.B.'s course; that would have been about nineteen fifty. Well I'll be blowed. Just think, we might have met fifty-odd years ago!

'That was about the time the Korean war started, I remember. The regulars enjoyed gloating at us. "You'll never get out now," they kept saying. They were partly right, too; just as we were expecting to be de-mobbed at the end of our eighteen months, Bevin, I think it were, stuck another six months on.'

'Oh-h-h dear!' said Elsie, rather amused.

Jane Fuller walked sedately into the room, making for the coffee table, and smiled across at Elsie. She had a rather deliberate manner with everything and, coffee in hand, tacked gracefully between the furniture, like an elegant yacht, to take the seat that Smiler had pulled over from the window for her.

'Thank you darling,' she said sweetly; she tended to address everyone as darling, through habit derived from the fashion world.

'And how are you today, my dear?' she

said to Elsie. 'Oh, did you remember to talk to Kathy?' she enquired before Elsie could reply.

'Yes, she's going to do it today,' Elsie assured her. 'I say, Jane, you'll never guess,' she added mysteriously.

'I'm sure I won't,' said Jane, putting her cup down in preparation for the coming revelation.

'Smiler was at Mercury,' announced Elsie.

'Really! Good heavens! When?' said Jane, doing her utmost to look impressed.

'Nineteen-fifty,' said Elsie, waiting for a reaction.

'B.C.' said Jane enigmatically.

'I suppose it was,' replied Elsie, meaning 'yes!' Before Charles.

Elsie was used to these situations when Jane, even after 40-odd years, still saw life in relation to her marriage to Charles.

Charles was a Lt Commander and a pilot in the Fleet Air Arm. Being drafted to Malta, on an aircraft carrier, his squadron had, on arrival, been flown off to operate from an air base on the island. The planes had been re-fuelled for long-range exercises to commence the following day, subsequent to a special briefing to be held that afternoon.

Charles, finding himself at a loose end for a while, decided to take his plane up for a quick tour of the island before lunch, unaware of the particular nature of the impending briefing.

Having obtained clearance from the duty controller, he taxied out to the runway, allowing himself the usual take-off distance, not forgetting the full fuel load. Being unfamiliar with the effect of the prevailing air-density at that time of the day, he started his run to take off and found that the plane was not reacting normally. The usual lift point failed to occur and, being by then committed, he opened the throttle to full in the effort to get off. The plane hurtled off the runway, with minimal lift, and failed to clear the on-rushing obstructions.

That was after two years of marriage and Jane hadn't looked at another man since. She stayed in the Service largely because of the support that Elsie provided and as an automatic way to carry on with life. When Elsie left the Service to get married three years later, Jane put her mind to making a career in the commercial world. She resigned her commission to join a fashion house and, using her service experience, worked her way to the top, exploiting her years of discipline to impress management with her uncompromising efficiency. The two women saw little of each other over the following 20 or more years, but remained in regular touch, mainly by correspondence.

Elsie's life had been quiet and contented,

married to someone who had spent almost his entire working life with a company supplying electronic harnesses, mainly to the defence industry. It was, in fact, through his association with Jane at Mercury, as a supplier, that they had first met

A few weeks after their 30th wedding anniversary her husband Billy underwent a minor operation and shortly after being discharged fell victim to a mystery complaint subsequently attributed to the hospital. No remedy being found, he died two weeks after re-admission. Thus, by the summer of 1987 Elsie found herself alone in the world again. Thereafter, visits were more often exchanged between Jane's London flat and Elsie's house in the country. After a further two years, Jane retired on her 60th birthday, selling the flat and her shares in the company, whereby she found herself comparatively wealthy.

Elsie persuaded Jane to share the house with her for a while, to allow her plenty of time to find a suitable property in the same area. As the months passed they gradually came to the conclusion that their best course would be for Elsie to put the house on the market while they explored the possibilities of finding a retirement home compatible with both their needs.

It was while attending a party given by some old church friends of Billy and Elsie that the two women were introduced to Daphne, with whom they developed an instant rapport. Daphne was still building up her clientele at the time and invited the pair to spend a few days with her, as her guests, to enable them to experience life in such a place. They readily accepted the offer, returning home after a few days to consider their impressions.

Two months later they became permanent residents at the Lodge and found their contentment, in all respects. Elsie was able to continue her association with her old church and as Jane, like the major, was nominally C of E, she would accompany Elsie on Sunday mornings; partly because she quite enjoyed the services and also because they felt it safer for Elsie not to be walking alone.

'What did you think of National Service? I believe most people thought it a waste of time, didn't they?' Jane asked Smiler.

'Well no, I wouldn't say that,' he replied, 'although it were a bit of a nuisance at the time, and as far as the Andrew were concerned, we weren't wanted anyway: they made that clear to us from the start; we were regarded as an unnecessary drain on the budget. I remember a lieutenant – I can hear him now, saying to us, "You people are costing the Admiralty two thousand pounds a year, each." That were a right fortune in those days, as you can imagine.'

'But you think that, on the whole, you enjoyed it, do you?' continued Jane.

'Oh aye, generally speaking; mind you, it depended on all sorts, like what kind of boat you were on; what the officers were like in their attitude towards us, and so on; but I think most of us thought of it as a positive experience. It changed your whole life and outlook; you could cope with things far better. I suppose that's partly what it was all about. Only an idiot could fail to gain from it in some way.

'You can usually tell when people have been in the services. They take things in their stride more. Nothing's too much trouble, "where there's a will, there's a way", and so on. I think it's because they've learned what's possible when things are done the right way and with the right approach. It were no good complaining that there wasn't time to do this or that; the PO knew exactly what was possible, and you very soon learned to do it. Once you got used to it, life wasn't difficult; they didn't expect the impossible. In other words, you learned to take things in your stride. You know what they say – "If you want something done, ask a busy person". Anyway, that's how I see it.'

'Were you a "sparker" or a "bunting"?' asked Elsie.

'V/S,' answered Smiler.

'Visual signals,' she confirmed.

'Aye. As you know, we were still flag hoisting and that sort of thing in those days. Semaphore and light flashing were still the day-to-day methods of signalling. Mind you, that were only the practical side of it; communication was a lot more involved than that. We had to be conversant with twenty-four different textbooks, for a start, including cryptography, which I thought was the most interesting aspect. Codex machines, based on the Enigma that we hear so much about these days, was the securest form of encrypted signalling.'

'Did you train at Mercury?' asked Elsie.

'No, we were sent to the signal school at Cookham Wood, next door to the Borstal school at the top of Rochester Hill, near Chatham. The camp was all Nissen huts, which were surprisingly cosy, actually. We arrived at the end of a blazing hot summer and were there for nine months, including a ferocious cold winter. There were a great iron stove in the middle of the hut to keep the place warm. We used to light it every night with lumps of margarine whipped from the galley next door. It was a different story though in the training huts which were unheated. In the typing room we sat in our greatcoats and hats and our finger tips were quite painful from constantly thumping the freezing cold keys.

'While the summer lasted, we would spend duty weekends on call, as it were, lying in our hammocks slung between a couple of trees close to the wire fence. We'd lie there in the sunshine watching the young offenders, as they call them these days, collecting up stones from the field the other side of the fence. What was done with the stones, I've no idea.

'The lads would stand and talk to us at times and we'd occasionally precipitate a riot by tossing a cigarette over. It was like feeding piranhas.

'The view across the Medway valley was beautiful; endless woods and fields rolling away to the horizon. I remember, there were a little airfield nearby where Tiger Moths would come and go occasionally. Now the entire view is housing as far as you can see and the little airfield is a civilian airport, or so they tell me.'

'I believe that was a WRNS camp at one time, wasn't it Jane?' said Elsie.

'It seems to ring a bell,' Jane replied with a trace of indifference.

'Aye, I remember them saying it used to be a WRNS camp, now you mention it,' Smiler added.

Jane stood up.

'I'd better get on with it or it'll be lunchtime before I get finished,' she said, smiling at the other two before gliding away.

'Did I say something out of place?' Smiler asked uneasily.

'No, don't worry,' Elsie replied, 'it's just that she prefers not to talk about those days too much,' and she briefly related the story of Charles. 'Don't worry, she won't be the least bit offended.'

'So!' said Elsie. 'Presumably you became an AB before you left?'

'Aye, it was as far as you could get in the time, unless you were singled out for a commission, if you had the academic qualifications, and were willing to serve the extra time.'

'So you were never likely to become a "three badger" then,' she quipped.

The term 'Three badge AB' was generally perceived and used in the Royal Navy, as one of mild disparagement towards those old salts who had remained in a low rank throughout their service, through limited ability or lack of ambition. The type was, however, often regarded as the salt of the earth.

His lack of ambition was definitive and self-evident, but in his defence it can be said that perhaps, very wisely, he had found his role in life and was content with it. He had absorbed his training and with a little extra effort had passed his Able Seaman's examination, which gave him a slight degree of authority over others without incurring too much responsibility.

His rank raised him from being the lowest of the low and established his self-respect. Furthermore, it gave him a considerable increase in pay, whereby he could afford to send a certain amount home to wife and family, while retaining sufficient for his simple comforts of beer and cigarette tobacco, of which he could draw two half-pound tins monthly, at six shillings a pound. He kept his head down, and by avoiding serious offence rarely attracted the attention of superiors, confining his misdemeanours to those of traditional expectation such as periodic bouts of inebriation occasioned by celebration of his birthday, or even that of his sovereign. Sustaining an unblemished record for a period of four years gained him a good-conduct badge to wear on his sleeve. For maintaining that order of virtue for the full 12 years of his service, his three badges proclaimed him both master of his trade and fully-qualified example of his sobriquet. He would most likely sign himself on for a further long term of service in order to continue the comfortable existence and benefits that he had accrued, not the least of which was the protection afforded by a munificent Service against any hostility of the outside world towards his person or reputation.

While the occupant of virtually every post

in the Royal Navy was held, by someone, to be the backbone of the Service; the lowly Able Seaman's role could not be deprived of its importance to the operation of any ship, and in his day, the three badge AB was synonymous with dependability.

Sadly, his kind have no further place in the modern world, where the ambition of mere contentment is despised in the voracious pursuit of parity. Possessiveness obscures the simple enjoyment of fundamental experiences and such happy souls as he no longer exist. Society has no room for them, and the navy of today depends on technically skilled personnel in all departments.

Smiler cited his own experience of meeting with just such a character who was stationed on St Mary's island at Chatham, where, consistent with his career as a stoker, his work entailed tending the boiler houses.

Sequential to his war service, he regarded himself as deserving of respite. Accordingly, by fortuitous acquaintance with and social cultivation of a critically placed contact in the drafting office, he had engineered an extended period of rest on the island, whereby he contrived to get virtually lost for a number of years.

No rota bore his name, no duty watch summoned his presence, while he further developed his skills at maintaining anonymity. He wore action working dress, known as number eights, comprising the tough blue shirt and dark blue-jean trousers at all times, save when going ashore to the pub or making the risky fortnightly trip to collect his pay of £6.13s. On those occasions he wore his fading number two uniform, taking care to wear a clean white lanyard, well washed blue collar, and freshly blancoed cap, in order to avoid critical attention. They were his passport to the outside world beyond the causeway.

All other kit such as spare boots and shoes, number one uniform, and other items regarded as non-essential, had been gradually dispersed through a ready market to raise additional funds when the need was dire. It was so long since he had been subjected to the worst of all day to day perils visited on naval ratings, namely the kit muster, that he would, in such circumstances, have been obliged to borrow a seamanship manual, to remind himself of what a kit muster should look like. Needless to say he had long since relinquished his own copy, to pecuniary advantage.

Smiler stood up, and took his leave of Elsie, saying, 'I think I'll go back and see if they've woken up yet, if you don't mind.'

'Not at all,' she replied 'I must go and tidy up before lunch, anyway. Thank you so much; I have enjoyed our chat; such a change to talk about those days again.'

Chapter 11

Insecurity

Thea Knightly-Brown was a slightly aloof person tending to be reticent towards her fellow residents, particularly where she judged them to be of a less worldly background than her own. Nevertheless, besides being an aunt of her old school friend, she was, as far as Daphne could judge, of a sufficiently democratic outlook to be accepted into the fold.

A degree of insularity had settled upon her, mostly as a reaction to the world she found around her on returning to these shores from Africa. She perceived that world as being sadly declined in graciousness and good order. Total emancipation had restructured society, removing all trace of deference, respect, humility and responsibility for self and others. Everyone appeared to have so much more money, without showing the smallest appreciation of it, or respect for it.

Avarice seemed to be the principle motivation throughout much of society, without relationship to just reward for effort and creativity. Executives who were declared by their fellows to be so underpaid that they must be granted a massive increase in salary in order to retain their vital services, made no explanation as to why such a pittance was acceptable in the first place.

She perceived a profound difference between the wealthy who genuinely made their money through their own endeavours, and were therefore entitled to every penny of it, as against those who sought to emulate them by mere contractual manipulation without obligation to industrious effort and moral responsibility. It was noticeable that the great philanthropists were to be found amongst the former.

Thea was utterly astonished to learn that there were those at the other end of the scale who would feel persuaded to buy a lottery ticket because the potential prize had risen from ten million pounds to thirty million. Would they not risk their pound to win ten million? Where did satisfaction lie if not in simple physical and mental delights? That money can't buy happiness is tritely said, and mostly true; but what must a rich man do to achieve the overwhelming joy experienced by a tramp who finds a five-pound note?

Such were the immediate impressions of the new Britain gained by Thea on her return. The revelations came to her as sobering realities after life in Africa to which news from home bore little relevance and seemed too remote to absorb through radio or television. She had seldom bothered to look at the English papers, to which she attached the same importance as to the *Reader's Digest*, believing the content to be politically and socially too tedious to bother with.

In her schooldays she had been quite a venturesome spirit and a natural leader of her circle of friends. It was she who organised the midnight feasts in the dormitory of eight girls. She who went into the village and out of bounds, beyond the post office, to acquire the melon and cider: the melon to be bored and filled with the cider, then stored for a day or two in the cellar under the boarding house. She was well acquainted with the cellar as that was where she kept two cages of white mice, with a view to breeding and selling them.

On the occasion of an atomic-bomb test, to be carried out during the early hours of the morning and widely predicted to bring about the end of the world, she organised such a feast to include any comestibles the girls could arrange to have sent from home. At the conclusion of the feast they all shook hands before getting back into bed, in case the worst should happen before morning. None was able to stay awake for long and the following day arrived as prosaically as ever.

In addition to the mice in the cellar, she kept silkmoths in a glass tank placed on a shelf in the common room. She was able to do so, because silk moths feed on mulberry leaves and there happened to be a white mulberry tree growing near the school swimming pool. When the larvae pupated, they span beautiful gold silk chrysalises. Thea would give one or two of them to close friends who would derive considerable amusement from picking off the thread to start it onto a pencil. Once started, it would wind on continuously covering the pencil from end to end with the brilliant gold silk, as the cocoon tumbled about on the end of the thread without breaking. Most of such activity was conducted surreptitiously below the desk during evening prep.

Her common room menagerie further extended to hosting a slow-worm, an adder and a number of newts; the housemistress being supportive of natural history matters, as instructive for all, though with some apprehension in regard to the possible escape of the adder.

Whether or not her approbation would have extended to harbouring mice on the premises was never engendered. Fortunately for Thea, access to the cellars was, in addition to the steps down from inside the house, also by an unlocked door on the outside, virtually hidden by the shrubbery.

Thea's parents were living a comfortable though hardworking life as proprietors of a rambling 16th century hotel and coaching inn in a small market town and were entertaining thoughts of retirement. However, shortly after Thea finished her schooling, her father fell seriously ill and died, leaving the business in the hands of her mother.

When her younger sister Frances finished school and went to work in London, her mother put the hotel on the market and took a small cottage in the town as a temporary residence. After a further six months, she accepted an old family friend in marriage, and went to live with him at Leigh-on-Sea, giving the cottage to Thea.

After a few romantic adventures, Thea met and married a farmer four years her junior. For many luxurious years they lived on his farm in Africa, possessing 20,000 head of cattle and much besides. Ultimately, political circumstances led to the loss of her husband in a violent dispute with natives. When her home was impounded by militant political elements, she returned to England leaving virtually everything behind, with little hope of recovering any of the estate.

Thea's mother had died in 1992 leaving each of her daughters a substantial sum of money, which in Thea's case was left on deposit in England, not being needed in Africa, which proved to be a great boon as matters turned out. She stayed with Frances for a few months until her niece Catherine happened to mention her friend Daphne Currer-Spriggs and, one thing leading to another, she became a resident at Anvil Lodge.

In Africa Thea was occupied with un-bridled social activity and had servants to do absolutely everything for her; even to pick up things from the floor. It was a way of life, having inescapable effects inevitably moulding those exposed to it, whatever their natural philosophy at the outset. Conse-quently, it was a harsh transformation for Thea even to live in Frances's home.

Living at Anvil Lodge, she had been in constant danger of forgetting herself and making demands on the staff that just wouldn't do. At times she had been very close to tears in her efforts to adjust, but managed commendably to avoid the tempt-ation to look for sympathy, especially from Daphne, for whom she bore the utmost admiration.

There was, however, one ear attuned to her plight and that was the major's. He was sufficiently acquainted with colonial life to understand that crossing the gulf between the two worlds was, for some people, akin to eschewing heroin and he was moved to make the effort to help Thea to adjust; if only by revealing that understanding which was, really, what she needed most.

They would often discuss the contrast in standards between the days of their upbringing and those of the present. One thing that seemed to make a strong impression on her was the sheer profligacy and waste that prevailed, particularly amongst the young and middle-aged. While the major tended to agree with her in general terms, he pointed out to her that in some instances there were rational explanations for its being virtually unavoidable. Global industry had developed such huge markets that amortisation of costs had reduced prices to the point where scarcely anything was worth the cost of repair, as replacement was so much cheaper.

The formulae of economics had become so inverted that people of the developed nations scarcely comprehended the meaning of terms such as waste and save. Everybody possessed just about everything; it was part of the moral decline, as he saw it. Sufficiency was just not recognised as a state of satisfaction.

'If you ask me,' he opined, 'every generation needs a damned good war to bring it down to earth, figuratively speaking. It would restore a sense of proportion, and appreciation of what they really had, and just what was of real value.

'Sooner or later, resources of energy and material must come to an end and, with demand constantly increasing, who could tell the outcome? While governments exhort the population to save energy, they countenance the occurrence of prolific waste of energy such as totally unnecessary street lighting. Standard lamps could be halved in number, halved in height and halved in power, with equal effect. Properly designed reflectors to direct the light onto the ground where it's required, instead of up in the sky and into bedroom windows where its intrusion can be an affront to householders, would be a profound step forward, in itself. It is a matter of fact that such measures were carried out many years ago by an American city as a result of intensive lobbying by astronomers, against light pollution, that the energy saved was equal to the entire consumption in Ireland. Furthermore, acceptable and pleasing colours as already demonstrated by a few enlightened authorities, could at last replace the miserable yellow lights used for generations, for economy, to the destruction of all other colour.'

Wanton waste of lighting energy was a matter close to the major's heart.

As Thea had opened the topic, he felt free to develop the subject further, saying, 'It's a revelation to drive along the M25 at night, not only to observe the vastly over-lit motorway system, not deemed necessary in the open country where no or little lighting exists, but also to reveal the extent to which office blocks remain a blaze of light, long after the occupants have left the buildings to the care of night watchmen, whose needs are probably no more than two or three lights per floor.

'Local authorities would no doubt defend their overblown budgets by specious arguments supporting their readiness to follow the recommendations of lighting manufacturers, by who knows what inducements? Commercial executives were content to regard company funds as more than adequate to deal with the cost of a few extra lights left on overnight. Their world was far too lofty to permit concern with the astronomical conservational cost to the country. Meanwhile the older generations persuade themselves that their contribution to conservation, by switching off any unnecessary light, is meaningful to the planet's survival.

'Nowadays everything is taken for granted,' he went on. 'Just imagine the effect of a paper shortage today; no more tissues or toilet rolls. No hard copy or newsprint. Loss of any simple commodity or service would seem catastrophic. Present generations would find rationing a great deal harder to suffer than did their forebears of sixty years ago, the great majority of whom were unaccustomed to any more than basic living.

'Think of the effects of a potato famine, not at all unlikely; or total loss of gas or electricity. I think a good many would soon lose their minds. We, at least, have seen the best as well as the worst of things and should make the most of life while we can.

'Sorry, old girl, not exactly cheering you up am I?' the major said, 'Let me get you something to drink.'

'Thank you, major,' she said with a smile. 'Do you think Ramiro could provide a Pimm's?'

'I've no doubt of it,' he assured her.

His support eventually enabled her to develop a positive attitude towards life and those around her, including the staff. Thereafter, her defensive mask was gradually dissolved, as the major coaxed her to smile again and eventually to begin to form friendships. Daphne was highly relieved to observe the change in Thea's disposition and was observant enough to guess that not a little of it was due to the major's ministrations. Had it not been for her allegiance to Thea's niece, Catherine, she would probably not have accepted Thea in the first place. Now she could report positively in her occasional letters to her friend.

Joan Collett, at the age of 66, was almost

the youngest of the community and was a relative newcomer. Fairly described as 'Lively, popular, and very active,' her ability to make friends easily, led to a heart-to-heart with Thea one evening after dinner. Their dinner companions having things to do, both retired to their rooms, leaving Joan and Thea to adjourn to the drawing room together.

Joan related her circumstances prior to arriving at Anvil Lodge.

'Like Gill and Maisie, I was a teacher,' she began. 'My husband, Steve, was lecturing at a university until he was diagnosed as having cancer, following treatment for a mole on his leg. He died in nineteen ninety. I carried on teaching until I was sixty and retired in ninety-eight. After four years of being on my own most of the time, I decided to look for somewhere like this, and here I am. I don't think I could have made a better choice.'

Thea told her story, concluding that she was as content as she could expect to be, but envied Joan her ability to relax and mix so easily with everyone.

'Oh, you've just lost it for a while; what have you got to worry about, with all your experience? You just need to reconnect that's all,' Joan assured her.

'Did you play any golf out there?' Joan enquired.

'Oh yes, quite a bit in the good days,' Thea replied.

'Don't tell me, you had your own course, eh?' Joan laughed.

'No,' said Thea, 'but there was a super club not far from us; I could be there in half an hour.'

'Well, I suppose it was nothing for you to drive fifteen to twenty miles for a round of golf,' Joan suggested.

'Good Lord no! it was sixty-three miles, door-to-door. I used the "Cessna", unless Brian wanted it, in which case it took me an hour and twenty minutes in the Mercedes or one of the Range rovers. We never thought it worthwhile to have two planes, few of our friends did either.'

'So! you flew here and there on your own, eh?' said the astonished Joan.

'Oh, yes! apart from Tuck.'

Joan's eyebrows asked the obvious question.

'Tuck was my little white Sealyham; I took him everywhere. We had eleven dogs, some hunting, some working, some just pets; but Tuck was special to me, poor darling.'

'Why, what became of him?' asked Joan.

'When the natives turned against us, they cut his head off; I found him draped over the fence, one morning.'

'How awful for you,' said Joan. 'How could they be so cruel after working for you so closely?'

'I don't think it was the house staff that were responsible, more likely some of the estate workers. They were rather childlike, really; reacting according to circumstance. Most of the time they seemed very contented, willing, cheerful, laughing at almost everything, provided we treated them fairly. They had an inclination to be naughty where they thought they could get away with it, although they expected one to be strict, generally speaking, and they had a considerable fear of losing their job.

'They were a happier lot, by all accounts, than servants were here in England; provided they weren't unsettled by activist strangers who would turn up from time to time trying to brainwash them with half-baked Marxism. However, I'm afraid they were not used to having convictions of their own, it wasn't really natural to them, so their minds were open and susceptible to all sorts of baleful influences.'

'Easily led, you mean,' said Joan.

'Absolutely.'

'I believe you're a golfer, aren't you?' Thea enquired.

'Rather!' replied Joan with enthusiasm, pleased to return to the topic without having to risk upsetting Thea with further memories. 'There are three of us actually; me, Tom Dangerfield, and George Townend. It makes things a bit lop-sided and awkward, unless we find someone at the club, each time. I've been hoping to talk you into joining us, ever since you said you played. What about it? I'm sure it's just what you need. Go on, say you will.'

Thea was drawn to the idea, but replied to the effect that she was too old and rusty to start again now and in any case her clubs were still where she'd always kept them, in the clubhouse, having far more on her mind than to recover them before returning to England.

'Nonsense,' said Joan, 'you're younger than the men are and clubs are no problem.'

'What about the men, they might have something to say about it?' Thea concluded.

'In other words you will?' said Joan, then, 'The men will be thrilled to bits, I can't wait to tell them.'

'Oh well! if you're sure,' said Thea, 'thank you for being so kind, Joan.'

Tom Dangerfield had been familiar with the old RAF golf course that nestles high in the Chiltern forest above Halton for most of his life, having during the late thirties followed wonderingly behind his plus-four'd father, who spooned and niblicked his way round the course. Later, in his twenties, Tom would play on Sunday mornings; paying his green fee at the RAF guardhouse before driving the mile or so up to the course to tee off at six o'clock when the sun was up already warming the greens.

Occasionally, a deer would step out from the trees to join the families of rabbits grazing on the long lush fairways. He would complete the nine holes by eight o'clock, coming off as other players were queuing up to tee off. There was no clubhouse, the only building being a small shack for the green keeper's gear.

Later again, the old course was handed over to civilian care, and profound changes ensued, including construction of an opulent new clubhouse, with subsequent extensions, and a gradual expansion of the course from nine to eighteen holes.

A taxi pulled into the club car park, one morning, to deposit Tom, Smiler, Joan and Thea for their first game together.

'First things first,' said Joan, leading the way through to the lounge where she introduced Thea to Molly Haine, the stewardess. 'Is the secretary in?' asked Joan.

'Not yet,' Molly replied. 'I do hope you're going to join us, Thea,' she continued in her immaculate cultured voice.

'If they'll have me,' Thea replied, smiling.

'Don't worry, if they can take these two, you have nothing to worry about,' Molly said, nodding towards Tom and Smiler.

'Have you a handicap?' she continued.

'Not really, I haven't played for a few years, I'm afraid.'

'What were you playing off last, Thea?' Molly went on.

'Oh, I believe it was about six,' she replied, to a stunned audience. 'I was on three, at one point, but that was in my younger days.'

'Oh my God,' said Joan, 'what have we let ourselves in for?'

'We?' Tom queried.

'Coffee, on the house?' Molly offered, trying not to laugh.

'Good girl, Molly,' answered Tom and they seated themselves at a table by the window, overlooking the eighteenth tee.

'I was playing at a course up north, once,' announced Smiler, 'and I was on the short tenth, looking at the green right down below. There was nobody with me so I thought, I'll take my time on this one; these short holes are never as easy as they look. I'll get well under it and really whack it up with a pitching wedge. I must have caught the ball too far back and it shot off about ninety degrees to the left and disappeared over the hedge, right across the road and hit the chimney of the house opposite; then it came straight back over again, down to the bottom and bounced up onto the green. I were down in three; I couldn't believe it and nobody else has since.'

'These things only happen when you're on

your own,' said Tom. 'I was playing the ninth at Chorleywood once. Drove off down the narrow bit of fairway and sliced into a tree on the right. The ball hit the middle of the tree about twenty-five yards down and came straight back, stopping right where the tee piece had been. I played it again without a tee and without moving my feet.'

'How is Daphne?' Molly called across from the bar.

'Very well; busy as ever,' replied Joan.

'Give her my love; she hasn't been over for some time now,' Molly added.

'I expect she will when the weather's warmer, though I don't think she'll ever have time to take up golf seriously.'

Thea rented some clubs and a trolley for the day from the shop. Joan suggested that Thea might like to take a handicap averaging the rest of them, which was 18, she herself being 16, Smiler 20 and Tom 18. All agreed and they made their way to the first tee. It was further decided that Joan and Smiler would play Thea and Tom, to balance the handicaps.

Despite the unfamiliar clubs and shoes, a few practice swings were sufficient for Thea to regain some of the old feel and she stepped forward to place her tee, being the last to drive off. The other three had each placed a ball equally within short-iron distance of the green. Taking a three-wood,

Thea waggled it twice behind the ball and slowly drew the head back up to the end of its arc and after a trace of pause began the descent, accelerating downwards as her hips turned to pull the club. The head swept through the ball, with a click, sending it soaring upward into the distance above the left side of the fairway; at last dropping down to bounce once before the green, and pitch-up to roll past the flag, coming to rest three feet beyond, and two hundred and fifty yards from the tee.

'By!' said Smiler.

'Ooooh!' said Joan.

'How about a little wager?' said Tom.

'You'll be lucky,' said Smiler, and they set off down the fairway, all smiles and none bigger than Thea's.

They played nine holes before coming in for a not too heavy lunch, followed by a further nine in the afternoon.

At the end of a very entertaining match, won by Tom and Thea, portending a considerable adjustment to her handicap, they reassembled in the bar lounge for a very merry session while waiting for the taxi and a noisy ride home. The feeling of well-being attained by Thea that day had a profound effect on her life at the Lodge thereafter.

Chapter 12

Coming Clean

Tracey was noticeably preoccupied with something and would be seen standing still gazing out of the window or into space, which was not characteristic of her at all. It would not be long before Mrs Robertson or Daphne would notice her behaviour. As it happened, Kathy was the first to spot that something was amiss. Tracey was at the bottom of the stairs holding a tray and lost in thought.

'Are you all right, darling?' Kathy enquired, feeling some responsibility for the girl's welfare.

'Yes, thank you, Miss,' Tracey replied, as her gaze cleared.

'Come into the office,' Kathy commanded gently, leading the way in. 'Sit down for a minute and tell me what's worrying you.'

'Nothing, really,' Tracey replied unconvincingly.

'Of course there is,' said Kathy. 'Is it something to do with your boyfriend?' she added, tuning in to familiar territory. Tracey coloured slightly.

221

'What makes you say that, Miss?' she asked.

'I know about these things, darling; something's wrong, isn't it,' Kathy coaxed.

'Not really,' said Tracey looking puzzled.

'Then what are you worrying about?'

Tracey struggled with her thoughts for a few seconds before saying, 'He wants to get married.'

'And you don't?' Kathy ventured.

'I'm not sure,' came the reply.

'Oh dear!' said Kathy. 'Listen to me, Tracey, he may be madly in love with you, or he's just being a man, I don't know, but it's beside the point. You mustn't think of it as a great adventure that will probably be all right. You have got to snap out of dreams and face reality. If you have got to ask the question, "Am I in love?" then the answer is simple. No! you are not; you'd jolly well know if you were, I can assure you; you'd be behaving a lot differently from the way you are at the moment. Do you understand me?' said Kathy in a sympathetic tone.

'I think so,' Tracey replied.

'Well, I hope you do, because this is the most critical time in your life and you can't afford to play at it!

'I don't mean to be unkind, darling, but so many people reach this point and for lack of good advice they allow themselves to be drawn into marriage, or something like it, without a proper foundation, and when it all goes wrong they find themselves well and truly stuck with it. They take a chance, thinking, oh well, if it doesn't work out we can just separate or get divorced; but believe you me it is never that simple. However hard-nosed about it they are, their lives are certainly spoiled if not ruined. If you want to lead a happy life, you have to get it right in the first place.

'Tell me, what happens when you hold hands with him?'

'I don't know what you mean, Miss.'

'You don't have to keep calling me Miss, call me Kathy. You do hold hands do you?'

'Sometimes,' said Tracey, with some bewilderment.

'Well!' began Kathy again. 'If you hold hands every time you meet, and you both get a warm surge of feeling through your fingers and you automatically squeeze them tighter, then, perhaps, you're in love; if not, then you can't be; there's just nothing there. Do you understand me?'

'I think so, Miss – Kathy.'

'Few parents teach their children the most important facts of life, which have less to do with sex, and more to do with emotions, which they seem to find more inhibiting to talk about. At the most critical time in their lives, children are left to find heir own way through it all without knowing what they

223

should really be looking for. Being in love, and how to recognise it, is what their happiness really depends on if they are to avoid throwing away their future. Too often it's only the lucky ones who find their own way, by chance.

'Love is a form of magnetism,' said Kathy. 'Marriage is right when the two magnets are the right way round; they slam together and nothing can separate them. If they're the wrong way round, marriage just forces them together, by artificial bonds, without which they would just fly apart. That's what a bad marriage feels like, secret desperation to break free. Only a bad marriage needs bonds, which is why so many people find themselves trapped for life, by their conscience. They may be miserably discontented, but they go on sacrificing the rest of their lives to it for the sake of the families, quite apart from the economic difficulties involved in separation.

'What do your parents think about it?' asked Kathy.

'Dad never wants to talk about that sort of thing; he never knows what to say anyway. Mum just thinks I'm too young,' replied Tracey.

'No, you're not too young; you're a grown woman; you're just not ready yet. I'm afraid lots of parents are not sufficiently sympathetic towards their children when they're most needed to be. When things consequently go wrong, all they can say is, "You made your bed; you lie in it". For goodness' sake don't quote me at home,' Kathy added.

It was a lot for Tracey to take in, but she felt relieved and liberated by the perspective gained from Kathy's words, being clearer in her mind, and with a better idea of her true feelings.

'So, how do you feel about it all now, darling, worse or better?'

'Much better, thanks,' she said and, smiling, gave Kathy a hug, picked up the tray, and disappeared back towards the dining room, with a renewed spring in her step. Kathy, in truth, was feeling a bit drained by it all and slipped along to the drawing room to collect the cup of coffee she was about to fetch when she found Tracey by the stairs.

Needless to say, the telephone was ringing as she returned, and stopped, of course, as she lifted the receiver.

'Blast!' she muttered, hoping it was nothing important.

After a few moments and a sip of coffee, she thought to herself 'Of course' and dialled 1471. She recognised the number given as the golf club, and returned the call.

'Ah, hello Kathy,' said Molly. 'Are you and Geoff doing anything on Saturday week? Sorry it's a bit short notice.'

'In the evening, you mean?'

'Yes, I'm having a small party here,

eightish onwards. Can you come?'

'Well I'm O.K. and as far as I know so is Geoff, I'll have to check, of course. What's the occasion, something exciting?' Kathy asked, with enthusiasm.

'My birthday actually.'

'Ooh, lovely. I'll give you a ring about nine tonight if that's all right.'

'Perfectly, darling, speak to you then, bye-ee.'

Kathy put the phone down and glanced at the wall clock. There was time to go through Ramiro's wine list and make up the order before Daphne came in to sign things.

The laundry van swept past the office window and on round the cobbled drive to the service door next to the kitchen to collect and deliver the day's load. Between the kitchen and the cellar room, a stone-flagged passageway led from the wide back door, past the cellar room and the general storeroom doors and beyond. Facing the storeroom door was a revolving access to the kitchen, which served extremely useful and varied purposes as a staging point.

The opening was four feet wide, having a door, pivoted vertically in the middle, with three semi-circular shelves on one side. The shelves permitted either the loading of meals from the kitchen, for distribution to residents' rooms, or for stores from the storeroom to be conveyed to the kitchen; the half open position allowing adequate width for normal passage to and fro.

Thus could meals be conveyed onto trolleys in the passageway, and via the service lift, to the guests' rooms above, at the greatest convenience to both kitchen and room staff. Beyond that, the passage turned right into an area containing the service lift to the first and second floors, and a door discreetly marked cloakrooms, visible from the main hall through an arched opening to the left.

Mrs Dorothy Parsons, known to residents and staff as Dot, was entrusted with all matters pertaining to room servicing, as distinct from room service which was part of Mrs Robertson's operations. She had dominion over the store room, the contents of which related to her specific duties, in addition to certain kitchen requisites, such as cleaning materials, paper goods and so forth. These she dispensed to Robbie's requirements, without hazard to their cordial relationship, which was delicately tuned to the acceptance of Robbie's marginal seniority.

Dot was assisted by two girls from the village, one of whom, Alison Plant, worked only in the mornings unless specially required. It was she who received the laundry, signing the delivery note and ensuring that the collection note was properly signed by the driver whose non-stop suggestive chatter was defused by her demoralising silence, as advised by Angela Plumton, her full-time workmate. When the room servicing was completed, she was sometimes seconded to assist with room service.

The major's room, being the only one on the ground floor apart from the adjacent guest room, was usually serviced first, being the nearest on the morning route. Furthermore, the major was reliably up and about in the morning, allowing the girls an early start on their circuit of rooms.

While Angela was changing the towels for the major, one morning, she couldn't resist broaching a matter that had been a topic of discussion from time to time, during the short debriefings that Dot held round her desk in the storeroom, at the end of each morning.

'Your towels are always so clean and dry compared with other people's,' she was emboldened to observe to the major, calling from the bathroom. 'It's as though you don't use them, though I'm sure you must do.'

The major, who was sitting at his window seat reading the *Telegraph*, lifted his nose from the paper, to reply, 'No, No, never use 'em, at least not very often,' he confided. Ever ready to impart advice, he went on,

'The secret, if you can call it one, is to make proper use of the flannel. Despite the general notions of the typical thicko male, who regards them as cissie, a good thick flannel is, in fact, a first rate tool, not only for efficiently clearing the muck off your skin, in the first place, but also for instant drying afterwards. Continually rinsed in hot water, and thoroughly wrung out, a flannel will dry your skin in seconds, leaving you warm and clean. Your body heat instantly evaporates any residual dampness. Unlike a flannel that can be continually wrung out, a towel soon becomes a saturated useless lump; rather like me on Saturday nights,' he added.

'You do make me laugh, Major,' said Angela, giggling as she changed the towels over.

'You take my tip, dear, forsake the towel and use the flannel; whether you're washing, bathing or showering; not that I make much use of the bath, apart from curing aches and pains. Shower's the best ticket, you mark my words; quicker, cleaner, hotter and takes a fraction of the water.'

'My dad always has a shower, and so do I, but Mum never does. She likes her bath.'

'I expect so; most older women do, apparently,' said the major. 'They always think of reasons for avoiding the shower. It's a ceremonial business,' he continued. 'They lock all the doors and windows, pull all the curtains, turn on the radio and wallow for half an hour, before rising up from the tepid water to drag it all off with the towel.'

'Yeah! that sounds like my mum all right,' she agreed.

The major made no further comment, allowing the girl to get on with her work.

'There you are, Major,' said Angela. 'Clean face towel, hand towel, and bath towel. I'll try your flannel business,' she added as she left the room.

She couldn't wait to apprise Dot and Alison of her boldly acquired explanation of the major's way with towels.

What extraordinary logic guided some women through their lives, the major mused. The concept of the face towel was a good instance of feminine concerns. Of all parts of the skin, could any be hygienically less important than the face, or more important than the hands? Yet, without diminishing the undoubted importance of the face, as the centre of cosmetic attention, it had to be observed that it seemed abhorrent to a woman either to use a hand towel to dry her face, or to desecrate a face towel by drying her hands on it.

He was reminded of a particular occasion in his childhood which typically illustrated the point. He was in company with friends and siblings at a tea party when they were all told, by a strict parent, to go up and wash their hands nicely, before sitting down for tea. Up in the bathroom they found themselves bereft of a towel.

The cry from the top of the stairs, 'Mum, there's no towel,' was met with the reply from the bottom, 'Here, you can use this old one, if it's just for your hands; it's got to go in the wash anyway.'

That was by no means his only experience of similar thinking. He had, for instance, witnessed the utter distraction of a lady of the house when a face towel had fallen to the floor, whereas a hand towel would cause no such concern at all. Trivial as these matters might seem, they had their significance, none the less.

In the major's view it was very much a matter of what the eye doesn't see. He had observed how ladies of all ranks would, while eating, rid themselves of any stickiness on their fingers by rubbing their hands together, like flies, until it had all magically disappeared.

It was not impossible, he supposed, that applying such emulsions to the skin could prove a positive benefit, scientifically, but no woman would be persuaded to do so on conscious principle.

Similar effects applied to the common practice of cleaning kitchen surfaces by wiping them over with a damp cloth, which in effect did no more than spread the accumulation of culinary detritus evenly over the surface as a transparent layer left to dry off with the texture of a ploughed field, when viewed from a low angle.

Angela's departure brought the major's mind back to current affairs. At twenty past ten that morning he was due at the dental surgery for his six-monthly examination. He had managed to preserve the appointment card since the previous visit, which was a matter for self-congratulation as far as he was concerned, having missed the previous occasion and insisted on paying a nominal fee for failing to turn up.

As he drove the Bee along the drive to the road, he found Madge Russell walking briskly ahead. Pulling alongside her, he pressed the switch to lower the window.

'Hello, Madge, can I give you a lift any-where?'

'Good morning, Major,' she said brightly. 'That really is kind of you, I was going to catch the bus into the town. Are you going that way?'

'I am indeed,' replied the major. 'Hop in, old girl,' he said, reaching across to open the door.

'Thank you so much,' Madge said, getting in and pulling the door to.

When she was settled and the seat belt clipped in, he set off again, turning left into the road.

'It's a lovely car, Major, you must be very pleased with it,' she said, smiling at him.

'It'll do, I think,' he replied, modestly. 'How are things going with you, Madge?' he enquired warmly.

'Actually, I've had another letter from Bernard,' she said. 'There's to be a post-mortem on poor Ivy and he's obviously very displeased about it. It seems that he protested, but the doctor is adamantly dissatisfied over something; there's talk of the police being involved, and heaven knows what; otherwise the funeral should have been on Thursday.'

'Ah, perhaps that blackguard is due to get what he deserves, after all,' said the major.

'I shall be so glad when it's all over and she can rest in peace,' Madge said wistfully. 'But I mustn't bore you with it all, you were so patient before.'

'Not a bit of it, my dear, you must tell me if there is anything I can do to help.'

'Oh, that is kind but I don't think there would be.'

'Nonsense, my dear, presumably you've got to go down there for the funeral at least; I wouldn't dream of letting you go on your own; we are all your family now you know. Don't worry, I'll drive you down and I'll bet I won't be the only one to go, you'll see; assuming you don't mind, of course.'

As they drove on, he raised various matters relating to Ivy as delicately as he could, prompted by his experience when his aunt died at Chesham. By the time they arrived in the town, Madge felt as though she had been led into a different world; she was overwhelmed at having someone willing to share her burden in the way Hugh would have.

She glanced at the major with a feeling she would not have cared to interpret, but was in fact, something slightly more than admiration. He responded to her gaze warmly and his eyes seemed to her to positively dance, with disconcerting effect; she wondered if he was aware of their power to affect a woman; if he were, it suggested that he was taking an interest in her and that she dismissed as fanciful in the extreme.

'Where can I drop you off?' asked the major, glancing sideways at Madge.

'Anywhere here will do for me,' she replied. 'I've only got to walk to the dentist's.'

'Well I'm damned,' said the major. 'That's where I'm going; what time is your appointment?'

'Oh, not until eleven.'

'Well, I've got ten minutes yet, so when I've found a parking spot, we'll go to that coffee place across the road from the surgery and you can have a cup while you wait for your turn. By that time I'll be back and I'll wait there till you're out. Easy, eh!'

'Lovely,' she replied.

It was a long time since she had felt cosseted by anyone and she made the most of the feeling while she could, knowing that such occasions were all too scarce and brief. She knew that the mixed feelings she was experiencing could easily lead her into a situation that was fraught with pitfalls; wrong impressions could easily generate false assumptions in the mind, even at her age; she must be careful to avoid any fantasising where the major was concerned, despite being aware of his frequent glances at her, not all directed at her face.

She could only define her own feelings as potentially positive towards men in general, which allowed the possibility of someone approaching the equal of Hugh striking the right note perhaps, some day before she was too old to respond. In the meantime, she was very glad of the major's support, just when she needed it, and would allow herself to accept the relationship in whatever form it might take.

The return journey was cheery. Mr Harley, the dentist, had found nothing amiss with either of them, leaving them free of those concerns for another six months; which added to their sense of well-being as they span through the lanes bordered with emerging white thorn blossom tingeing the grey-green hedges. The sun sped along with them, flashing through the arching trees above, and splashed light on Madge's still elegant calves, stretched before her, further stirring the major's interest in his passenger.

He reached across and patted the hands clasped in her lap, as though to reassure her. His mind was principally on the imminent prospect of a pre-lunch appetiser in the sitting room, to round off the morning's activity. He decided that Madge had proved herself to be good company and deserving of some attention beyond the morning's excursion.

'Join me for a snifter before lunch?' he proposed as they turned into the Lodge drive again.

This sudden suggestion on top of the galvanising experience of the hand patting, which had caused a sensation like a knotted silk thread drawn up through her stomach, put a considerable strain on Madge's late resolutions and she was taken aback for a moment, giving the major cause to wonder if he was embarrassing her; perhaps she didn't drink, in the social sense.

In an instant of panic she touched his arm as she tried to rationalise her thoughts, sensing that perhaps the moment demanded a profound decision; did it or not? she wondered, not daring to expose her dilemma by prolonging the moment. After all, she thought, it was nothing more than a perfectly understandable and natural invitation. She found herself falling into the very trap she had resolved to avoid, moments before.

It did, however, reveal to her that she was vulnerable to any encouragement she might perceive in the major's attitude towards her. She therefore based her reply on the principle, realised long ago, that ultimate regret would reside far more in things not done in life, than otherwise.

She slightly tightened her grip on his arm and replied, 'Thank you, Major, I would be delighted to; shall I see you in the sitting room in fifteen minutes, then?'

Chapter 13

Decisions

Madge knew that she was about to dip her toe in the water where the major was concerned, unless she could bring herself to make a rapid decision to stop being silly and face the fact that she had no more than the trivial incidents of the morning on which to base any extravagant romantic notions. She told herself that she, at least, needed time to think before she allowed herself to be carried away by tenuous presumptions.

As they came through the entrance hall into the main hall Madge found it difficult not to betray a slight tinge of self-consciousness while exchanging smiles with Kathy and Daphne who, emerging from the office, had no right, she thought, to look at her and the major with quizzical expressions.

'See you later, old girl,' the major said cheerily, as he turned right into the corridor that led to his quarters, as he usually called his rooms.

She managed no more than a strangled confirmatory squeak and turned the opposite way into the lift to escape, momentarily at least, from further exposure.

Once inside her room, Madge kicked off her shoes and sat on the bed to think for a moment. She wondered what 'being true to herself' should mean; doing what she felt she really wanted to and just letting the future take care of itself, or dwell on her former resolve to remain faithful to the memory of dear Hugh whom no one could replace. Until today she never imagined such questions would ever occur to her. What was she trying to say to herself, that she was falling for the major? She couldn't answer even to herself in her present state of mind.

Until she had time to grapple fully with

conflicting thoughts, they would continue to revolve in her mind and just now there wasn't the time. Besides, she knew nothing about the major really, who did? No one seemed to know whether he was married or ever had been. She must be careful, she concluded. These sobering thoughts brought her to a calmer state of mind. Again she resolved to let fate unravel itself in whatever form it might.

She stood up, removed her suit and went into the bathroom. When she returned, she flung back the wardrobe doors and reviewed her options. She reached instinctively for her favourite dress which she reserved for occasions that justified its excruciating cost, which were few and far between. She paused with her hand gripping the hanger while she debated the effect of wearing it. Normally she would not particularly bother what she wore to lunch. If she did wear it, she knew it might be seen as artful since she would obviously be with the major, and conjecture would be off the ground. If she didn't, she knew she would feel dishonest with herself and why should she?

She snatched the dress off the rail and resolutely began the deliciously erotic process of pulling it down over the curves, of which she was justly proud. Again, to her amazement, she experienced the same resonating thread of excitement inside her that his casual touch had occasioned in the car. Looking at herself in the full-length mirror, she lost her nerve. He would surely regard it as too brazen and feel targeted; that would never do. It would be far safer to wear it at dinner on a suitable occasion when it would merely be seen as competitive, if meanwhile events ever justified it. No, she thought, it was far too exotic for midday but fun trying it on. She quickly changed into something engagingly smart, carefully adjusted her makeup to being simple but effective, and went down to join the gathering company in the sitting room.

Sam Willoughby was talking to the major about the enormous cost of tyres for heavy plant vehicles, explaining that huge as they were, they were nevertheless vulnerable and could be easily ruined by a simple wooden stake such as a broken sapling left in the ground. The topic had led on from the major's question about the use of dynamite in felling trees, which Sam assured him could be done neatly and accurately when used by an expert such as himself.

He was at home with heavy plant and machinery, being the stock-in-trade of the family business which embraced road haulage and site clearance on a large scale, including preparation for motorways and airports. During his National Service days he was a natural selection for the tank corps and so relished treating tanks like toys that he came close to making a career of it although on account of his size he found tanks a bit too cramped.

His wife, Joan, had died in a car crash two years before he retired and, like most of the others, he came to Anvil Lodge as much for company as anything else. Even at 72 he was still a big and powerful man.

The major was watching for the arrival of Madge and when her trim figure appeared in the doorway his face lit up with agreeable surprise which prompted Sam to turn his gaze towards her.

As she walked over to join them, Sam said, 'My God, is that our Madge? I don't know why but she looks different to me somehow.'

Madge was with them before the major could make a reply.

'Now, my dear, what would you like?' he said to her as he flagged down Ramiro.

'Do you think Ramiro could find me a gin and French?' she asked with devastating demureness, calculated to convey the meaning 'well here I am, what now?'

'He could, I'm sure,' replied the major as the boy appeared to take the orders.

'Ah, there you are, a gin and dry Martini for Mrs Russell, and the same again for us, please.'

Ramiro glanced at Madge for a second time before sidling away to his trolley. She was satisfied that she was achieving the desired effect on at least some of the males within range and hoped it would not be lost on the major who might perhaps be reserving his reactions as a defensive ploy; time would tell. She was beginning to feel a growing element of excitement in the strictly private game in which, she had to admit to herself, she was indulging.

'You'll stay with us for lunch, Sam?' said the major.

'Er, of course,' said Sam, who was mentally photostatting Madge.

He had assumed that he and the major were supposed to be together anyway, but realised that the case might be in some way different. He even wondered if he should suggest leaving them to it; but that could be presumptuous and perhaps make things worse.

'The major and I have been to the town this morning,' said Madge, seeing that Sam was mildly confused and entitled to a situation report of some kind.

'Yes,' said the major. 'Extraordinary thing, both at the dentist virtually at the same time. Picked up Madge in the drive,' he added. 'Reminds me, must have a word later, if you can spare a minute.'

'Time is about the cheapest commodity there is around here,' replied Sam. 'Just say the word.'

'Shall we go in?' said the major when they had finished their drinks and, steering Madge by the elbow, made for the dining room and selected a table.

'You do look nice today, Mrs Russell,' said Tracey to Madge.

'Doesn't she always,' quipped Sam.

'Oh, Mr Willoughby, what am I going to do with you?' she answered, giggling.

The major fussed with Madge's chair before sitting down.

'Looks as though we got back in nice time,' he observed as a sudden shower of hail clattered against the windows heralding the onset of the season's changeable weather.

Those on adjacent tables were noted by Madge to be stealing occasional glances in her direction while making visible side comments to one another, which confirmed as far as she was concerned that due to her circumstances she had been hiding her light under a bushel by neglecting her appearance, to the extent of probably seeming mousy and lifeless. If it was this easy to draw attention, what effect might she achieve if she put her mind to it.

Where the major was concerned, she decided it must be up to him from now on to consolidate their relationship, if he had a mind to, by declaring the fact to her in whatever ways he might. In the meantime, she was fairly sure that he was her man and she would enjoy the game of reeling him in, if he proved to be available; albeit without overt effort on her part. If he accepted her as the Madge he had known, hitherto, she would be sure of him, and would refine her act in due course.

Firstly though, there were things to establish before matters could develop any further. Firstly, she must slow things down, bearing in mind that apart from the major's solicitations of a few days ago in regard to Ivy, it was only three or four hours since fate had first appeared to be playing a part in their lives. Secondly, if those circumstances were to become meaningful, she had no intention of continuing to call him either Major, or L.-J. indefinitely. Accordingly, there was a need to extract a name from him on the next occasion of their being alone. She could probably find out easily enough anyway, but she felt it was his privilege to tell her.

As to his background, important as it was to her to know something if not all about him, that too she would expect to learn entirely from him in his own time and trust that it was enough to consolidate her confidence in him.

By the end of the meal Madge was feeling happier for the amount of thinking she had managed between the conversations. The major had shown more attention to her than normal courtesy required and she felt a growing excitement, which showed on her face and in her voice. Sam was beginning to feel convinced that something was afoot between them, but remained discreet throughout. When they retired to the sitting room for a smoke and coffee, Madge suggested that she should leave them to have their talk while she went into the drawing room and she left them before they could dissuade her.

Ramiro felt his shoulder cupped in a huge hand as he passed the sitting room and without looking round said, '*Si, Si* Meester Willoughby', and hurried into the drawing room, as Sam called, 'Two' after him.

Sam and the major entered the sitting room and adopted opposite armchairs with a small table between them.

The major drew his pipe from his side pocket and sat back with a contented look. Sam leaned back and smiling quizzically, winked at the major.

'You old dog,' he said quietly.

The major feigned surprise, arching an eyebrow.

'What's that, old boy?' he enquired innocently.

'Nothing L.-J.,' said Sam, not wishing to discomfit the major, who, he judged, was not inclined to talk about his situation vis-à-vis Madge.

'What's the problem you mentioned, L.-J.?' asked Sam.

'How would you like a day out?' said the major.

'When?' said Sam, with mild surprise.

'Not sure, soon,' said the major enigmatically,

'Where?' Sam further enquired.

'A funeral,' came the answer.

'Good God! L.-J. I know life can be pretty dull around here at times, but why not go to the races or something? I believe Kimble point-to-point is fairly soon. Or is there a beginning to all this that you could start from?'

'Sorry, Sam. You remember me mentioning Madge's sister Ivy, who died a week or so ago?'

'Ye-es!' said Sam. 'Hang on a minute.'

'Thanks, Ramiro,' he said as the tray was placed between them.

'Surely she's buried by now,' Sam said, frowning.

'She should have been, but there are complications,' explained the major, and went on to describe the full situation in regard to Bernard.

'Well, where do I come into it?' said Sam looking puzzled.

'Well, first of all, I told Madge that some of us would sort of rally round, so to speak, like a family, old boy, she has none of her own, and furthermore if things get out of hand between Bernard and me, I might be in need of support of some sort,' the major trailed off.

'You mean a bodyguard?' asked Sam incredulously.

'Well, not exactly, but if you were there it should be enough to deter him from any violence, which I must admit is as likely to be on my part as on his. Mind you, I've never seen the fellah; he's obviously a nasty piece of work but he could be a midget for all I know.'

'Well from what you've said, perhaps there could be some satisfaction in sorting him out,' Sam concluded.

'So, you're game, are you, old boy?' said the major hopefully.

'Why not?' Sam said. 'As you say, it's a day out!'

'Good man,' exclaimed the major.

'Who else is going?' Sam asked.

'Well, I don't know yet, old boy, hasn't really been time to think any further.'

'Why not talk to Joyce Kingham, she's a game sort and useful in any situation, being an ex-nurse and all that; and she'd be good company for Madge; I'm sure Madge would appreciate having another woman around,' Sam suggested.

'You're right, old boy, good thinking. Should make a good landing party,' the major concluded. 'Let's have a drink on it. Where's Ramiro got to? Brandy all right, Sam?'

'Just a small one, L.-J. Incidentally, sorry if I got the wrong end of the stick over you and Madge.'

The major grunted, but conceded no comment.

As suspected, there was no difficulty in recruiting Joyce to the venture, which the major engineered by casually suggesting a stroll in the grounds later that afternoon, to which she had responded with predictable eagerness, grasping the major's arm as they set off, as though in fear of him changing his mind.

It had to be, of course, that Madge was, at that moment, having a cup of tea with Joan Collett in the drawing room. Joan was pointing out of the window at the profusion of pink blossom on the peach tree as the major walked past with Joyce clinging to him like a vine.

'Hello-oo!' said Joan with a conspiratorial glance at Madge, unaware of the mild pang of emotion that was gripping her companion.

Madge was well aware of Joyce's uninhibited ways with the men and that she would be the same with any of them, but she nevertheless felt compelled to wonder why he was keeping such close company with her.

She forced herself to adopt a positive attitude towards the incident, putting her trust in there being no more to it than she hoped. Paranoia was going to be her undoing if she wasn't careful from now on: she could become obsessed with trivial signs and incidents that would have been entirely unworthy of attention before now. Joan continued her small talk, while outside, the major pursued his purpose with Joyce, concluding that all was prepared pending the where and when details, from Madge.

Over the ensuing days the major became aware that Madge had maintained her noticeably more attractive appearance, in a subtle, but reserved way, as though she was restraining an urge to break out of her shell. As she increasingly drew the attentions of the male residents, in such ways as readier discourse and attentiveness on their part, she also appeared to relate more easily to the females, often assuming the centre of discussions, as her full personality emerged.

The overall effect of Madge's rise in popularity was to make the major aware that he must better define his relationship with her and act upon it accordingly, otherwise he stood a real chance of letting her slip from his grasp, if in fact he could claim any grasp in the first place. All of which was of course, exactly in accord with her strategy.

He had, meanwhile, found his thoughts dwelling more and more on where she was, and what she was doing and, more frequently, whom she was with, while cautiously keeping his distance without being quite sure why.

His experience of women was not exactly lacking, although for various reasons, laudable or otherwise, he had never been tamed into marriage. While still in the army he had on occasion avoided hot situations by arranging postings too daunting for any bride and all in all had managed to lead a pretty independent life.

He was, however, beginning to see himself as a castaway and Madge as a passing ship that represented everything he was missing in life; she had appeared like a miracle as he was running out of years but she would soon sail on out of sight. If she felt the same way about him he was not going to find out by sitting around doing nothing. While propriety allowed her to indulge in gentle fishing, he would have to do the hunting.

After a week of uncertainty on both sides, the growing desire of each to be with the other was increased by the reluctance of either to reveal, by any tactile breach of decorum, the mounting fervour that existed between them. Madge was glad when she finally received a letter from the coroner's office informing her that agreement had been reached between the coroner and the police and that Ivy's body could at last be released to funeral directors. It was further stated that as Bernard was facing criminal charges, she was, for the immediate purposes, regarded as next of kin to the deceased.

Accordingly, she could if she wished nominate funeral directors or agree to that as well as other formalities, being handled by the authorities concerned. Should she require to, she could obtain advice and guidance from Mrs Diana Goodbody at the above address; an early telephone call was advised.

While she wondered about the extent of Bernard's misdemeanours, Madge would have preferred to remain in ignorance and sever all further involvement with her sister's background. She felt, though, that somehow the law would dictate otherwise.

Now that she had the letter, Madge could break the ice with the major directly and without artifice. She found the opportunity the following morning which dawned bright and mild. After breakfast the major emerged into the hall to collect his *Daily Telegraph*, but as he did so, Madge descended from the stairs into the hall. 'Good morning, Major,' she said brightly, 'I was hoping to catch you; I've heard from the coroner, perhaps you'd like to talk about it.'

'Of course, m'dear, in the drawing room?' he suggested.

'It's a lovely day, how about the garden?' she countered.

'Splendid,' he said, returning the paper to the pile on the table.

As they followed the path by the sitting and drawing room windows, she clung to his arm, saying, saucily,

'Two can play at this game, you know,' and, catching her meaning, he tilted his head back and laughed out loud, as though the moment called for a fanfare to the world.

This was the first time that they had actually physically touched together, and by her small initiative she fired an emotional rocket that soared away to burst into the multitude of pent-up feelings that they were both desperate to declare to each other and the world.

Madge felt like banging on the windows to make sure that everyone saw them, but both rooms were empty, for once. She tightened her grip on his arm, as though suddenly licensed to do so, and he reacted in confirmation by pulling his arm tighter to his side to trap the small hand; his first possessive gesture.

They sat on the old bench seat where they had met such a short time ago and she again produced a letter, which he quickly read through, before returning it to her, saying, 'Right, darling girl, don't worry about anything, just make the phone call and let them arrange it all for you if that's what you prefer.'

He explained the arrangements he'd made with Sam, and Joyce, and led the conversation back to the present.

'Now what about us?' he asked turning towards her.

Madge took his hand.

'What is the most important thing in your mind at this moment?' she said, looking him directly in the eyes.

Immediately she saw the scintillating gleam appear again and almost fainted from the effect. He felt the eloquent flow of energy from her soft warm hand.

'Well,' she said, forcing him to speak his mind, with no escape.

'I think you know that,' he said feeling helpless.

He had never before been in a situation quite like this. Bold romance in the early morning totally disarmed him, as she knew it would, and she could rely on the answers.

'So what are you going to do about it?' she demanded.

'By God, Madge, I've had no practice at proposing, I'm just damned well going to marry you,' he blurted out.

'Not without a name, you're not,' she said

with steely self-control.

At this, the major was utterly flummoxed – what could she mean?

'If you think for one moment that I'm going to spend my married life calling you Major, then it's all off,' she declared. 'So if you can stand the pain, tell me your proper name and I'll decide whether or not I can live with it.'

She imagined everything from Abraham onwards and would find her own if necessary.

'Tim,' he said, looking aggrieved.

'Tim?' she repeated with evident surprise.

'Well, what's wrong with that?' he demanded.

She burst into laughter and threw her arms round his neck.

'Oh, my darling, nothing at all,' she said, pulling herself tightly to him and he experienced the most sensuous kiss of his life.

When he was allowed to come up for air, she said, 'Darling, it's a lovely name, why does no one use it?'

'Damned if I know, nobody ever asks, I suppose,' he answered, sheepishly.

Since fate had thus far chosen to shield their situation from public notice, they decided to add zest to life for a short time at least, by continuing as far as they could manage, to exhibit a normal relationship. Once the funeral was behind them, they would announce their plans to everybody at an appropriate time of their own choosing, if possible. Meanwhile, their restraint would be maintained by unspoken agreement to preserve the old-style virtues that characterised their backgrounds and would enhance their ultimate union.

Madge telephoned Mrs Goodbody, and had a long conversation during which she was told that Bernard was for the high jump, as Diana Goodbody had put it. Madge was invited to drop the Goodbody from the conversation, and further learned that Ivy's affairs had been investigated with persistence, by the police, as the extent of Bernard's activities unravelled.

It seemed that, by bullying Ivy into signing papers she didn't really understand, and insisting on a joint account, Bernard had worked his way through her capital. By failed ventures and gambling, most of the money was already lost. His arrest was imminent and he would almost certainly be in custody before the funeral. The house was to be sold to discharge debts outstanding, which meant that Bernard would be destitute by his own hand, when he was finally released from prison.

Madge requested a burial service, to be held at the small church that Ivy had attended whenever she was allowed to. The date was set at Friday the 31st of the month.

With the further assistance of Diana, Madge commissioned a memorial stone for the grave, to be fitted as soon after the funeral as possible. Consequent expenses in that respect that the estate failed to cover, she would gladly undertake herself.

Chapter 14

Consequences

The axiomatic profundity that 'Nothing should be too anything', having indisputable veracity, but no fathomable conversational use, stood like a folly in the landscape of the major's mind, where it had existed since its inception through idle contemplation on a subject long forgotten. It remained there immutably awaiting purpose while he entertained the patient hope that it would eventually find some inspired application and decorate a conversation with the richness of meaning he felt it deserved.

While he dozed in the warm sunshine outside the French window, his freewheeling mind was giving that literary ornament a further dusting; and as reality merged into fantasy, at the edge of consciousness, delusion assumed the mantle of rationality. In an intoxicating moment of revelation he grasped the holy grail of enlightenment. Full meaning and purpose was illuminated for one joyous instant before the world began to spin round with a rushing noise of increasing loudness and confusion threatened to tear him away from his euphoria. He struggled to articulate definition of the precious something, striving to hang on to the words as they gradually dissolved into gibberish. He woke up with a violent start, as though discharged from a chute; the noise suddenly displaced by the sounds of reality.

He blinked in the strong sun that had tightened his face unpleasantly. His attention was drawn by the whirling whistle of four red kites gyrating above the meadow, as they played together. Also, the telephone was ringing.

He levered himself out of the deckchair and reached for the receiver just inside the door.

'Llenots-Jones,' he said, sleepily.

'Are you all right, darling?' said Madge.

'Yes, old girl, just nodded off for a while, that's all; lovely to hear your voice, anything up?'

'I've got some more news, when can we talk?'

The major ruffled his hair, as though to

clear his mind a bit.

'Why not come round, we'll go for a walk if you like,' he suggested.

'Lovely, sweetheart, I'll just change into something suitable and I'll be round in five minutes.'

Damned awkward, he said to himself, as he changed his shoes. Both he and Madge wanted to keep a low profile but they couldn't ignore each other for an indefinite period; the strain would be too much, at least it would be for him. Women seemed to have more restraint than men.

When Madge arrived, dressed in a shirt and slacks, he looked up, and they set off arm in arm, obscured from the rest of the house by the great bushy rhododendrons, and headed for the gate and the open fields beyond. Before Madge could begin to talk about her news, the major wanted to clear up their situation in regard to their being together.

'I really don't think we can keep up the pretence for long, old thing,' he began. 'It'll have to be one thing or the other, and I think it would be impossible to continue to ignore each other now, don't you?'

'I agree, darling; it will only take the smallest incident to convince everyone that we're close. I think we just have to accept that fact and allow the idea to sink in gradually. We don't have to make any announcements yet, just appear to be friendly,' she concluded.

They reached the stile, which he crossed and waited for her, standing with his arms ready to assist her. She climbed over and stood on the lowest bar, smiling; then reached for his neck, letting her body fall against him; her weight round his neck. She clung for a while, feeling she could walk on top of flowers.

He lowered her to the ground, as she said, 'You'd better not look at me like that at breakfast, Timothy darling.'

'Now tell me what you've found out,' he said, putting an arm round her waist and steering her along the path.

She recounted everything that Diana had revealed to her.

'So, we've got just under a week then; I'll tell the other two,' he said. 'After that we can start thinking about the future; I can't see any point in waiting more than practically necessary, to get "wed", as Smiler would put it.'

'Absolutely not, darling, my hormones are overheated enough as it is,' she said, laughing at his embarrassment.

'O.K., old sweet; tell you what, let's announce it on Saturday, shall we? It's formal dinner night, first Saturday of the month and all that.'

'Already!' she exclaimed. 'I can't believe

it's a month since the last time, when poor Ramiro got into all that trouble.'

'You know what has occurred to me?' said Madge, as they walked on slowly. 'No one at the lodge is married, apart from staff that is.'

He pondered the remark, realising the questions raised by it.

'Well, we must talk to the C.O. straight away; we can't leave her in the dark; it wouldn't be fair.'

'Of course,' she interjected.

'There's more to talk to her about than I realised,' he went on, looking at Madge. 'I've really no idea as to whether she has any kind of policy in regard to married couples. I've never given it the slightest thought beyond, perhaps, vaguely assuming that the question never arose.'

'Oh dear,' said Madge, looking at the major archly, 'perhaps she'll just throw us out.'

She lifted her shoulders, and grinned at him. She didn't really care what happened to them, it was all too exciting, anyway.

'Well, I'll tell you what I think,' he said. 'I think we should be on the outside anyway. I think we should find somewhere to live and be on our own for a few years at least. What do you think?'

'Absolutely, darling, how deliciously exciting; let's start looking right away.'

She pulled tighter on his arm.

'First things first, old girl. I think we must talk to the C.O. before doing anything else. In the meantime, I suppose we ought to be getting back for lunch, if we want any.'

By chance, the major found both Joyce and Sam in the sitting room at lunchtime and arranged for the four of them to sit together for lunch. Sam and Joyce both confirmed their availability on the following Friday, the 31st. Sam was slightly disappointed that they were not likely to encounter the awful Bernard and felt that his role was diminished by the fact, but assured himself that their presence would be greatly appreciated by Madge.

Madge thanked them for their support, reaching across the table to grasp the hand of each.

It caused some surprise on their part when she said, incautiously, to the major, 'And where would I be without you, dear Tim?'

Sam's face lit up with eager curiosity.

While looking at Joyce for reaction, he exclaimed, 'Tim?' and before anyone else could respond, the major looked at him directly, and pre-empting further questions, said, 'So what? You never asked.'

Sam was perfectly satisfied with the reply, thinking no more than, 'ask a silly question...'

'If this is a game, can anybody play?' said a wide-eyed Joyce and then, looking at an expressionless Madge steadily for a few seconds while her mind ticked over, engaging the full power of feminine intuition, she began to smile faintly and without conveying the slightest import to either man, her face, like a brass band in a silent film, was a deafening interrogation to Madge, who returned the look with a bland gaze and an almost imperceptible nod. Putting a hand to her mouth to mask the grin that was spreading across her face, Joyce sank back in her chair, her eyes twinkling with excitement.

It was helpful to their mild subterfuge that Madge and the major were forming a close enough friendship with both Joyce and Sam that they were frequently all together, giving rise to no more speculation over any one of them being with any other.

Kathy, leaning back in her chair and gazing out of the window, was mentally reviewing the party at the golf club, on Saturday. Molly Haine had celebrated her 53rd birthday, and had enlivened the proceedings at the outset by using the occasion to announce her engagement to a prominent member of the club whose means were known by everyone to be very extensive and the wedding of the year was predicted. She confided to Kathy that the guest list would include not only Kath and Geoff's daughter Karen, and Daphne, but also Tom Dangerfield, Joan Collett, Smiler, and Thea.

The party had been a huge success, continuing until somewhere around three in the morning. Kath, in her full glory, was of such stunning attraction that the other women present were incapable of disguising their apprehension whenever their men came within range of her lethal perfume.

Geoff feared that the odds of her staying with him were growing more tenuous by the day. Apart from the physical magic, her riveting personality was the essence of his being hopelessly drawn to her and the need for drastic action on his part, if he was to secure her, seemed paramount.

What was needed, he decided, was something to precipitate her overt committal. Their outings invariably concluded with the decision as to where to end the day and begin the next; his house or the cottage. This sometimes hinged on his daughter Karen being at home or otherwise.

Karen was rapidly developing a life of her own and spending more and more time away. On this occasion, she was staying with a university friend in London for a long weekend, so Geoff's rambling, split-level bungalow was decided upon.

Mrs Cross, the housekeeper, would arrive at nine o'clock in the morning and seeing Geoff's car in the drive, would call through from the sitting room, 'Are you two going to get up today?'

Mrs Cross had grown to love Kathy like a daughter and was desperate to see the two of them properly together, as she called it, and frequently chided Geoff to do something before Kathy lost her faith in him.

Above the music of the last dance of the evening, Geoff said into Kathy's ear, 'Why are we going on like this, Kath? I can't keep on living without you. Sell the cottage and move in to our place.'

She clasped her hands behind his neck and leaned back at arm's length. Studying his face, which was lined by a desperate expression, she decided there and then that he was the future, as far as she was concerned.

She arched an eyebrow and replied, 'Why should I? I'm only forty-two, with my own home, the whole world beckoning, and you say, move in with us,' she said, emphasising the 'us'.

As she maintained a stern and critical expression, he began to think that this was the end. He had gambled on the wrong horse and it had fallen at the first hurdle. He tried to hang on to the shattered exchange; desperately thinking of some fragmental fact that might salvage the situation.

'Karen is renting a flat in town next month,' he said, almost weeping with frustration. 'Another few weeks that's all, and I'll be on my own.'

Her expression remained unchanged, as he searched frantically for inspiration. Kathy could bear the agony on his face no longer.

She pulled herself into him with tears forming in her eyes and, placing her head against his shoulder said, softly, 'Forget the cottage, darling, just take me home.'

That was three days ago. A knock on the office door brought Kathy back to the present. She opened the door to find the major poised to knock again.

'Major, do come in.'

'Ah, don't want to keep you, m'dear; looking for the C.O. actually.'

'Oh, she's out for most of the afternoon I'm afraid. Can I do anything for you?'

He thought for a moment, then replied, 'Ah, bit personal, actually.'

'I see,' said Kathy, 'I'll tell her as soon as she returns, if you haven't seen her first, of course.'

'Right ho! thanks, m'dear,' and before retreating, added 'How are you, anyway? Must say you look very happy.'

'Oh, I certainly am, thank you Major.'

'Jolly good, give my regards to Geoff, won't you?' he said turning away. Before Kathy could close the door, he looked back at her, saying, 'Perhaps I ought to tell you though, bit of a long story really.'

Kathy widened the door, saying, 'Come in and sit down, Major. Would you like a cup of tea, I'm about to have one.'

'Very kind, m'dear,' he said and sat down as she closed the door.

'Fact is,' he began, 'Madge Russell's sister, Ivy, died recently, and some of us are taking her down to the funeral on Friday.'

'That's very kind of you all,' said Kathy. 'Is it very far?'

'It's a small place in Somerset; two hours' run more or less I should think,' the major said and briefly outlined the situation, explaining Madge's need of support.

'It's good of you to tell me, and helpful to know where residents are if possible, just in case of emergencies,' said Kathy while ringing through to the kitchen to ask for a pot of tea and two cups.

'I don't suppose it's necessary, but if you did want to, you could presumably contact us through the funeral people,' the major suggested and Kathy wrote down the name and location of the company.

Kathy was vaguely wondering why the major was telling her all this, rather than Madge Russell herself, whom she knew to be a very competent person; but the thought didn't fully register.

'Would you like me to tell Mrs Currer-Spriggs about it?' she asked.

'By all means,' the major replied, adding

'though I still need to see her privately, you understand.'

'Of course,' said Kathy. 'I'll leave a note in her sitting room, she always goes in there first when she returns.' Kathy treated the major to a radiant smile. 'Will you have another, Major?' she offered, taking his empty cup.

Daphne's ageing cream Mercedes swept up to the front entrance and, leaving the keys in the ignition, Daphne walked briskly into the house and into the sitting room. She pushed her coat back over her shoulders, deftly catching it behind her as it slid off, and cast it over the back of a chair. Her eye had caught sight of the note on the small table as she came in and, snatching it up, she flopped back into the armchair for a quick rest before going in to see Kathy and Robbie.

'The major craves an audience, *tout de suite*, K.,' she read.

That's rather frivolous of Kathy, she thought, not for the first time that week, putting it down to approaching spring perhaps. She ordered tea from the kitchen, adding a request for Ramiro to come and put her car away. It would not take him long to see to it, she knew; he loved to be seen at the wheel of the Mercedes and he would drive slowly past the windows round to the stables' yard. Then she dialled the major's room number, her curiosity mounting by the second as somewhere deep in her mind she nurtured a seed of romantic affinity with him.

There being no reply, she waited for the tea to arrive and diverted Tracey to the office, following her over.

'Thanks for the note, dear,' she said to Kathy, 'he's gone to ground somewhere at the moment. Any idea what it's about?'

'He didn't give me a clue,' she answered, 'but there is something else he asked me to tell you, though.'

She went through the details of the coming Friday's trip to Somerset.

'Ah, that probably accounts for their coming in together when we saw them.'

'Oh yes, I suppose so,' agreed Kathy.

'I thought it would be nice to send some flowers to the funeral. What do you think?' said Kathy. 'From everyone here, I mean,' she added.

'Oh, yes indeed, I'm sure she would very much appreciate it. She's such a nice person. She told me all about her sister Ivy the other week, you know; it was all very tragic, it would be nice to do something.'

'Oh well,' said Daphne, 'do you need me for anything else, dear?'

'No, I don't think so, Daphne, everything is under control; I'll take care of the flowers; I can get all the details from the funeral company.'

'And I'll take care of the major,' said Daphne, with a wink, and went off to see Robbie.

She was returning from the kitchen and about to enter her rooms across the hall from her sitting room when the major came through the entrance hall.

'Ah,' they both exclaimed.

'There's time for a chat now if you like,' said Daphne.

'Oh, thank you,' he replied and she gestured towards her sitting room.

They settled back in armchairs, as the major searched for opening words.

'Perhaps Kathy has mentioned the funeral on Friday,' he began.

'Yes, she told me all about it just now,' Daphne replied. 'Poor Madge, now she has nobody at all.'

'Well, not exactly,' said the major coyly, 'she has me now.'

'You!' said Daphne, looking puzzled, and assuming that he must be referring to the funeral trip or something.

The major braced himself for what he knew would come as a startling surprise to her.

'We're getting married,' he said beaming. 'And we think it best to find a home of our own for a few years.'

Daphne's mind reeled as the words took effect. She was shocked, firstly by the abruptness of the revelation and then by the realisation that it mattered to her. The major was surprised by the way she was reacting but said nothing, while she disciplined her thoughts before forcing herself to formulate appropriate words in reply.

'You know each other that well?' she asked incredulously, aware of her heart thumping.

The question had little meaning she knew, but she resisted the several others she was tempted to put.

Judging by her tone and expression, the major deduced that Daphne was not only affected by the announcement, but that her reaction was clearly an emotional one. Could she possibly have been nurturing hopes of a closer relationship developing between them? he wondered and searched his mind to recall anything he might have said to her earlier that would precipitate the notion.

Anxious as he was to discuss the various implications of the situation, as the purpose of his visit, he didn't know what to say. Now, other questions were coming to mind; how would he account to Madge, for Daphne's attitude towards him, if she found it difficult to conceal?

This was a situation that the major could never have dreamt of and he was desperate to escape from it somehow. He was unable to look her in the face and felt himself blushing with embarrassment. Daphne found the strength to put her feelings into perspective, wondering where so much emotion had come from and knowing that it must be controlled there and then. She stood up suddenly, causing the major to do the same.

'My dear, I wish you all the joy in the world, you both deserve it,' she said putting her hand forward to shake his, squeezing it rather too hard. 'You must both come and see me as soon as possible to discuss details. Perhaps you could manage coffee in the morning, eh?'

The major, nodding agreement, could see the emotion in her eyes as she effected a smile, and impulsively embraced her, before leaving her alone with her disillusionment.

Daphne sat down again, sapped of her customary good spirits. After several minutes of contemplation she sat up straight and resolved to pull herself together. Being lachrymose was not her style and, after all, it was not as though she had actually lost anything. Gradually she began to feel a little ashamed and hoped she hadn't made too bad an impression on the major. She would present a jollier aspect to him in the morning.

She lifted the telephone and buzzed the office number to see if Kathy was still there, to join her for a cheering drink. Reg answered, saying that Kathy had just left and was on her way to Dr MacDonald's house.

Daphne poured herself a large sherry, rang Robbie and arranged to have dinner brought to her room.

On Wednesday morning Madge joined the major in the sitting room in order to discuss and prepare themselves for the forthcoming meeting with Daphne. He warned her that any apparent discomfiture on Daphne's part would be on account of her having heard so suddenly that she was about to lose two of her older residents.

As they entered her sitting room at the agreed time, Daphne advanced on Madge with outstretched arms, and beaming with pleasure embraced her with the utmost affection.

'Do sit down, my dear, and you, Major,' she said gesturing towards the settee.

Sitting forward and upright in her chair, Daphne was wholly enthusiastic towards their plans, insisting that the ceremony and reception arrangements be left in the hands of herself, Kathy, and Robbie. The whole event could be accommodated in the Lodge, including the ceremony if required. The couple's sole concern would be in fixing a date, which in turn depended on their finding a home that she hoped would be not so far away that they would lose touch with all their friends at the Lodge.

Did anyone else know of their plans yet?

Daphne enquired. With the possible exception of Joyce who had probably guessed, they were aware of no one.

'When will you announce it?' she said.

The couple looked at each other for a moment, and Madge said, 'We had thought that we would announce the engagement on Saturday, but we now think it better to find somewhere first; then we can announce a wedding date at the same time.'

'Well, that seems to be that then,' Daphne concluded. 'Thank you for telling me everything; and you will give us as much notice as you can, won't you?' she said, standing up. 'I hope it all goes well, on Friday,' and to the major, 'Make sure you bring them back safely.'

'Of course, m'dear,' he replied, as he rose from his chair to grasp her hand warmly, expressing their thanks, before departing.

Many of the residents including the major, were on Geoffrey MacDonald's register of patients. It was the major's custom to present himself at the surgery for a chat and check over about every six months. While his next appointment for that purpose was not until the coming May, he nevertheless felt it might be prudent to go fairly soon, just for peace of mind, if not out of duty to Madge. He accordingly secured an appointment for the coming Thursday, at eleven forty-five.

'What's up with you, L.-J.?' said Geoff, as they shook hands, and he gestured towards the empty chair.

'Nothing at all as far as I know,' said the major, 'at least I sincerely hope not.'

'You going to tell me something out of the ordinary then?' Geoff asked.

'You could say that old boy. You know Madge Russell, don't you?'

'Yes, she's one of mine, nothing wrong with her I'm glad to say, strong as a horse a week ago anyway. Why do you ask?'

'Because we're getting married.'

'My dear chap, that's absolutely splendid news,' said Geoff, pumping the major's hand. 'You couldn't have made a better choice, she's quite delightful. So that's what it's all about, eh? Now you want a check-up as well do you?'

'As well as what?' enquired the major.

'Oh, God,' said Geoff. 'Spoken out of turn, haven't I?'

The major looked puzzled still.

'Sorry L.-J., I meant, as well as Madge.'

'So you mean she had a check-up a week ago?'

'Well, I shouldn't have said anything really, but no harm done I hope.'

The major started to laugh quietly. She must have booked in a few days before that, so it was before he made his idiotic proposal, he thought to himself.

'Right,' he exclaimed, 'let's get on with it then. By the by old boy, you won't say anything to anyone yet, will you?'

'I'll make a bargain with you,' said Geoff. 'I'll say nothing about your wedding provided you say nothing about mine.'

The astonished major leapt up and returned the handshaking complement, laughing with delight.

'My dear chap, I'm so delighted. When will you announce it?'

'Ah, that you'll have to wait and see,' said Geoff.

'Fair enough,' said the major removing his jacket.

'Right as rain,' said Geoff at the end of his examination. Your pulse coincides with a seventeen year old's.'

'Flattery,' grunted the major.

'Not in the least, you've nothing to worry about, I assure you. If anything, you're in slightly better condition than I am but that's not too surprising, in this job.'

They wished each other good luck and the major left the surgery, standing on the pavement outside for a moment contemplating his good luck, good fortune and good health. No man could have felt more contented. He called at the Esso garage at the end of the town and filled the tank ready for the trip the following day, then had his hair trimmed before returning to the Lodge.

Chapter 15

Outcomes

'I can't say I've ever heard of Woodington,' said Sam at breakfast on Friday morning, 'though I don't know Somerset that well.'

'It's only a small village,' said the major. 'I should think it will take us about two and a half hours but I don't want to cause Madge any worry so I suggest we set off about nine o'clock. That will give us three and a half hours, time to stop on the way and to find the place once we come off the M5.'

'More tea or coffee anyone?' asked Tracey.

'No thank you,' they chorused.

'Well! I think if everyone's finished, we should make a move,' the major said, looking from the two women to Sam.

'I'd like another piece of toast,' said Joyce, 'but I'll take it up with me.'

'Don't drop bits of marmalade on the floor then,' Sam teased.

'Where's the Bee?' he asked, looking at the major.

'Ramiro's bringing it round to the front. It's eight twenty-five, now. Let's say five to, out the front,' the major suggested.

They all agreed and stood up.

'Have a safe journey,' said Tracey, waiting to clear the table, as they filed out of the dining room to go and make ready for the day's expedition.

Joyce and Madge took the back seats for easier women's chat, while Sam took charge of the map. They stopped for a break at the last service station on the M4, before sloping onto the M5 and running down to the A39, at an easy 60 m.p.h. Once they neared Glastonbury, Madge began to recognise landmarks and was able to guide them to Woodington with very little trouble.

The major drove, as directed, up a rough track signposted 'To the XIVth Century church' and pulled up on a gravelled area by a low brick wall supporting green-painted railings. Just beyond the wall was a notice board with gold lettering on a black background. 'Church of St George, Woodington Parish, Vicar: the Reverend George Watts,' was the principal information conveyed.

They got out and stretched their legs.

'Not too bad,' said the major looking at his watch. 'Twelve fifteen; quarter of an hour to go,' he added.

There was one other car parked nearby, having what Sam thought to be a rather ostentatious aerial fixed to the roof by a large rubber base.

'We might as well go straight in and be

sitting down,' said Madge.

As they walked through the gateway into the churchyard another car drew up and out stepped a rather smart but sombrely dressed woman, by herself.

She hurried up the path clutching her hat, to catch up with them; putting her hand forward to shake with the nearest of them which happened to be Joyce, and smilingly announced, 'I'm Diana Goodbody.'

'How do you do?'

'Joyce Kingham,' said Joyce, taking her hand.

'Oh! you must be Mrs Russell,' Diana said moving towards Madge, 'I'm so very sorry about your poor sister; thank God she's at peace at last.'

'It's awfully good of you to come,' said Madge, shaking hands and introducing the others.

They went through the porch and Sam gripped the heavy latch ring of the ancient door. It stuck for a second before suddenly flying up against its metal stop with a loud hollow bang. With the noise reverberating round the church, they passed through the doorway into the slightly musty atmosphere of the aisle.

Three men were sitting in a pew half way down the left side. The outer two were in dark well-worn suits and ties; the central figure was bearded and casually attired.

Tom and Joyce led the way down the aisle towards the cleric waiting to conduct the service. Diana, Madge and the major followed them to the front. As they passed the three curious visitors Madge gasped and clutched at the major's arm.

'It's Bernard,' she whispered.

They took their seats and waited a few minutes as the sounds of further activity could be heard coming from outside. The door opened again and the coffin was borne along the aisle to be placed on a catafalque. As the bearers withdrew, two attendants came forward and placed on top of the coffin, first an exotic assemblage of flowers with a card from Madge; and then a beautiful elaborate wreath. Madge wondered whom the wreath could be from. She began to weep quietly.

Diana placed a hand over Madge's and whispered, 'I came in case you were alone; I'm glad you are not; I don't know why your brother-in-law is here, I wasn't expecting it. I'm sorry.'

The service proceeded and the coffin was finally carried out, followed by the small party. The little procession made its way through the churchyard, through a gate and into a small cemetery on the hillside where a grave had been prepared.

The wreath and flowers were removed before the coffin was lowered into the grave.

Placed on the grass beside the grave, the tributes were then visible to Madge who, reading the words on the wreath: 'With deepest sympathy from all residents and staff at Anvil Lodge', turned to the major with eyes streaming. He put his arms round her, remaining silent.

'So thoughtful,' she said, burying her face in his coat.

Ivy was buried in a peaceful spot overlooking the valley; a beautiful place they all agreed afterwards. When the interment was completed, the small group turned away to leave the sextons to their work.

The two men had held Bernard back from the vicinity of the grave, and as they started to walk away, Bernard grinned at them, causing Madge to break into uncontrollable sobbing.

Boiling with rage, Sam suddenly made a dash towards the three. He was an intimidating figure and Bernard, in common with all bullies, was an abject coward when dealing with men. Guessing the intentions of the huge figure advancing upon him and fearing the worst, he started to flee for his life. While the escorts were not expecting him to be troublesome, they had removed his handcuffs during the service and had no control of him.

As the furious Sam shot past them, gaining on his loathsome quarry, Bernard, like terrified prey, felt the massive hand gripping his shoulder and span round with a sickly leer of fright. He found himself lifted clear of the ground and held aloft. Expecting to be hurled away, he was, instead, dropped to the ground and then dragged along by one ankle back to where his keepers waited impassively with handcuffs ready.

The senior of the two shook Sam by the hand and thanked him profusely for his bravery in assisting the police by capturing an escaping prisoner. He also explained that Bernard was there as of right while not being the least interested in the service beyond the excuse to be out of prison for a few hours. His late behaviour would be fully reported and would almost certainly contribute to his ultimate sentence.

Joyce was rooted to the spot, astonished at Sam's display of heroic masculinity and was unable to take her eyes off him for several minutes. They watched the car drive away as one of the policemen could be seen speaking into a microphone. It was the last that any of them would ever see of Bernard.

They took their leave of the Rev. Watts with much thanks and the major begged Diana to join them for 'a spot of lunch' somewhere. She gladly accepted and was able to recommend a coaching inn near Glastonbury, not far from the coroner's office where she worked.

During an excellent and more than welcome lunch, and with the funeral behind them, the general mood of all changed to one of conviviality and satisfaction with the day's outcome. When Diana was apprised of Madge's engagement to the major she was overjoyed at the news and delighted at the promise of an invitation to the wedding. By the time they parted, she and Madge had consolidated a lasting friendship with mutual undertakings to remain in contact. Thus was concluded a pleasant gathering before the Bee was turned towards home.

Sam, having no further navigational role, conceded the front seat to Madge at the instigation of Joyce who suggested that it seemed more appropriate. As they drove off she settled back with a tingle of satisfaction to spend the next two or three hours re-kindling her arts of subtle seduction, to weave magic effects on the unsuspecting Sam. The day being Friday and the rush-hour early, the return journey took three hours, bringing them back to the Lodge at six o'clock.

Seeing the party arrive outside, Reg emerged from the office to meet them as they trooped into the hall.

'Good day?' he enquired generally.

'Very good indeed thanks, Reg,' replied Sam.

'Oh, Major,' said Reg, 'Miss Summers

asked me to give you this as soon as you come in, sir.'

'Thank you, Reg,' he replied, taking the envelope from Reg.

'Shall I get Ramiro to put the car away, sir?'

'No, don't trouble him now, I expect he's pretty busy at the moment, I'll see him later.'

'Right you are, sir,' said Reg, stepping back into the office resisting the compulsion to salute.

They dispersed somewhat wearily to their rooms, Madge declaring that she was going to lie down and do nothing for at least an hour and would not be down for dinner until the last moment, in view of the late copious lunch.

When he reached his room the major sat down and opened the letter from Kathy.

'Geoff told me of your wonderful news, I hope you don't mind, though I suppose the fact that he has told you ours makes up for it. Anyway, I know it's frightfully short notice but could you and Madge possibly come to my cottage this evening for a little celebration drink? I feel we really should do something together and, besides, there is something important we would like to discuss with you both. Don't be upset if you can't make it but please phone me a.s.a.p. Regards, Kathleen.'

The major was most intrigued by the last, enigmatic comment, but wondered if Madge would feel too tired for a further outing. He phoned her straight away and read the letter to her.

'Well what do you think, old sweet?' he asked.

'I can't think of any reason to not go,' she said enthusiastically, 'but if you'd rather not after all that driving, my darling.'

'No. I'm game if you are; I'll phone her and find out what time they would like to see us and then phone you back.'

'All right, darling,' said Madge, putting the phone back on its bedside base.

Kathy had been working in the garden since she arrived home, in an effort to catch up with some of the odd jobs that had mounted up even during the winter but were never urgent enough to deal with at the time. Now that spring was emerging she thought that she must make an effort before things started to get out of hand.

The sun had set gloriously through the trees and the light began to diminish. She was raking up the results of her toil when the telephone started to ring. She dropped the rake and hurried across to the kitchen door, reaching inside to lift the phone off the wall.

'Hello,' she answered brightly.

'Hello, Kathy?' enquired the major.

'Oh, it's you, Major. How did you get on today?'

'Went pretty well, really; everyone's having a bit of a rest at the moment. What time would you like us to come, we were all planning a bit of a rest and a late dinner, as a result of a rather large and late lunch,' he replied.

'Oh, I am glad you can come. Why not skip dinner, have a rest for an hour or so, then come round about eight and we'll have supper later on, eh? and to save worrying about driving, I'll get Geoff to pick you up on his way here.'

'I say, that's absolutely splendid,' said the major.

'Good. I'll tell Geoff to collect you about ten to eight then. Bye!' she said, ringing off.

With the visit confirmed, she telephoned Geoff to discuss what they needed to be bought on his way over to the Lodge. She then returned to finish clearing up in the garden, amazed at how much darker and colder it seemed in the short time she had been indoors.

She returned the tools to the small brick outhouse that served as a garden store. Filling the log basket from the stacks of logs heaped along the back wall, she locked up and walked awkwardly back with the load into the kitchen, glad to be in the warm again. Her next priority was a glass of gin

285

and Italian, before making and lighting a log fire in the sitting room. With all the mucky jobs done she went upstairs for a quick shower and to dress for the evening.

The major reminded himself that he had been dying for a 'snifter' ever since their return and, after telephoning Madge, he called Sam suggesting they meet in the sitting room for a quick one. Ten minutes later he was feeling distinctly refreshed by a large gin and tonic as he explained to Sam that he and Madge had been invited to dine out. They talked about the day's events and the major thanked Sam for his support.

They parted at seven o'clock and the major returned to his room. He had arranged to see Madge in the hall at ten to eight and duly presented himself in time to visit Reg in the office, where he gave the car keys into Reg's keeping with the request that either he or Ramiro might find the time to put it away. Reg stiffened up.

'Don't you worry about a thing, sir, just you leave it all to me.'

'Oh, that's nice,' said Madge as they drove up the narrow lane a few yards to where Kathy's cottage among the oak and beech trees had nestled for 350 years.

They turned left into a short drive that cut into the sloping grounds and led up to a double garage. The drive was lighted by wrought-iron lanterns flanking the black-timbered gateway, supplemented by an antique street lamp placed at the top of some stone steps leading up the bank from the drive to the garden.

Geoff retrieved some shopping bags from the boot before locking the car and, with the car keys between his teeth, nodded them towards the steps. At the top, a stone path curved away up the lawn to the door of the cottage where Kathy stood waving and smiling.

Madge was enchanted by the pure English charm of the place. Green shoots were visible on the ramblers clinging to the flint and brick walls around the leaded windows. The light from the windows cast an emerald tinge across the lawn and revealed faint yellow swathes of daffodils emerging in the darkened flowerbeds. A quiet sound of water splashing and tumbling over stones betrayed the existence of a spring stream somewhere on the far side of the gardens beyond the cottage.

'What a magical home you have,' said Madge as she embraced Kathy.

'Isn't it lovely?' said Kathy, leading the way through to the long low sitting room. 'Do sit down,' she said, taking their coats and motioning them towards the acres of warm coloured chintz.

They settled back into the luxurious

depths and gazed around the ancient beamed room. A huge open inglenook fireplace formed one end wall, in the middle of which a blazing log fire, surrounded with antique iron cooking apparatus, imbued the atmosphere with luxurious charm. Madge felt as though she was visiting paradise.

Geoff came in through the dining room, from the kitchen, with a tray and glasses of champagne.

'Here's to us,' he said standing with an arm round Kathy.

'To us!' they chorused.

'Now!' said Geoff sitting down in an armchair and pulling Kathy onto his lap. She ruffled his hair and kissed the top of his head as he continued, 'Tell us what you can about your plans.'

'Well,' began the major, 'first of all we need to find a place to live; until we've solved that problem there's not an awful lot we can say is there, old sweet?' he said, looking at Madge, who shook her head in confirmation.

Before he could continue, Geoff raised his hand, with the comment, 'Say no more, old chap; it could be that you don't need to look any further. Kath and I have been talking about it today and if you don't think it's interfering too much we think we might have the answer to your problem.

'When Kath moves out of here to come to

my place, which will be very soon, this place will be available more or less lock stock and barrel. We would be prepared to offer the option of buying it if you wanted to; or you could rent it, either temporarily at a very modest rate or permanently at an agreeable one. Whichever you decided, it would be far cheaper than what you're paying between you at present.

'As you can imagine, of course, if we put this place on the open market it would be gone for the asking price before we could get home again. What do you say?'

Madge was utterly stunned by the suggestion. She could not at first believe what she was hearing; it was as though she was listening to a fairy story and being made to believe it. As her mind struggled to accept the reality of a seeming miracle, she looked at the major with bewilderment. He could see that to decline the offer would destroy Madge's dreams, beyond all consolation.

'I don't know what to say, old boy, or how to thank you both; this is all beyond our wildest dreams,' the major said. 'We will be absolutely delighted to take you up on it.'

'Excellent,' exclaimed Geoff, dumping Kathy on the floor without ceremony and leaping up.

'Now we can really celebrate. Where's that bottle?'

'You brute,' said Kathy, hauling herself up

from the floor as he went back to the kitchen.

She crossed to Madge and put her arms round her.

'I'm so glad, Madge darling; I know you'll be very happy here.'

Geoff returned and poured the rest of the champagne into the women's glasses.

He turned to the major winking archly, saying, 'Sorry old chap.'

'Let me show you round,' said Kathy taking Madge enthusiastically by the hand and leading her off into the dining room.

'What do you call it?' asked Madge as they went.

'The locals call it Rosemary Cottage, which suits me well enough and the post always finds it,' said Kathy.

Geoff looked at the major and grinned.

'Let's have a proper drink, shall we? I've managed to get an eighteen-year Glenmorangie at last.'

'By God, Geoff, now you're talking,' said the major, glowing with satisfaction. 'Then you can show me the garden while I have a quick pipe,' he added.

'By the by, Geoff, when does Kathy plan to move, any idea?'

'As soon as you like, Tim, you're virtually waiting on each other,' Geoff replied, to the major's surprise.

'Well, I suppose that will be as soon as

Madge wants to get married then,' said the major.

'Absolutely, just say the word, I dare say Kath would like a day or two to pack a few things, but that's all; she won't bring much; no point. You'll have absolutely everything you need, "as is!", so to speak.'

As they strolled round the garden, the major said, 'We'll need a taxi, to get back. Can't have you taking risks on our account.'

'Not to worry L.-J., Kath's organised something, just relax and make the most!'

'It's been a very long and memorable day for Madge,' said the major, 'she'll go out like a light when she finally turns in.'

'What an extraordinary week this is,' he thought puffing contentedly on his pipe.

After supper they returned to the sitting room and chatted till Madge could keep awake no longer.

'Wake up, old sweet,' said the major. 'It's high time we were off,' and looking at Geoff said, 'I'll phone for a cab if you don't mind, old boy.'

'Don't worry,' Kathy said, 'I told Reg to stand by for a call. If you've no objection he'll come and pick you up in the Rover. Will that be all right, Tim?'

'Well played, Kathy,' he answered.

And so they returned to the Lodge at the end of a long and most gratifying day.

Chapter 16

Conclusions

Being a frequent overnight dreamer, the major was subject to certain recurring themes, welcome or otherwise. As it happened, during the night subsequent to the visit to Kathy's home, his slumbers found him, as on other occasions, in company with a crowd of people in a largish room. As usual, he suddenly remembered that he had the ability to raise himself off the ground, or floor in this case. 'Ah yes!', he thought to himself, 'I know! I shall astonish everybody by demonstrating my ability to defy gravity.'

And so by maintaining concentration on the conviction of its possibility and eschewing all 'Icarian' doubts, he had only to press down with his toes to start himself off the floor. He began his ascent in the fashion of a lifting rocket, projecting himself slowly upwards to indulge again in the exquisite sensation of weightlessness and unfettered flight.

He continued his rise from standing before the fireplace to clearing the heads of the assembled company and assuming the relaxed horizontal attitude of a reclining God, set off to cruise around the room close to the ceiling. He had on other occasions ventured to dangerous heights out of doors and could recall passing along a busy street at roof top level without ever forgetting to maintain the necessary concentration to avoid a disastrous plunge.

Three times he circuited the room, inviting the amazement and delight of those below. It was, however, common to all such occasions that he never succeeded in attracting from the company even the smallest degree of attention or admiration of his prowess; neither could he later remember any sort of finale.

There was, however, the single and gratifying fact that in his conscious life he could fully recall that unique sensation of leaving the ground; much superior, in fact, to the near orgasmic moment we all recollect of first keeping our feet on the pedals of a bike. Furthermore, there lurked in the depths of his psyche the suspicion that one day, if only the conviction were strong enough, he might yet achieve the phenomenon in reality, which perhaps accounted for the dream's recurrence.

The major usually remembered his dreams and had sometimes wished he'd kept a record of them, together with sketches of the places and descriptions of the many people he had met who, despite their very distinctive appearance and character, remained unique, bearing no resemblance to anyone he had ever met in reality.

In addition to recurrent themes common to many people, such as falling from high places and leaden-legged pursuit, he frequently found himself quite unable to remember whereabouts in a car park he had left his car, or even where the car park was. Psychologists would no doubt place all manner of interpretations on such themes and circumstances; but, then, couldn't we all?

Despite his overnight adventures, the major awoke on Saturday morning at a reasonable hour and felt sufficiently refreshed to get up and make a start to the day. He hoped it would be a relaxing one, with the monthly party to look forward to in the evening. There was, of course, a lot to talk over with Madge, and Daphne should be informed of their further advanced situation, as soon as possible. He wondered how long it would be before Madge woke up. He finished shaving and dressing and was about to dial Madge's number but thought better of it. It would be a pity to wake her up after all she had coped with the previous day. He would carry on to breakfast and wait till she contacted him, which he knew she would do as soon as she surfaced. He was about to leave when there was a discreet tap on the door.

'Come in!' he called and Ramiro put his head round the door.

'Good morning, Major,' he said and with a secretive look proffered a note towards the major.

'Well come in, man,' said the major, taking the envelope and eyeing Ramiro who had assumed the furrowed brow of a person entrusted with information of a most sensitive nature.

The major glanced at the contents.

'Thanks, old boy,' he said as a dismissal to Ramiro who was hovering just inside the door wondering if he would have a further part to play in the intriguing situation of the major's appearing to have a liaison with a lady. He withdrew, closing the door without a sound and stole away.

'Tim, darling,' the note said, 'I am going into the town to the hairdressers. I know it's a bit early but it was the only time they could fit me in today, when I phoned on Thursday. I know you would have taken me but I hoped you would have a nice long lie-in after all you did yesterday. The taxi is collecting me at eight-thirty and I should be back by eleven. I'll see you in the drawing room for coffee. I'm almost dying with excitement. Love, Madge.'

'Well, well, what a girl, I would have

thought she'd sleep till midday,' he thought as he closed his door. He walked along the short corridor to the main hall to pick up his paper and go in to the dining room. Kathy had just arrived and was about to enter the office to take over from Reg.

'Good morning, Tim,' she called across, giving him a dazzling smile. 'How are you this morning?'

'First class, m'dear, how else after last night?' he answered with a return smile.

'Just dashing for some breakfast, I'll pop in for a word after,' he added.

'Lovely,' she said and went on into the office.

'Good morning, Reg,' she said, brightly. 'Do you think you could possibly stay for the morning. I've got to see Mrs Currer-Spriggs for a meeting when she returns.'

'No trouble at all, miss, stay all day if you like,' he volunteered.

'Well, why don't you go to the kitchen and have a jolly good breakfast and then have a sleep in the spare room until I need you?'

'Very good, miss, thank you very much.'

'Thank you, Reg, you're a real treasure.'

'I say, L.-J., you're looking chipper this morning,' said Tom Dangerfield as he looked up from the large table where he was having breakfast with Tom Beardmore, Jim Witherspoon, Sam, and Sandy Balfour.

'Mind if I join you?' asked the major.

'Actually, we were hoping you'd appear,' Tom replied.

The major settled himself as Tracey crossed the room.

'Good morning, Major. You'll sit there, then eh? Your usual, is it?'

'Good girl,' he replied.

'You keep your ear to the ground pretty well, L.-J.,' said Tom. 'We were just saying there's an odd atmosphere to the place at the moment, as though something's up; somebody knows something that we don't, I'll be bound. Any ideas?'

The major's gaze swept round the table.

Sam's face was expressionless apart from an enigmatic wink and even he wasn't too sure of why he was doing it.

'What makes you think so?' the major enquired innocently. 'Perhaps because it's party night,' he offered.

'By the way,' said Sandy, changing the subject, 'how did you get on yesterday?'

'Very well actually,' the major replied, 'if you can say that about a funeral. What would you say, Sam?' he said looking at Sam.

After a momentary pause Sam returning the major's gaze with a slight grin, replied, 'It had its satisfying moments I must say.'

The substance of that comment was to be revealed to all throughout the day as Joyce retailed in as dramatic terms as she could contrive to anyone willing to listen, the encounter between Bernard and the heroic Sam, the latter being now firmly placed on a pedestal by the doting Joyce.

After breakfast the major tapped on the office door.

'Come in,' said Kathy and he entered, surprised to find Reg still there.

'Do sit down, Tim,' she added.

'Good morning, sir,' said Reg, just returned from the kitchen. 'I'll carry on as arranged then, Miss.'

He backed out and closed the door. 'I've asked Reg to stay for an hour or so while I have a discussion with Daphne,' Kathy explained. 'She's out for the moment but I'm joining her for coffee about ten-thirty. I must talk to her about our plans to get married; I won't mention the cottage or anything to do with you and Madge for the moment, of course.'

'Actually, we had similar things in mind,' said the major, 'we'd like to talk to her as soon as we can; Madge is at the hairdresser's at the moment; says she'll be back about eleven.'

'Yes, I know,' said Kathy, to his surprise.

'How does she know that?' he wondered, convinced that women were telepathic.

As if in answer to his question she added, 'She told me on Thursday.'

'We're hoping to see the C.O. as soon as we can today, we think we ought to keep her in the picture as things are warming up so quickly,' the major said anxiously.

'Well, she'll be rather busy today, of course, perhaps we could see her together; after all you and I have no secrets anymore, have we?'

'Kath, you're a genius,' he said. 'Can I leave it to you to arrange?'

'Of course!' she said. 'I'll see her as arranged and, if agreeable to her, you two can join us when Madge comes back, I'm sure Daphne won't mind.'

'Right,' said the major, turning towards the door. 'You're going to be frantically busy coping with everything today; the best thing I can do is get out of your way I think; let me know what's arranged and I'll see you later, I'll be in the sitting room till Madge returns.'

In the sitting room the major found Muriel Lewis enjoying one of her two cigarettes of the day and talking to Tom Dangerfield. Tom beckoned him to join them.

'No golf today, Tom?' the major asked.

'No, Smiler has gone into the town for a haircut; said he'd been saving up for one. Thea and Joan have gone to the club for some ladies' event or other.'

Tracey appeared looking for employment, being freed from the dining room for a while, Robbie telling her to freelance in the reception rooms, to assist Ramiro.

'Can I get you a nice cup of coffee, Major?' she asked.

'That would be most acceptable, m'dear,' he replied.

'I'll just go and get you one then. Biscuits?' she added.

'Just one perhaps.'

'Are you a sportsman, Major?' enquired Muriel.

'Can't say I am really,' he answered. 'I came to the conclusion long ago, that the sports field can be a frustrating place for the novice. I tried many things that appealed to me; cricket, bowls, sailing, archery, etc., all with the naive intention of taking part, as time and fancy afforded; but that's not the way things go at all.

'I once took a fancy to bowls and joined a club. The members were all very kind and helpful, and I dare say I would have become a tolerably good player but soon found that one was expected to turn out regularly twice a week and serve on the tea rota, etc, which is perhaps all very laudable and necessary for a club to function efficiently, but hardly the same as being able to enjoy a quiet game when in the mood and free to do it. So that didn't last.

'The same applied to archery, where one was expected to turn out on both days every weekend of the season on pain of death.

Golf is much more tolerant of the individual, whose casual needs are well catered for provided he avoids two things: weekends and competitions with experts, who will continually declare penalty points for all sorts of obscure misdemeanours on the part of irritating novices.'

The major paused for breath, whereupon Tom interjected with, 'You exaggerate surely.'

'Perhaps a little, I often do, but it's my experience nevertheless.'

'What about cricket then?' Muriel threw in.

'As far as the game is concerned, I enjoyed playing and not without some success. I developed a curiously deceptive form of bowling which enabled me, on one occasion, to take three wickets in one over. In my youth I played best in the slips, perhaps owing to much practice with the slip-machine at school. However, contrary to the historical adage that playing the game counts above winning, in which the concept of sportsmanship is supposedly enshrined, nothing could be farther from the truth in my experience; certainly not in the areas below county level.

'The idyllic village green cricket can be the scene of blatant selfishness and arrogance on the part of the leading lights of the club who will exhort the least gifted members of the so-called team to make sure that they turn up on Saturday or Sunday to show team spirit, only to find, as usual, that they are twelfth man for half the game and at long stop for the other.

'Needless to say that when the master batsmen have stuck to the wicket as long as they possibly can for the glory of winning, they will declare the match before the lesser players get a chance at the crease. The same applies to fielding; the best bowlers keep the ball in order to win the match, some of whom appear to think that the object is to sportingly take the batsman's head off. It's the team that must win, at the expense of the individuals.

'Say what you like, cricket can produce the best of sportsmanship perhaps, though I can't see how; while it can certainly bring out the worst. The game is too often governed by the elite who will be seen in a small huddle between overs deciding the fate of everyone else. Do these heroes give any real thought to their excesses? While I can't say that I've suffered personally, having developed some skill at school, I have witnessed such behaviour many times over the years so I don't say these things lightly,' the major went on.

'I think most of the blame lies in the abysmal rules of the game, which could so easily be rearranged to the benefit of all the players. There are occasions when the rules are adjusted, in response to such realisation, on a local basis, but it shouldn't be necessary for players to spend the whole season with a small share of the game.'

'Blimey!' said Tom, 'Perhaps the rules have changed since our day, L.-J.'

'I'd like to think so,' said the major.

'Football is a more civilised game than cricket, at least it used to be. We played soccer at school although there was a move, some years ago, to change to rugger; largely suspected of being for snobbish reasons, but it was rightly defeated.'

At ten twenty-five, Kathy appeared in the doorway. The major excused himself and went across to her. 'Any time you like,' she said, with a smile.

'Well done, m'dear, and many thanks.'

She went off to see Daphne and he rejoined the discussion.

At about that time, George Townend emerged from the pseudo-Edwardian facade of the gentlemen's hairdresser's. Haircuts always seemed such singular occasions, not that he had a great deal to sacrifice, but he nevertheless half expected comment from everyone. In the days when the difference was more obvious, it was customary for everyone to make silly comments, as he himself did to others without the least notion as to why.

It was like being at school in his day when wearing new socks with short trousers was always subject to comment. New socks were of paramount importance, to be chosen with care if ridicule was to be avoided in regard to the clock pattern selected. It was the one item of clothing to which parental control seemed to be sensitive and understanding, conceding final selection to the wearer in recognition of the considerable pride involved. Parents of that era would have felt well contented had they been aware of the appalling financial suffering that lay in wait for their successors in regard to such items as footwear labels.

George ran his forefinger round the inside of his collar in an effort to remove the inevitable stray hair that the brush had missed as always, with irritating result. The fresh early spring air felt uncomfortably cold against the newly exposed skin. How unlike his first major loss 55 years before, when he and his fellow conscripts were brutally exposed to the relentlessly hot sun of mid-summer, having most of their carefully nurtured locks removed, in a trice.

That was a moment of truth that had hung over them from the minute they had shambled through the gates of HMS *Royal Arthur*, one of the many 'Stone Frigates' as the Naval shore establishments were known, on what must have been the hottest day of a very hot summer.

Having arrived at Corsham station with their small cases containing the final symbols of civilian freedom, the 30 or 40 victims of National Service summons assembled outside the station in one '******' great heap, to await further directions.

After a few minutes, a large naval lorry drew up and what appeared to be an officer got out and rushed into the station. It was one of those occasions when the natural leaders of men manifest their presence by bold example.

'That's obviously for us,' pronounced just such a paragon and, heaving his attaché case over the tailboard, clambered in followed by all who were happy to consider themselves led.

When the lorry was fully lined with sitters, and bonding had commenced, the tailboard crashed down violently and the officer thundered, 'Git art,' while thumbing over his shoulder towards the road.

With the usurpers of his vehicle suitably ejected, the tailboard was slammed back up by the authority whose rank was now coming into question in the minds of the confused group.

A sailor in a faded blue collar appeared from the station saying, 'What's up, Pots?'

'Take this "******" lot up,' ordered the

Petty Officer Telegraphist, returning to the driving cab.

'Orr "******" me, Pots,' exclaimed the tar, but received no further comment.

As the lorry roared off along the dusty road, the hapless sailor glowered at the waiting crowd and greeted them with, 'Shut up, all of yer. You can call me able seaman, if you must speak, otherwise just follow me and keep in to the side of the road.'

So saying, he led his charges through the afternoon heat with coats over their arms and cases swinging low until, after a long and mainly uphill tramp, the dazzling white main gate of H.M.S. *Royal Arthur* came into view. As they passed through into the camp, they were appalled to see, on all sides, necks and shoulders red raw, whose owners' repeated jibes were, 'Wait till Phoebe gets you!' The ominous threats occasioned early and anxious enquiries from the new arrivals, which were met with a derisive, 'You'll see,' adding to the mounting apprehension.

Most were soon convinced that Phoebe must in some way be connected with the raw state of their forerunning fellows. In fact, the inflammation was due to the rigours of rifle drill, while in summer dress which consisted of the thin, white-front, a sort of blue trimmed short-sleeved, neckless, linen shirt.

The rawness was the result of the continual impact of an 11-pound rifle onto virtually bare shoulders whose skin, like the whole neck area, was red from sunburn. Phoebe, subsequently proving the greater threat to their persons, being the contract barber who appeared to derive the utmost satisfaction from removing as much of the men's remaining self-respect as her brief required, which was almost all of it.

Reflecting on the extremes of life, George Townend pulled his tie tighter to gain the optimum warmth of his collar and set off in search of a taxi. Just near to the old town market hall in a lay-by marked 'taxis only', he found his transport. The driver was absorbed in a newspaper which was spread over the steering wheel while he reclined in the pushed-back seat.

'Wake-up, Sid,' George commanded, rapping on the window.

'Ullo, Smiler,' said the driver, grinning and winding down the window. 'What brings you into town this lovely morning?'

'Mind your own bloody business and let me in; it's cold,' replied Smiler.

He walked round to the other side and got into the car.

'Sorry, mate, I'm booked,' announced Sid with an awkward look.

'Hell's bells!' said Smiler.

'Don't worry, my mate will be back in a

minute, he's only taking someone to the station; sit there till he comes if you like; at least till my fare turns up; she won't be long now.'

'Thanks Sid,' Smiler replied.

'Going back to the Lodge are you?' Sid enquired.

'Aye,' said Smiler.

'Hey, Come to think of it, that's where my fare's going; she's one of your lot, I had to pick her up this morning; you could be in luck, mate.'

'Who is it?' Smiler asked.

'I was just trying to think of the name,' answered Sid, 'I've got it written down here somewhere. Ah! Here she comes now; nice pair of pins too. Hello, she looks different somehow.'

Smiler got out of the car quickly.

'By, it is you then, Madge, you look...' he was about to say younger, but thought perhaps it was the wrong expression to use. 'Terrific!' he concluded.

'Well, thank you, Smiler,' she answered.

'Hello, Mr Coombs,' she said, looking at Sid, with a hint of inquiry.

'Ah, Mr Townend is waiting for my mate,' he explained.

'Oh, I see,' said Madge, with some amusement. 'Shall we all go then?' she said, waving Smiler back into the front seat and getting into the back.

Daphne raised her head to look through the window at the sound of the taxi crunching to a stop.

'Ah, this looks like Madge Russell, now,' she said quietly, resembling a ripple of distant thunder. 'Oh, she seems to have collected Mr Townend on the way,' she added, before returning her gaze to Kathy. 'They won't be in for a few minutes,' Kathy said, referring to the major and Madge. 'I expect she will go to her room before she finds Tim and then they will need a little chat to prepare themselves; she hasn't seen him today yet.'

'Of course,' replied Daphne.

So that's his name then, she thought, with a slight pang that others should learn before she did.

'Everything smooth for this evening, dear?' she enquired.

'As far as can be at this stage,' Kathy answered with a smile.

'It will be lovely to have you and Geoffrey here,' said Daphne. 'Everyone will be thrilled at your news; I can't wait.'

Kathy avoided any reference to Madge and the major's late situation and plans, leaving it entirely to them to reveal what they might in their own way.

Madge, feeling satisfied with the apparent effect of her outing, left her room and went down to find the major. On the way to the

309

drawing room she glimpsed him through the doorway of the sitting room and made her way across to join the group. The two men stood up as she approached and she motioned them to sit.

Both seemed lost for words, and Muriel carried the moment away from them by saying, 'Madge, you look wonderful; what have you been up to this morning?'

Madge smiled shyly.

'Thank you, Muriel,' she said quietly, 'just been into town for one thing and another.' Switching her look to the major, she said, 'I'm sorry to be late, perhaps we should go in straight away, she might be getting a bit impatient.'

'Yes, m'dear, perhaps you're right.' He rose to his feet, saying, 'The C.O.'s invited us to coffee, she's anxious to know all about yesterday. Sorry to dash, you two. See you later, eh?' and steered Madge to the door.

'Darling, I think I'll just go across and see how Reg is managing,' Kathy said to Daphne. 'I'll only be a minute or two.'

'Yes, off you go dear.'

Kathy opened the door to find the major with hand raised to knock.

'Come in, come in,' called Daphne, all smiles.

'Won't be a sec,' said Kathy, as they came into the room. 'Do sit down, Madge, and you, Major,' said Daphne, waving them towards the seductive armchairs.

They sat together on the settee and at last felt free to hold hands.

'You must be dying for a coffee, Madge, or have you had one already?'

'Please,' said Madge with emphasis.

'I must say you're looking radiant, my dear,' said Daphne, placing a table ready.

She noticed that Madge was wearing no more than basic make-up. Clearly she had been expertly groomed.

'Now,' said Daphne, 'tell me how things went yesterday; did you get down there without difficulties?'

Between them they conveyed the substance of events, including Sam's contribution which she found most amusing.

'Well, I do hope you feel contented that you've done all you can for poor Ivy, such a pity she didn't have the few years of peace that you hoped for. But now you must think of yourself and the future. Where have you got to with your plans? You obviously have things to tell me. What did you want to talk about? Gracious, I sound like a school mistress, I'm so sorry.'

She was interrupted by Kathy's return from the office.

'Reg is in his element,' she announced, 'I'm beginning to fear for my job!' she laughed.

'I'm glad you're back,' said Daphne,

'before we go any farther, would you all please me by having lunch with me?'

They all looked happy with the suggestion.

'That's awfully good of you,' said the major as they all nodded agreement.

'Oh splendid,' said Daphne, reaching for the telephone. 'Ah! Robbie, I'm sorry to be a nuisance today of all days but could you possibly send in a light lunch for four, say about one o'clock; it is important; I'll leave it to you to choose something nice,' she said, glancing at everybody for approval. 'Thank you so much, dear.'

She put the phone down, stood up, hands together, and said, 'Sherry everyone?' When all were furnished with a glass of sherry, Daphne resumed her seat and raised her glass, saying, 'Here's to the future, I wish you all every happiness.'

'Thank you darling, and the same to you,' said Kathy.

'Hear, hear,' said the major.

'Now,' began Daphne, 'where do we go from here; have you found anywhere yet?'

'Shall I?' Kathy said, looking at the major for agreement.

He nodded vigorously, glad of the offer.

'In a nutshell, darling, whenever Tim and Madge are ready, I shall move in to Geoff's house and they will move into mine.'

'As soon as we're married,' the major

added quickly, for Madge's comfort.

'Good heavens! So simple, so perfect,' said Daphne with astonishment. 'Does anyone else know about it all?'

'Well, no, not yet,' the major replied. 'We shall be jolly relieved when it's common knowledge, actually.'

Kathy again took the initiative saying to Madge and the major, 'Daphne has kindly agreed to announce our engagement at the party dinner tonight and I wonder if you would like her to make it a double event by doing the same for you. I'm sure she would if it suits you both.'

Madge squeaked with delight and hugged the major.

'Wouldn't that be marvellous, darling?' she said to him, her eyes shining with excitement. 'Would you really?' she said, looking at Daphne, 'we'd be so grateful.'

'Of course, my dear, nothing would give me greater pleasure,' said Daphne, adding, 'I think we can look forward to a memorable occasion.'

They continued to discuss details of the arrangements for another half hour until a discreet tapping on the door was answered by Daphne calling out, 'Who is it?'

'Angela, mum.'

'Oh yes, come in, dear.'

The door was pushed wide before the major could reach it, and Angela steered a well-laden trolley over to the corner of the room. She moved the folding screen to reveal a dining table with six chairs and proceeded to set out the lunch.

'Ramiro will be in in a minute with the wine, mum. I've left the sweets and everything on the trolley, and Cook says, no need to rush; it's all cold and she hopes everything is all right,' said Angela as she departed.

The major held the door open as she passed through, pushing it to as he caught the whispered, 'Thank you, sir.'

Her exit was immediately followed by a further knock on the door heralding the arrival of Ramiro with his trolley.

'Come in,' called Daphne and the major swung the door inwards again before he had released his grasp of the handle.

It was only that morning that Ramiro had conveyed the secret message to the major from the very lady who was sitting before him now. Something was definitely 'up' he concluded.

'Madge dear, would you like anything before lunch, a dry white wine perhaps?'

'Thank you, Daphne, that would be just right,' Madge replied.

'Same for me, darling, please,' said Kathy.

'How about you, Major?' said Daphne.

'Any chance of a G and T, Ramiro?' the major asked.

'*Si*, Major, I bring specially,' said Ramiro,

winking grotesquely, as assurance that he was the major's man.

The boy's gone completely barmy, the major thought.

Ramiro applied himself to dispense in order of instruction, pouring the white wine for Madge first. As he presented it to her, standing square on before her seat, he appeared to her to be endeavouring to communicate telepathically. His expression was clearly weighted with meaning but totally incomprehensible to her as he strove to convey to her that she and the major could not be in safer hands than his. Madge was relieved when he passed on to Kathy, who was served with a look verging on dismissal.

Daphne glanced at the wines provided for lunch and registered her approval; Ramiro was learning and proving his value, she thought.

'Thank you, Ramiro, I'll phone through if I need you again,' she told him.

He pushed his trolley to the door, with a sideways, man of the world smile, as he passed the major and departed.

'Peace again at last,' Daphne purred, smiling. 'So, we've settled the matter of engagements very nicely. Have you decided anything in regard to wedding arrangements?' she asked, looking at Kathy and Madge in turn. 'I wouldn't want you to feel obliged to use the Lodge if you have preferable ideas,' she said.

'Well, as far as we're concerned a short civil ceremony and a reception somewhere is all we want,' said Kathy. 'But I must say that Molly has been trying hard to persuade us to have a reception at the club, as she is going to do, though her own will be on a grand scale.'

'And what about you two?' said Daphne to Madge and the major.

'Well, much about the same really but we would feel much more at home if the party could be here, wouldn't we, old sweet,' said the major, patting Madge's hand.

'Yes, darling, I certainly do, provided it wouldn't upset any of the other residents.'

'Don't you worry about that, dear,' Daphne assured her. 'I can't think of anyone here who would miss a free party, anyway.'

At the mention of the word free, the major said, 'We would appreciate having an idea of costs in order to make some timely provision, you understand.'

'Oh major, how could you imagine having to pay for anything. I refuse to be deprived of the pleasure of doing it all as ... as my wedding present, so there, that's it and all about it; all I need to know is the date!'

She wished she had as easy an answer to what she would do in Kathy's case, and hoped Kathy was not feeling overlooked by the gesture. She made a mental note to talk to Molly Haine about it.

'Daphne, my dear, I really don't know what to say.'

The major struggled for words to get himself decently out of the overwhelming situation. He looked helplessly at Madge who, knowing that everything was settled, just leaned over and kissed him.

The major who had been anticipating a relatively stressful interview demanding cognitive input on his part, based on little more than the hope of inspiration in what he viewed as a predominantly feminine realm, felt as though he had been lifted up and carried across some rapids and set down again on a safe shore. He would willingly have extended the notion to one of waking up at that moment in the future when he would find himself in the cottage with Madge and all the intervening frippery over and done with. He was, however, gratified by the knowledge that after this evening there would be no further necessity for restraint between them, in public.

'I suggest we have some lunch now if you feel ready for it,' Daphne said with an enquiring look.

'Sound idea,' the major replied, standing up eagerly.

'Ooh! Robbie's excelled herself,' said Kathy as they approached the dining table.

'Geoff is picking me up this afternoon;

we're going to collect an engagement ring,' Kathy confided to the major over lunch.

By God, he thought to himself, hadn't thought of that. It would tidy things up if we did the same. He looked at Kathy with an expression of thanks for the hint. She smiled knowingly.

An hour later, Reg announced the arrival of Dr MacDonald.

'Geoff is here,' said Kathy, 'I'll have to go if you'll excuse me, everyone.'

'Of course dear, I expect he's in a hurry,' Daphne answered.

Kathy returned to the table to collect her bag.

'I'll see you all later,' she said; and to Daphne, 'I should be back in an hour or so, darling.'

'Right ho,' Daphne said with a smile.

The major drained his cup of coffee, rose from the table and said to Daphne, 'Thank you so much, my dear, absolutely splendid lunch but I think we must be getting on too; lots to be done. Thank you again for everything; we'll see you before dinner as usual.'

He turned to Madge and said, 'Ready, old sweet?'

They took their leave of Daphne and Madge started towards the stairs to go to her room.

The major took her elbow, saying, 'Just a sec, old sweet, before you go up. What do you say we go into town and find an engagement ring? You could wear it tonight, eh.'

Madge glanced round the hall, then threw her arms round his neck and kissed his cheek.

'Darling, what a lovely thought; I'll see you here in ten minutes.'

Chapter 17

Contentment

Madge sat at her dressing table, looking at the gold ring on her finger.

'Dearest Hugh, I'll never forget you,' she thought. 'We had such wonderful times together.' She turned the ring several times as tears welled up and a small ache formed in the back of her throat. Easing the ring off, she placed it in the open jewel box to be treasured as long as she lived. The bath had been filling for some time; she got up to turn it off; glad of a reason to break the mood. She switched on her favourite recording and, removing the rest of her clothes, left the bathroom door open to hear the romantic strings dreamily playing.

The time slid by, drawing closer to the

moment when she would be openly engaged to Tim. It was time to begin the rest of her life and she was resolved to make the most of her second chance of living to the full. At the age of 62 she knew she still had the skin and looks to turn heads. As instructed by the beautician, she was careful not to let bathing undermine the morning's work for that extra special look.

On returning to the bedroom, the slow, exciting process of preparing the effect of optimum allure began. She sat down again at the dressing table and as she worked she felt the erotic threads inside her, charging the excitement to an almost unbearable pitch. She was amazed that she could still feel like it, as though she were 20 again. Finally, she advanced to the wardrobe and once again slipped the hanger off the rail. This time the dress would be exactly right. It slid down over her skin, hugging her body, without leaving the smallest crease. The final touches of make-up produced a jewel-like effect without hint of vulgarity and she emerged from her room, like a final instar butterfly taking wing.

As usual, dinner was timed for seven thirty; the staff were at full stretch, chivvied more than usual by Robbie. An air of anticipation of something special about the proceedings pervaded all. Angela and Alison had been recruited for the evening and Dot

Parsons had put herself at Robbie's grateful disposal as extra supervision.

In the sitting room Ramiro, who had been accorded the assistance of Angela for distribution of drinks, was all agog when at ten past seven Kathy arrived with the doctor. Guests were rarely seen at these events and he lost no time in transmitting the intelligence to Tracey by means of Angela ostensibly fetching more water.

Kathy, in emerald, was radiant as always; both figure and dress were overwhelming in their own right; but together they presented a fountain of beauty at which the menfolk could drink all night whatever their age. As the youngest male present, Geoff could indulge his pride in her without fear of challenge and had never in his life felt happier or more relaxed.

Daphne made her appearance at seven and contrived to speak to everyone as they came in. They all detected the atmosphere of anticipation, but of what, they had no notion and were quite content to absorb their pre-prandials with growing excitement and noise for its own sake.

The major appeared to be high-spirited but somewhat nervous, which drew concerned comments from his companions. His glances towards the door became more frequent with the minutes passing, and no sign of Madge. Smiler, standing tall among them, his snow-capped summit freshly groomed, was immaculately attired in a new dinner suit, necessitated by inexorable midriff expansion finally defying all further means of making ends meet. The detested cummerbund, suffered for the last two years in order to disguise the curious palliative devices employed, finally drove him to do something about it, and he wondered why he had endured the situation for so long. Probably, he concluded, because it had been his third dinner suit, was top quality, and he'd assumed that it would see him out.

He had gone all the way to Jolliffe's, in Sid Coombs's taxi, several times for fittings. Now at last he felt tidy and relaxed and counted it a good job done. He prided himself in being tidy and shipshape, as often observed by Angela when doing his room.

'A tidy ship is a safe ship,' he would say to her. 'No good being like a midshipman's sea chest: everything on top and bugger-all handy,' he once said to her.

She had rushed away shrieking with laughter and come very close to incurring the sack when she used the expression to describe Dot's store room.

Meanwhile, the conversation was on the topic of bores and boredom, which led him to proclaim that in his opinion, 'listeners were the best entertainers', since they allowed a companion to indulge in his favourite topic, and always left him with the impression that he'd enjoyed a good conversation. The major, however, in his distraction, cast a poor light on the assertion, proffering only occasional grunts of affirmation.

They were standing behind a tall armchair which currently harboured the irrepressible Joyce who was ever hopefully exercising further ploys towards the consolidation of Sam's interest in her. She presented his late exploits in progressively more dramatic terms and his reputation was reaching heroic proportions. However, much as he liked Joyce, his modest, quiet nature led him to wish that she would tone it down a bit. If she did but know it, he would be much more responsive toward her were it not for her excesses and he rather hoped that someone would enlighten her accordingly.

A hush swept over the room when the first gong sounded and as if it had announced her arrival, the mesmerising figure of Madge in glittering blue was framed in the arched doorway. The major turned his head instinctively towards her and for the first time in his life experienced a sensation that he had only heard about, as his legs gave way at the knees, and he gripped the top of the armchair to save himself from collapse. He was staggered in every sense by the magical vision of Madge at her best.

She was aware of the sudden silence her

arrival had occasioned, and colouring slightly, forced herself to keep moving towards Daphne, who met her with a hug while whispering, 'Oh, my dear you look absolutely wonderful, Tim will be so proud of you. Let me get you something to drink, I think you need one to settle your nerves a bit.' She beckoned to Angela to take care of the order and steered Madge towards the major, handing her over, saying 'Would you mind taking care of Madge for me when we go in, Major?'

Robbie glanced at the large old clock that ticked away remorselessly on the kitchen wall, defying all argument or protest at its uncompromising authority. Satisfied that all was ready, she dispatched a nervous Alison to the hall to bash the gong properly and not too timidly. At the sound of the final gong, cigarettes and pipes were extinguished; Sandy regretfully stubbed out his cigar, wondering if it was still respectably long enough, should he be noticed recovering it later. The migration to the dining room began; glasses were left on the table provided near the door, as they all filed out chattering on in conclusion of their conversations.

In the dining room, the long table was richly decorated with flowers and candles flickered in their candelabras placed at intervals. Wines were on the table ready, as were the starter dishes. In front of each place was a glass of champagne. At the head of the table, the first two places on each side bore discreet reserved labels.

Kathy and Madge came in ahead of Geoff and the major followed by Daphne and finally Ramiro who pulled the double doors to behind him. When the doors closed, Reg, watching from the far end of the hall, opened the office door and out trooped four figures, in dinner jackets, and carrying musical instruments. They had been briefed as to where to place themselves in the hall and had merely to await their cue for striking up with the repertoire approved by Daphne, to accompany the meal, and for background music afterwards.

'Who knows?' she said to their leader. 'There might even be some dancers.'

Having closed the doors, Ramiro took station behind Daphne, ready to render polite assistance with her chair, before commencing his duties with the wine; for which purpose he had coached Angela, as his assistant, in the art of pouring. He would take care of the red and rosé, and she the white. Daphne waved Kathy to her left, and Madge to the right, to take the end seats with their partners beside them. When all were settled at their places, she motioned everyone to be seated. All eyes were upon her as everyone guessed that a moment of revelation had probably arrived. A pin would have fallen to the floor with a clatter.

'My very dear friends,' she began, doing her best to pitch her voice as high as she could manage. 'When I opened this place for business, I thought of it very much as a business, without the vaguest ideas that it would lead to anything more than that. I was careful in my choice of residents, with compatibility between them an overriding principle upon which to base the best chances of success. I don't believe that I deceived myself in that assumption.'

'Hear, hear' called someone, and a murmur of approval rippled along the table.

'What I didn't anticipate, at that time, however, was the extraordinary depth of attachment that would evolve not only between themselves, but also between them and my wonderful staff to whom I owe so much.

'I am sure that many if not all of you must have guessed that this evening was to be a special occasion. I can tell you that it is, in fact, a unique event in more ways than one. It is hoped that what I have to tell you all is not already known to you, since those concerned have done their best, with the utmost restraint, not to reveal the facts until now.

'I am doubly honoured, having been

invited to announce the engagement of my oldest and closest friend Kathy, to her handsome doctor, Geoffrey MacDonald.'

At that point the room erupted into wild applause with much banging of palms on the table, even some attempts to whistle.

'Good old Geoffrey,' 'Well done, Geoff,' were heard among other enthusiastic calls, as the tumult looked like continuing unabated.

Daphne raised her hand, and the noise tailed off.

'Not only that,' she continued, 'but...' she paused for effect during which time Joyce Kingham, who had been wide-eyed at the revelation, suddenly realised what was coming next; at least she hoped she did, and clapped her hand to her mouth while instinctively grabbing Sam's arm with the other and froze with anticipation.

'Also,' continued Daphne, 'the engagement of the major and our own dear Madge Russell.'

The uproar which followed took even longer to subside.

When she finally regained some control, Daphne, with prior agreement announced that the two men would like to transact some business of their own. They both stood up, and while Geoff slid a large emerald ring onto Kathy's finger and, tilting her chin up, gave her a gentle kiss, the major drew from his pocket the token of his commitment in the form of a ring with a row of three sparkling diamonds. Lifting Madge to her feet, he placed the ring on her proffered finger and held her tight, to roars and sighs of approval which soon turned to persistent demands for a speech.

The two men sat down leaving Daphne still standing. She waved again for silence before lifting her glass of champagne saying, 'Will you all now join me in wishing these wonderful, lucky people, many, many years of perfect happiness together? Madge, Tim, Kathy and Geoffrey.'

They all stood for the toast, repeating the names and sat down again.

'I rest my case,' said Daphne and sat down amid laughter and long enthusiastic applause.

The major leaned towards Daphne and said, 'Thank you so much, my dear, Geoff and I would be pleased to respond but perhaps after the meal would be the best time.'

She agreed, and called out, 'Please start, everybody,' and with an instant decision, added, 'At the end of the meal, we'll have an interval of ten minutes, before returning for coffee and liqueurs, smoking permitted, to give the doctor and the major the opportunity to say a few words to us.'

She turned to Ramiro and nodded. He opened the double doors slightly, put his arm through with thumb upward and the orchestra began to play, to the surprise and delight of the diners.

Conversation was loud and enthusiastic. Ramiro used the doors as a volume control when the music was overcome by the level of conversation. Tracey and Alison worked hard to keep everyone happy with the service. Angela was enjoying her unaccustomed task under Ramiro's direction, which she regarded as a form of promotion and was determined to make a good impression on everyone, in the hope of a more permanent role in that direction.

The ladies were impatient for a closer examination of the engagement rings, while the men whispered their envies of the major. All apart from Sam and Joyce were completely taken by surprise at the revelations, which afforded endless discourse throughout the meal.

At the conclusion of the meal, Daphne rose to propose the 'loyal toast'. She suggested to Madge and Kathy beforehand that they would be wise to avoid being besieged throughout the interval by disappearing, instanter, to her private rooms on the ground floor, which they gratefully did, leaving Geoff and the major to the inevitable storm of backslapping and whimsicalities as the company broke up for the interval.

A series of soft rapid taps on the gong

informed the diners that it was time to return to their seats for the remaining formalities. The orchestra switched off for their own interval and refreshments. When the last diner was seated, coffees and brandies were served. Daphne, when all seemed settled once again, rose to her feet and the hubbub subsided.

She simply said, 'Ladies and gentlemen, Dr MacDonald,' and sat down again.

Geoff rose to much applause.

'Thank you, Daphne,' he began. 'Thank you for so much, including the opportunity to speak before the major. I dare say I could follow him into battle with all confidence, but I certainly couldn't follow him after one of his masterly speeches.'

'Nonsense,' the major called out amid the laughter.

Geoff went on, 'I can't recall the last occasion that I was so nervous; nothing has ever seemed so daunting, apart perhaps from asking my beautiful Kathy to marry me.' He looked down at her and she put a hand up to touch his cheek.

'Aah,' said the women, in unison along the table.

'However,' he continued, 'there is not an awful lot that I can say, beyond expressing our sincere thanks for your hospitality this evening and for receiving our news so graciously. As to the foreseeable future, our lives will carry on much the same as usual I should think; Kathy will still adorn your daily lives and I shall continue to see most of you, as more or less resident GP.'

At that point, a spate of table patting and clapping broke out for several seconds.

'Thank you,' said Geoff. 'Meanwhile, we hope that you will all be able to join us for the reception following the formal cere-mony; think of it as doctor's orders, if you like. We expect to confirm the wedding date as three weeks today.'

'Where?' Smiler called out.

'The reception will be at the golf club,' replied Geoff, readily.

'Count me in then!' shouted Tom Danger-field to some laughter.

'Before I'm trapped into giving away too much, I think I should now respectfully give way and hand over to the real man of the moment, the one and only L.-J., our old friend the major.'

Geoff, then sat down to further lengthy and noisy acclamation. Daphne allowed a few minutes for replenishment and chatter before nodding to the major that he had the floor. He took Madge's hand and gave it a gentle squeeze, before rising to his feet, clearly affected by the moment as he was received with equal enthusiasm. He gathered his thoughts and began.

'Ladies, gentlemen. Sitting here this evening looking back over a lifetime of experience during a somewhat raffish career, and having visited many parts of the world, I can recall no incident singular or in sum whereby I have earned or justified this moment in life. I find myself suddenly and inexplicably endowed with the greatest rewards that any man could hope for at any point in his life, never mind at my age.

'At a time when I thought myself content to spend my remaining years as a rusting old bachelor, along comes Madge out of the blue, beautiful and full of love and devotion. How can a man deal with so much happiness? I suppose the answer is to make it spread over as many years as possible, which I fully intend to do.'

He took a sip of brandy as his words were greeted with a murmur of approval.

'We each had our reasons for choosing to come here to spend our retirement and I suppose that chief among them is the need for company and friendship. And how indeed we have succeeded in that purpose. As our dear hostess has already intimated, this is a unique occasion, partly because hitherto we have all been single residents. Although Madge and I will soon be married, that situation will continue because we intend to live in a home of our own for as long as we can look after each other.

'In that, we have had the astounding good

fortune to have been offered Kathy's magnificent cottage when she moves to Geoffrey's beautiful house. We will therefore be able to move straight in with everything we could need, as soon as we're married. We learned all this only last evening when Kathy and Geoff kindly entertained us for the purpose of suggesting the move.

'As you know, yesterday was a very long day for both of us, but we could never have anticipated such a gratifying culmination to it. Kathy will move as soon as we are ready to move in, which means that we can be married more or less straight away.'

The news was received with gasps of astonishment and delight.

The major continued, 'It therefore remains to reveal that Madge and I will be married in two weeks' time and through the great kindness of the C.O., the reception will be held here.'

A great roar of approval followed the announcement and it was some time before the major was able to bring his oration to a close.

'It is our sincere hope that, as we shall be living nearby, Kathy's cottage is only a few minutes' drive from here, we shall continue to see our old friends whenever you can find time to call on us.'

While he was speaking, the staff had quietly slipped in including Tracey and Alison, carrying discreetly concealed bouquets for the three ladies.

'In conclusion,' the major continued, 'I would like you all to join me in a toast to our gracious hostess. May she long preside over this happy home and enjoy that contentment which she continually seeks for others.'

He raised his glass, as all, including the staff, raised theirs, and loudly proclaimed, 'Daphne.'

The publishers hope that this book has given you enjoyable reading. Large Print Books are especially designed to be as easy to see and hold as possible. If you wish a complete list of our books please ask at your local library or write directly to:

Dales Large Print Books
Magna House, Long Preston,
Skipton, North Yorkshire.
BD23 4ND

This Large Print Book, for people
who cannot read normal print,
is published under the auspices of

THE ULVERSCROFT FOUNDATION

... we hope you have enjoyed this book.
Please think for a moment about those
who have worse eyesight than you ...
and are unable to even read or enjoy
Large Print without great difficulty.

You can help them by sending a
donation, large or small, to:

**The Ulverscroft Foundation,
1, The Green, Bradgate Road,
Anstey, Leicestershire, LE7 7FU,
England.**
or request a copy of our brochure for
more details.

The Foundation will use all donations
to assist those people who are visually
impaired and need special attention
with medical research, diagnosis
and treatment.

Thank you very much for your help.